PAUL GAMBLE

THE KNIGHT'S ARMOR

BOOK 3 OF THE MINISTRY OF SUITs

FEIWEL AND FRIENDS

NEW YORK

A Feiwel and Friends Book
An imprint of Macmillan Publishing Group, LLC
175 Fifth Avenue, New York, NY 10010

Our books may be purchased in bulk for promotional, educational, or business
use. Please contact your local bookseller or the Macmillan Corporate and
Premium Sales Department at (800) 221-7945 ext. 5442 or by e-mail at
MacmillanSpecialMarkets@macmillan.com.

Library of Congress Cataloging-in-Publication Data
Names: Gamble, Paul, 1975– author.
Title: The knight's armor : Book 3 of the Ministry of SUITs / Paul Gamble.
Description: First edition. | New York : Feiwel and Friends, 2018. | Summary:
    When twelve-year-old Jack Pease and his partner, Trudy, operatives of the
    Ministry of Strange, Unusual, and Impossible Things, try to find Trudy's
    mother, who is being held prisoner by an evil scientist named Mr. M, they
    uncover a nefarious scheme that involves the legend of King Arthur, Merlin,
    and the Excalibur.
Identifiers: LCCN 2017041737 | ISBN 9781250076847 (hardcover)
Subjects: | CYAC: Adventure and adventurers—Fiction. | Merlin (Legendary
    character)—Fiction. | Arthur, King—Fiction. | Scientists—Fiction. | Belfast
    (Northern Ireland)—Fiction. | Northern Ireland—Fiction. | Science fiction. |
    Humorous stories.
Classification: LCC PZ7.1.G353 Kn 2018 | DDC [Fic]—dc23
LC record available at https://lccn.loc.gov/2017041737

Book design by Liz Dresner

Feiwel and Friends logo designed by Filomena Tuosto

First edition, 2018

10 9 8 7 6 5 4 3 2 1

mackids.com

To Holly and the team at Feiwel and Friends.
Without them this book would not exist and
you'd just be staring at your hands.
And people would start to talk about you.

PROLOGUE

Many years ago scientists came up with an idea called "chaos theory."[1] Simply explained, it means that even the smallest thing happening in the world could have an enormous effect. So, for example, if a butterfly flapped its wings on one side of the world, it might cause a tornado on the other side.

However, in coming up with this theory, the scientists have missed the point almost entirely. The question they

---

[1] Scientists claim that chaos theory arises from complexity and uncertainty in the world. However, the real reason chaos theory arises is because scientists needed an explanation as to why so much of what they claimed to be right, turned out to be wrong. In a more honest world, all scientific papers would be finished with the sentence: "And this time we're almost sure that we've gotten it right. . . ." (Although generally, they wouldn't have.)

should be asking is what on earth has made butterflies so angry that they go around flapping their wings knowing that they could be causing destructive tornadoes and hurricanes.

But if you stop for a minute and think about the life of a butterfly, it is relatively easy to see what makes them so angry, vicious, and misanthropic. Although adult butterflies are considered beautiful, throughout their adolescent "caterpillar" years they are continually told that they are hideous-looking and that the only saving grace is that they'll "grow out of it." This treatment is psychologically scarring. Imagine if, on your eighteenth birthday, your parents went around your house collecting all your school photographs and saying that they were going to burn them because frankly, up until you became an adult, you were an extremely ugly creature. You can imagine how this gives butterflies severe self-esteem issues.[2]

On top of that, the actual metamorphosis from caterpillar to butterfly is more traumatic than the average person can imagine. If you want to know what it feels like to change into a butterfly, you can achieve it by going into the closet

---

[2] If you think humans have high levels of social pressure, think about what it's like for caterpillars. Butterflies are always appearing on jewelry, tattoos, or the logos of charities and companies. But the poor caterpillar hardly gets any attention at all. In fact, in the one book I can remember about a caterpillar the author seemed to be suggesting that it needed to worry about getting fat, because that book only seemed to talk about how much it was eating.

under the stairs, switching off the light, and then trying to assemble a hang glider.[3]

And if all that were not enough, when nature was designing the butterfly cocoon, it made something of an oversight by not including any toilet facilities. This means that when the butterfly finally breaks its cocoon and flaps free, it has been struggling around for several days in its own poop and wee. If you study butterflies, you will know that after they free themselves from the cocoon they must wait for some time as they slowly dry off their wings. Any lepidopterist worth her money will tell you that at this stage it is vital not to sniff or otherwise inhale the aroma of the butterfly.

Given the difficult struggles that the butterfly undertakes to emerge into the world, it is little wonder that it becomes incredibly bitter and spends its remaining time on earth flapping its wings madly, zigzagging this way and that, and generally attempting to cause as many destructive hurricanes as possible.

Keeping in mind that, according to chaos theory, a single wing flap can cause a tornado, we can consider ourselves very lucky that butterflies do not unite in their hatred of the world and undertake a synchronized wing-flap—imagine the kind of destruction that would cause.

Thankfully, butterflies rarely group together and cause

---

[3] On second thought, it's probably best if you don't try this. Even if you do manage to get the stupid thing together, it's almost impossible to get it out the door afterward. (Incidentally, this is also why Harry Potter never made an attempt to escape from the Dursleys by hang glider.)

this kind of devastation. Mostly because even butterflies can't stand the smell of other butterflies that have just escaped from the cocoon.

On the morning this story starts, Jack Pearse saw a butterfly on his way to school. *That's pretty*, he thought to himself. Sadly, he did not think on the matter any further. He certainly didn't wonder if someone was going to force thousands of butterflies to flap their wings together, causing tornadoes that would tear the world apart.

Not that anyone was doing that, of course. Although there was something not altogether dissimilar going on. . . .

MOTHS
LACK OF PLANNING

Over the years some people have claimed that in addition to being afraid of butterflies flapping their wings all together, we should also be concerned about moths.

Ministry operatives can be reassured that they should not lose sleep over this. Moths are not well organized enough to achieve such a feat. Of all the flappy insects in the animal kingdom, moths are the least methodical.

This is easily deduced from the fact that moths get up in the middle of the night and then spend their time flapping around in circles trying to find the nearest light source. If only moths took the smallest amount of time to plan and schedule their activities, they would buy themselves alarm clocks, get up in the morning, and then not have to flap around at all, but rather just lie in the sunshine enjoying themselves.

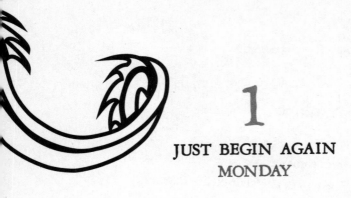

1

JUST BEGIN AGAIN
MONDAY

It was Monday morning and twelve-year-old Jack Pearse sat on the playground wall outside school with his friend Trudy Emerson. Jack was feeling both tired and confused.

The reason he was confused was that he didn't know whether to feel happy or sad. In many ways, he should have been happy, as in the last two weeks he had managed to save the entire country from both a maniacal pirate who had wanted to turn Northern Ireland into a sailing ship, and also an insane Atlantean queen who had wanted to sink the country to the bottom of the sea.

Jack had heard from some of the boys who played on the school football team that scoring a goal gave them a bit of a "buzz." However, Jack deeply suspected that that buzz wasn't quite as intense as the one you got from saving an entire country from evil supervillains.[4]

Jack's buzz was somewhat marred by the fact that Trudy's mother was still missing. In their recent adventures they had discovered that the queen of Atlantis had kidnapped Trudy's mother and she was now being held prisoner by an evil scientist. And worse, the queen had refused to tell them exactly where.

It was confusing not knowing whether to be happy or sad. Jack considered that maybe he was "sappy." But then decided that wasn't really a word he wanted applied to himself.

Not being sure what kind of mood you were in was quite stressful and tiring. Jack yawned loudly and stretched his arms. "I don't think I've ever been this tired. Although that might just be the cumulative effect of all the concussions."

Trudy stretched her arm. She hadn't needed to put the sling back on,[5] although the arm still ached a little when the weather was rainy. Which in Northern Ireland meant that it

---

[4] Jack is right about this. It is also the reason that you never see superheroes playing sports. Because after Superman had diverted an asteroid from destroying the planet you can imagine it'd be slightly anticlimactic to be applauded for scoring a touchdown. The other reason superheroes generally don't play sports is that if they were wearing shorts and a T-shirt, people would notice their tights poking out the bottom and their cape hanging out the back—which would be a dead giveaway.

[5] Trudy had injured her arm in their previous adventures when it had been stabbed by a giant mole and then hit by a flying bone fragment from a steam dinosaur. If the last sentence seems slightly odd to you, it

ached almost continually. "Well, you're going to need to start counting a lot of sheep, Jack. I need you well rested. We've got to find my mother this week."

Jack nodded. "I've been thinking about this. And I'm sure we can figure it out. We just have to think about the clues we've gotten so far."

Trudy fixed Jack with a stare. "You always figure these things out. I know you can do it again."

Jack was cheered by his friend's confidence. "I know I can too. I just need to focus, concentrate, and avoid getting distracted. . . ."

Jack's best friend David ran over to where they were sitting. "You want to see this, guys—Edwyn just had an allergic reaction to a peanut and it's turned him into a monster!"

"I never should have said that thing about not getting distracted," Jack muttered.

"A peanut allergy?" asked Trudy.

David nodded. "I think so; he's just swollen to twice his normal size and started smashing things. Someone said that it was a peanut allergy from a chocolate bar he'd been eating."

"This sounds like the kind of thing we should take a look at," Jack said.

Trudy frowned. "All right, but only as long as you promise that we'll get back to thinking about how to find my mother after this."

---

might be a good time to buckle up your seat belt, as this is going to get a lot weirder before we get to the end.

"Promise." Jack turned back to face David. "Lead on! Take us to the swollen Edwyn."

David nodded and managed to run almost halfway across the playground to the school entrance before he fell over in a tangle of limbs.

It took them considerably longer to get into the school than it should have. Although David was enthusiastic about leading them, he was as good at running as penguins were at tap dancing.[6] David fell down with such alarming regularity that at sports day while other kids participated in a race called the hundred meters, people watching David referred to it as the eighteen-bruises race. For David, a bruise was not only a medical ailment, it was also a measure of distance.

However, even before they got to see Edwyn, they came across something very strange indeed.

---

[6] I know what you're thinking, but that was an animated penguin. And I'm pretty sure they skimped on the research for that film because it wouldn't happen in real life. (Unlike everything in this book.)

MEASURING DISTANCES
USING THE KING'S MEASUREMENTS

You will almost certainly have noticed that many measurements are named after body parts. For example, distance is measured in "feet" and a horse's height is measured in "hands." And if something is absolutely tiny, it is considered to be a "hair's breadth." Those of you who have studied history will realize that this is because all measurements used to actually be based on the length of body parts of the king or queen.

This was one of the reasons that kings were mostly large men.[7] Large men tend to have big feet—and people liked a king with big feet because it meant that when they were buying things they got more for their money. If you bought six feet of cloth when you had a king with size seventeen shoes, as you can imagine, it was a much longer piece of material.

[7] Remember this; it becomes important later on.

The use of a king's body parts as measuring devices stopped for two major reasons. First, because kings got bored with hanging around marketplaces all day. There isn't much point in being a supreme monarch if you end up as nothing more than a glorified regal tape measure. The second reason is slightly more unpleasant. Although the people liked having a regal unit of measure, they didn't particularly enjoy the actual measuring process. After all, when you have bought a large amount of fabric to make a beautiful dress, the last thing you want to hear is "You look absolutely lovely in that outfit, just a pity about the aroma of foot odor."[8]

Some people doubt much of the above explanation, but it is clearly true. After all, why else do you think that kings and queens in the old days were always referred to as the *ruler* of a country?

---

[8] It's also interesting to note that sometimes smaller objects were measured in other body parts. Such as the nose. Obviously, during the cold and flu season this was especially unpleasant. In the olden days this conversation was often heard in marketplaces:

"Hey, that banana looks very unripe to me."

"Actually, the reason it isn't as yellow as it should be is that the king has a shocking flu at the moment and took a bit longer than normal measuring it."

2

MERCHANDISE
AND MONSTERS

"Get your Static merchandise here! T-shirts with the logo of the hero Static."[9]

After being employed by the Ministry, Jack was used to seeing strange things. However, this was more bizarre than most. One of their classmates, Dawkins, was standing behind a large table on which sat piles of branded baseball caps, hoodies, stickers, and badges.

In the last two weeks, Dawkins had become convinced that he was a superhero. He called himself "Static" and his

[9] If you're wondering what the logo of the hero Static looked like, it was basically a bolt of lightning inside a triangle—like the electrical warning sign you see on the outside of power stations. Except changed in a few subtle ways so that when I finally get around to merchandising it myself, I won't get in trouble with copyright-infringement lawyers.

superpower was the ability to build up static electricity shocks due to his school uniform being made almost entirely of polyester. Dawkins was sure that the ability to generate small sparks of static electricity was right up there with firing laser bolts from your eyes or being able to walk up walls. Jack was equally sure that it wasn't.

As they walked past Dawkins's stall he smiled at them. "You want a Static hoodie, don't you? What would you be? Boys medium? What color? Navy blue? I don't think you'd be adventurous enough to go with red. . . ."

"Dawkins," said Jack, grimacing, "I do not want a Static hoodie. I will never want a Static hoodie." Jack paused for a minute and then he spoke slowly to ram the point home. *"No—one—will—ever—want—a—Static—hoodie."*

A third year wandered up to the table. "Can you give me a Static baseball cap, a set of the Static badges, and a medium green Static hoodie? Ohh, and I'll take a small one in red for my little sister." Dawkins bundled the customer's purchases into a bag and money changed hands. Dawkins turned to Jack with a rather wide grin on his face. "And I believe you were saying something, Jack?"

Jack wasn't sure how to respond to Dawkins's gloating, but luckily the sounds of crashing from farther down the corridor gave him a good excuse to leave. "I'm afraid we've got to go and try to deal with a potentially deadly nut allergy. Otherwise I would have loved to stay and talk about your Static merchandise," Jack said, as he followed David and Trudy away from the Static stall.

The crashing and smashing noises seemed to be coming from halfway up the corridor.[10] Jack couldn't help thinking to himself, *Here we go again. . . .*

"What on earth is that?" asked Trudy. It was a very good question.

Whatever it was, it was certainly very scary, and other pupils were running down the corridor pushing past Jack, Trudy, and David. It looked as if the cause of the kerfuffle was something that until recently had been Edwyn.

Jack couldn't help thinking that if Edwyn had just had an allergic reaction to a peanut, he must have been extremely allergic to peanuts. Or alternatively he might have eaten the world's largest peanut.

The last time Jack had seen Edwyn he had been a small, slightly annoying schoolboy who had a tendency to get bullied. Now, it was difficult to be sure that the creature smashing up the corridor was in fact Edwyn. Although it looked vaguely human, every inch of it was swollen and bulging. The creature looked how Jack imagined it would look if you found the world's largest bear, shaved it, and then pumped it up using a pneumatic airline. And it was also probably as angry as the world's largest bear would be if you shaved and then inflated it.

"I think I preferred him before the allergic reaction," Jack whispered to Trudy.

---

[10] Jack had counted David's falls on their way to the classroom. The distance worked out as eight bruises and one minor contusion, as the crow flies.

"Well, it was certainly preferable to him being an enormous, dangerous, muscled brute," Trudy agreed.

Jack stared at the Edwyn-creature. The school uniform it had been wearing was torn to shreds. The only way they were sure that this was still Edwyn was that the swollen face still had a slightly stupid look, and attached to one of the tatters of blazer that remained draped across the creature's shoulder was the small *Static Rules* badge. Edwyn had declared himself Static's greatest fan ever since the erstwhile superhero had rescued him from a crowd of bullies.

Jack knew that this was exactly the kind of thing that he was meant to deal with as a Ministry operative. However, because he was a Ministry operative[11] he also knew that it was exactly the kind of thing that would probably end up being painful and potentially causing his uniform to get ripped again. "Look, he doesn't seem to be doing any harm," Jack noted. "Perhaps we could leave him and the swelling will go down after a while. That's normally what happens with allergic reactions, isn't it?"

Trudy arched an eyebrow. "Does this really look like an allergic reaction to you?"

David had taken a muesli bar out of his pocket and was munching on it. "It's his own fault."

"What?" Jack asked.

---

[11] Jack and Trudy were both members of the Ministry of SUITs (Strange, Unusual, and Impossible Things) a semisecret government agency that dealt with were-creatures, the Loch Ness Monster, and anything that the normal authorities felt was too odd for them to bother with.

"He shouldn't have been eating junk food. Especially not when he could have gotten one of these for free." David waggled his muesli bar, bits of which crumbled and fell on the floor.

Jack was confused. Partially he was wondering why David was suddenly against junk food, but he also wanted to know precisely who was going around and giving out muesli bars for free. "Someone's distributing free snacks? Why would they do that?"

Trudy jabbed Jack in the ribs with an elbow, which at least was a change from punching his shoulder. "Focus, Jack! I appreciate that you have an overwhelming sense of curiosity, but let's try and focus on being curious about one thing at a time." Trudy pointed down the corridor to where the Edwyn-creature was roaring. It reached out and smashed the door to a classroom, splintering it with his enormous fists. The children who had been hiding inside the classroom scattered backward.

Trudy took a step toward the Edwyn-creature. "We can't leave Edwyn like this. If he carries on like that he's going to hurt someone."

Jack tutted. "Sometimes it's almost as if you like trouble."

Trudy turned to Jack and grinned. "I do."

"Can't we just wait until a teacher shows up?"

Trudy shook her head. "You know that teachers never come out of the staff room until five minutes before roll call."[12]

---

[12] This is true; generally teachers spend as much time in the staff room as possible. The reason for this is simple: The one thing that teachers

Jack sighed. "I suppose you have a plan?"

"Half a plan." Trudy smiled.

"Does your half a plan involve battering Edwyn?" asked David.

Trudy frowned and shook her head. "No."

It was Jack's turn to arch an eyebrow. "Really? You've changed."

Trudy punched Jack in the arm in annoyance. Evidently she hadn't changed that much. "I can't attack Edwyn—whatever's happened to him to turn him into that half-kid, half-monster isn't his fault."

"So what are you going to do?"

"I'm going to let him try to hit me."

"What?"

"I said TRY to hit me. I'm going to use The Speed so I should be able to dodge him. If he's trying to hit me, he won't be able to attack anyone else." The smile dropped from Trudy's face and her eyes turned slightly watery. Jack knew she was thinking of a sad thought. Trudy seemed to have an endless repository of sad thoughts that she could draw on. And the sadder they were, the faster it enabled her to move. That was the power of The Speed.[13]

---

love most of all in the world is complaining about having to work with children. And you can only do that with other teachers. Because if you complain to children about having to work with children, they tend to get rather miffed.

[13] If you haven't read the first two Ministry of SUITs books, you may not be aware of the awesome power of The Speed. Have you ever noticed

Trudy blurred down the corridor toward the Edwyn-creature. The Edwyn-creature turned away from the classroom door, suddenly fascinated by the blurry shape that was streaking toward him. At the last moment Trudy jumped and somersaulted over the swollen creature's head. She effortlessly twisted past the two fists it threw up in the air trying to hit her.

"Shall I try using The Speed as well?" Jack called down the corridor after Trudy.

Trudy only managed to half shrug as she was ducking under punches the creature was now aiming at her. "No, I'm only providing the distraction here. You need to come up with one of your strange ideas so we don't have to hurt Edwyn. Something to cure this allergic reaction."

"My ideas. Right." Jack felt slightly under pressure. It was first thing on a Monday morning and his brain hadn't fully gotten into gear yet. Also, it was hard to think properly when an enormous monster was trying to murder one of your best friends. This was probably why teachers were so strict about not allowing homicides during exams.

"I don't suppose you have any ideas, David?"

David crunched on his muesli bar for a minute. "Not

---

that when you are having a bad time (at the dentist, taking exams, or visiting old, dull relatives . . .) that time seems to slow down? This is because it actually does. Ministry scientists have discovered that negative emotions cause the time around you to slow down. Correspondingly, if you concentrate on your sad thoughts this enables you to move at incredibly fast speeds. But only if the thoughts are *really, really* sad.

really. I have a cousin who gets really bad allergic reactions. She has this syringe thing that gives her injections of epinephrine—that counteracts the allergy."

"Brilliant—can you go and get the syringe from her?"

"No problem." David handed his schoolbag to Jack. "Hold this. I'll go and get the syringe now. I should be back by Thursday."

"Thursday?" Jack asked quizzically.

"Well, yeah, my cousin lives in Canada."

Jack sighed. "I don't think that's going to be soon enough to help."

Trudy was keeping the Edwyn-creature at a distance—occasionally it leapt forward, but she was far too fast for it and merely crouched to the side or rolled through its legs.

"Jack, we really need that solution quite urgently now! It's only a matter of time before I get tired or he gets lucky." As if to underline the point, one of the Edwyn-creature's fists lashed out, missing Trudy's face by an inch or less.

Although Jack was concerned about Trudy's well-being he was also slightly put out. After all, you couldn't just pluck good ideas from the air.[14] "I'm sorry, Trudy, but I'm afraid that I've been remiss in my contingency planning. I didn't anticipate a peanut-inflamed Edwyn attacking us."

"Less talking. More thinking!" Trudy panted. "I can't keep this up forever."

"Yes—you're right," agreed Jack. "I'll do my best to think of something."

---

[14] Jack is wrong about this.

David crunched on his muesli bar. "Basically that epinephrine stuff is just adrenaline. Pity you couldn't figure out a way to get Edwyn excited—that'd probably have the same effect."

And it was then that Jack plucked a brilliant idea out of the air.[15] "Back in a minute," he chirped as he bolted down the corridor.

MINISTRY OF S.U.IT.S HANDBOOK

ALLERGIES
THE ANIMAL KINGDOM—HONEYBEES

We are all aware that allergies are prevalent amongst human beings. However, humans are one of the most self-centered of all the species and therefore rarely concern themselves with the plight of other animals. The truth is, of course, that animals suffer from as many different allergies as humans do. Some pet owners, for example, will be aware that dogs are allergic to chocolate.

Of course, the effect of an allergy on an animal's lifestyle depends on both the allergy and the type of animal affected. An aardvark with a

[15] I told you that he'd been wrong about this.

wheat allergy will live a largely unaffected life (aardvarks mainly eat ants, and although ants live in extremely organized and structured societies, their baking skills are somewhat limited). If, however, you are a cat with a cat hair allergy you have a choice between continually having to wipe your whiskers or alternatively praying for the onset of premature baldness.

Interestingly enough, the animal with the most unfortunate allergy is the humble honeybee. Most honeybees have hay fever—an allergy to pollen. This is bad because bees absolutely love the smell of flowers. Therefore, on a pleasant summer day a bee will leave the hive and find itself drawn to beautiful flowers—but after going for a quick sniff they find their little bee eyes running and their little bee noses sniffling. Naturally enough, the bee will then fly erratically back to the hive as it is barely able to see. You will see bees flying in a strange back-and-forth pattern, rather than traveling in a more sensible straight line[16]—this is because they can barely see or breathe.

[16] It is also why people use the term "as the crow flies" rather than "as the bee flies," If someone gives you directions "as the bee flies," they're sending you on a much longer journey than you really need to go on.

So, what happens to all the dribble from the bees' noses, you ask? I suspect you already know the answer. They put it in little hexagonal containers to get it out of the way. Some of you may be asking why your local supermarket chooses to call it honey rather than "Bee Mucus." The reason of course is simple—if they called it Bee Mucus, they would never sell so many jars. And asking a visiting relative if he would like some Bee Mucus in his tea is considered to be something of a social faux pas.

With even a small amount of thought it is apparent that honey is nothing more than mucus despite the fact that some people claim that honey is food for bees. If honey was bee food, then why on earth would bees (a) continue to make it just to be stolen, (b) allow beekeepers to take it away, *and* (c) not be perpetually starving to death. If you have been stung by a bee you will already know that they are more than capable of defending themselves if someone was actually stealing their food.

The truth is that bees find it hilarious that people come to take their mucus away. In many ways it's the same feeling that dogs get when they notice people following them around with those little plastic bags.

3

THE NEXT TOP SUPERHERO SIDEKICK

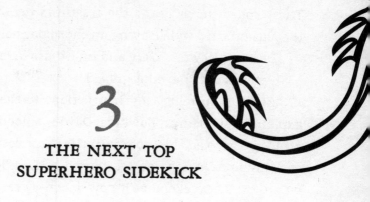

Jack arrived back two minutes later with a reluctant Dawkins in tow. David was just finishing his muesli bar.

"You do realize that you're costing me a fortune in merchandising sales?" complained Dawkins.

Jack pointed down the corridor to where Trudy was still distracting the Edwyn-creature by ducking and slipping past its punches. "That's Edwyn, your biggest superfan. He's had some kind of allergic reaction."

Dawkins's eyes widened as he looked at the rampaging creature. "That can't be. . . . No, wait, it is. I sold him that badge earlier."

"The only way we can counteract the allergic reaction is to get him excited."

Dawkins paused to consider. "Or perhaps if Static was here he could fight him. Static's pretty amazing, you know."

The Edwyn-creature swung one enormous fist at Trudy. Trudy rolled under it and the creature's fist smashed into the plasterboard wall, leaving an enormous hole.

"Do you still want to try and fight?" asked Jack.

"Perhaps not." Dawkins gulped.

"Right, then follow my instructions to the letter." Jack explained his plan to Dawkins. Dawkins nodded and took off his blazer and shirt to reveal the Static costume he was wearing underneath. Jack suspected he had been working on it over the weekend as it now actually resembled a real superhero costume. Dawkins/Static had managed to get hold of an old blue leotard of his mother's and decorated it with school ties. Over this he wore a pair of darker blue shorts. His chest had a yellow triangle emblazoned on it with a streak of white lightning down the middle. Static's mask was still made of school ties, but it had been neatened up and didn't look as ragged as it had before. The polyester cape was actually quite neatly sewn and hemmed. If it hadn't been for the odd cuff and pocket patched onto it, you would never even have realized it was made of polyester school shirts.

"Now are you ready, Daw . . . Static?" Jack asked, correcting himself quickly.

Dawkins placed his hands on his hips and assumed a heroic pose. "I am Static, the Spark Knight, the Shocking Trooper, the Lord of Lightning. I was born ready."

"Guys, any . . . time . . . now . . . would . . . be . . . great." Trudy panted. She looked up to see whom Jack had brought with him and was predictably disappointed. "Static? Really?

You know that he isn't a proper superhero, Jack—don't you?" While she spoke, the Edwyn-creature saw an opportunity and leapt forward and grabbed her with both hands. The creature effortlessly lifted Trudy above its head and prepared to throw her across the corridor. Jack pushed Static forward.

"Now say what I told you to say! Loudly!"

Static shouted at the top of his voice, "MY NAME IS STATIC. I AM A SUPERHERO—BUT I HAVE DECIDED THAT I NEED A NEW SIDEKICK.[17] THEREFORE I WILL BE HOLDING SIDEKICK AUDITIONS IN THE SCHOOL GYM AT LUNCHTIME TOMORROW—ALL COMERS WELCOME!"

Jack hoped that this would be enough. The Edwyn-creature had turned and was staring at Static. After a second, the creature dropped Trudy to the ground. She sat up and rubbed at her elbow but seemed to be mostly unharmed.

The Edwyn-creature shivered. It took a step toward where Static was standing and pointed with one enormous

---

[17] Some of you will have read Book 2 of Ministry of SUITs and will therefore know that Static already had a sidekick called Volty. If Volty had heard this speech, it might well have made him jealous except for two key facts: (a) Volty was a hand puppet; (b) at the moment Volty wasn't with Static because he was at home going through the spin cycle on the washing machine after Static had gotten some Heinz ketchup on him.

More superheroes should look into getting machine-washable sidekicks. Sidekicks are always getting dirty from being beaten up and dragged through mud, so it's a lot of fuss if they're "dry clean only."

hand before rubbing its eyes. Jack could see that the black pupils of its eyes had expanded like saucers. The Edwyn-creature seemed to be getting smaller, the swelling subsiding, the muscles shrinking. Slowly the Edwyn-creature took two steps forward and then it collapsed. As it lay on the ground it looked as if someone was letting the air out of it. It was gradually returning to a more normal Edwyn shape.

Trudy hauled herself up from the ground. "Okay, Jack, this is the bit where you glibly explain how that worked."

Jack tutted. "Trudy, I never thought I'd hear myself saying this, but sometimes you take all the fun out of being smug."

"Get on with it."

"It's simple, really. The thing Edwyn loves most of all in the world is Static, so when he heard that there might be an opportunity to become Static's sidekick, it caused adrenaline to surge through his veins. And adrenaline's basically the same thing as the epinephrine they give to people to counteract allergic reactions."

Jack and Trudy walked over to where Edwyn lay in the ragged remains of his uniform. Static was cradling Edwyn's head, kneeling in a heroic pose,[18] and shaking his fist at the ceiling.

---

[18] Not sure if you've ever actually tried kneeling in a heroic pose. It's really not as easy as it first seems. But it's very good for your core strength and therefore an ideal pose if you're trying to build up a six-pack. This means that standing in heroic poses will tighten your abdominal muscles and tone your arms. Which is the reason why heroes are generally so awesome-looking and ripped.

David wandered over and stood beside them. "Is Static angry with the ceiling for some reason?"

"I will not let this lie, Edwyn!" Static yelled in a most heroic manner. "I will gain revenge on whoever did this to you! I will hunt them out and destroy them! Mark my words."

Trudy turned to Jack. "Have you marked his words?"

Jack nodded. "I have, I really have. But do you think he's realized that it was a snack containing a peanut that did this to Edwyn?" Jack bent down and picked up a half-eaten chocolate bar that was lying on the floor beside the unconscious Edwyn. "Essentially Static has just sworn vengeance on a Snickers bar."

"Let's hope he hasn't bitten off more than he can chew." Trudy looked down at Edwyn in his ragged uniform.

"What are you thinking?" Jack asked.

"Not much," said Trudy, "except we should probably be glad that they make underpants out of material that can stretch."

Jack nodded in agreement.

ADRENALINE
Use as a Medicine

Everyone knows that adrenaline is a naturally occurring chemical in the body that can boost your energy and levels of excitement. More interestingly it is also used quite widely as a medicine—but that isn't the only use that it has.

For example, if you have an asthma attack you may be given adrenaline as a treatment. The brilliant thing about adrenaline is that not only will it help stop the asthma attack, but it will also make you a *lot more excited* about being a bit wheezy.

PEANUTS
WHY THEY CAUSE ALLERGIES

Over the years, many people have wondered why peanuts cause allergic reactions. Ministry scientists have discovered why this is. It is interesting to note that peanuts are sometimes used in the manufacture of dynamite.[19] Of course they need to be refined, poked, and distilled by scientists before this happens. But nonetheless it also means that peanuts must be very slightly explosive. Therefore, when people have an allergic reaction to a peanut, it is just a very small explosion taking place inside them—causing them to swell up and turn red.

Ministry scientists have expressed concerns that if an evil scientist were to genetically modify peanuts to make them even more explosive than normal, there is the potential for the explosions to be so large that they would cause someone to swell up and change into a monster. However, we are confident that no one would be evil enough to do such a thing.

---

[19] They really are. I mean . . . look it up; it's on Wikipedia and everything.

4

BLOOD TESTS

As usual, some of the school's teachers arrived on the scene shortly after everything had been sorted out. Jack, Trudy, David, and Static, along with the now barely conscious Edwyn, were herded toward the school nurse's room. Partly because the teachers wanted to make sure they hadn't sustained any injuries, but mainly because they wanted to make sure they weren't going to sue the school after being attacked by a monster.

Even though Edwyn was still groggy and unwell, Trudy couldn't help herself from chastising him. "You know, if you're allergic to peanuts you really shouldn't be eating Snickers."

Edwyn stared at her blankly. "But I'm not allergic to peanuts. . . ."

"There's something very strange going on here," Jack said.

"And unusual," agreed Trudy. "I've seen people swell up because of allergies. But I've never seen them swell up so much that they turned into rampaging monsters."

"I have no sympathy," said David. "You shouldn't be eating chocolate bars anyway. These are much more healthy." David took another muesli bar out of his pocket and began munching on it.

"Where are you getting all these muesli bars from?" Jack asked.

David raised a quizzical eyebrow.[20] "Didn't you guys see the posters around the school last week?"

"No, David," Jack explained calmly, "we were too busy saving Northern Ireland from being sunk to the bottom of the sea to notice anything on the school bulletin boards."

"That's a big problem of yours—you tend to get wrapped up in silly little things and miss what's important in life." David took a piece of paper from his pocket, unfolded it, and passed it to Jack. It was a poster explaining that a media company was coming to the school to hold auditions for extras in a fantasy film called *The Once-Forgotten King*. "What does a fantasy film have to do with health food?"

David frowned. "Well, fantasy films are all about dragons breathing fire, people dodging boulders and hitting other people with spiky implements. You need to be in pretty

---

[20] For the sake of full disclosure I feel I should tell you that David's quizzical eyebrow was his left one. His right eyebrow was reserved solely for when he smelled something funny.

good shape to do that kind of thing. The film company has agreed to supply free healthy snacks to the school so all the extras looked buffed up."

Static grabbed the leaflet from Jack. "Let me look at that—I might try for an audition."

Jack shook his head in disbelief. "This doesn't make any sense. People don't get fit just by eating health-food bars— you have to exercise as well."

Trudy snapped her fingers under Jack's nose. "Don't you start thinking about this, Jack—we're supposed to be focusing on finding my mother—remember?"

"That's unfortunate," David said, "because apparently the film people are really keen about helping kids to be as healthy as possible. They've actually set up a model farm on the playing fields where you can learn about organic foods that are good for you."

"What?" Jack was surprised. Although setting up model farms was exactly the kind of pointless thing that adults did, it seemed very strange that a film company would care so much about the health of potential extras. "There's something very odd going on here."

Jack would have asked more questions, but at that moment the nurse came over to them brandishing a large hypodermic needle.

"What's that for?" Jack gulped.

The nurse smiled in an unreassuring way. "Since your friend had such an extreme reaction, we're testing you all for allergies."

Jack winced as he rolled up his sleeve. "Blood tests . . ."

Trudy laughed at Jack. "Is the big, brave boy scared of needles?"

Jack shook his head. "Not at all. Actually, I quite like needles. You can use them to sew or knit and all sorts of useful things. The bit of it I don't like is when people start sticking them into my body."

Static spoke to the nurse. "Why do *we* have to have blood tests? I mean, it was only Edwyn that had the weird allergic reaction."

The nurse stuck a needle into Static's arm and he winced. "Everyone in school will be having them. We need to confirm you don't have any allergies. Also, we're doing a general health check on your vitamin and iron levels—just to ensure that everyone's eating properly."

David took a piece of paper out of his pocket and held it in front of the nurse's face. "I have this note from my parents that says I never have to participate in blood tests."

"Why not?" Jack asked.

"You know that I'm always falling down steps and stairs and getting bruises? I do it so often at home that my parents have gotten an inflatable rug[21] for the hall."

Jack indicated that he was aware of David's interesting and comprehensive collection of bruises.

"As it turns out a bruise is basically a little bit of internal bleeding. Every time I have a bruise that's a little bit of blood leaking out of my veins and collecting under my skin."

---

[21] It was actually just a blow-up mattress, but to make David feel special his parents had pretended it was a specially ordered inflatable rug.

"But. . . . you get a lot of bruises, David."

"Yeah, I know," David said, smiling. "I was at the doctor's not so long ago and he said that he reckons that there's more blood in my bruises than there actually is in my veins—so I'm excused from getting blood tests. The doctor says I'm a medical miracle."

"There's certainly something special about you," Trudy agreed.

Jack turned to Trudy. "Maybe we could . . ."

Trudy stood up. "No!"

Jack slumped down in his chair. "I was only going to suggest . . ."

"You were going to suggest that we go and look at the model farm to see if there's anything odd about it. But if we start investigating that, we won't have time to find my mother."

Jack squirmed. He knew that Trudy was right, but he also knew that something odd was going on with the school. A film company arriving was odd enough, but one that was worried about the health of the pupils was very strange indeed. "Trudy, you know what I'm like. No matter how hard I try I'm going to want to figure out what's going on at that model farm. I'll just nip over there at recess and have a quick look. Then after school we can really start thinking about finding your mother."

"Fine," Trudy said quietly. "You can go and look at the model farm . . . by yourself." Trudy turned and left the nurse's room without another word.

ACUPUNCTURE
Its Effectiveness

Many people within the Ministry have argued over whether acupuncture is actually effective. There are two schools of thought on this.

The school of thought that feels that acupuncture is ineffective is called the "hedgehog school." The school of thought that believes it to be effective is called the "cactus school."

The hedgehog school points out that hedgehogs are almost continually undergoing acupuncture with needles sticking into them. And yet hedgehogs seem to be very unhealthy creatures indeed. They are constantly getting squashed and injured. In fact, in some places little hedgehog hospitals have been set up to take care of them as they are so constantly sickly.

On the other hand, the cactus school points out that cacti also have a penchant for acupuncture and they are among the world's hardiest plants, almost impossible to kill and often living in the worst conditions, such as bone-dry deserts.

The Ministry has no official position on acupuncture. However, the Minister himself has noted that his grandmother used to sew patchwork quilts as a hobby. As it transpired, she wasn't very good at this and was continually pricking her index finger with the needle. The Minister says that although he is reluctant to draw a conclusion from this, he can't help noticing that his grandmother's index finger never got ill. [22]

[22] If you ever get a chance, it's worth asking the Minister to show you his grandmother's collection of patchwork quilts. They really are beautiful, although the intermittent splatters of blood are slightly off-putting.

5

SHOCKING CHANGES

As Jack and David wandered across the playing fields toward the model farm, they noticed that there were workmen in the street erecting a series of new electricity pylons. "Look at that."

David wasn't sure why Jack was so interested. "They're just electricity pylons."

"That's what worries me," Jack said. "Two weeks ago we were getting wind turbines; last week it was natural gas. And both of those things were just excuses to try and take over Northern Ireland. So, you'll understand why I worry when I see a new power source being attached to the school."

David chuckled. "Jack, you're beginning to get paranoid about everything. There's nothing unusual about electricity pylons. You see them everywhere."

Jack looked up at the pylons. A flock of birds had arrived and were roosting on the wires that were strung between them. Jack wondered why birds found electricity wires so comfortable. After all, it only seemed to be pylons that you saw them roosting on. They never clustered around tight-rope walkers in a circus or on clotheslines. He couldn't help wondering if something strange had always been going on with pylons.

Jack noticed that one bird in particular seemed different from the others. It was black and white with a splash of red on its forehead. While the other birds were relatively relaxed, this unusual bird seemed to be looking about, scanning the ground as if it were trying to find something. But what could it possibly be looking for?

Jack and David continued walking to where the model farm had been set up. Half of a rugby field had been fenced off over the weekend. The fencing was made of white wooden slats and was eight feet tall, preventing anyone from seeing inside. However, before David and Jack even walked into it they could tell that it contained something from the countryside—mainly because of the smell.

Jack felt nervous—first Edwyn's bizarre "allergic" reaction had turned him into a monster, and now there was something hidden from view on the playing fields. Strange things were happening . . . again. He was also worried that Trudy wasn't there with him. He understood why she'd been angry that they weren't focusing on searching for her mother, but Jack couldn't help himself when it came to his curiosity. Telling Jack not to be curious about something was like telling someone wearing a plaster cast not to feel itchy. It didn't help—in fact it made it worse.

David had offered to come with Jack, but that wasn't very reassuring. Although David was one of Jack's best friends he wasn't much use when it came to backup. When Jack thought about his recent adventure he realized that he and Trudy had complementary roles. Jack with his curiosity got them into dangerous scrapes; Trudy with her amazing acrobatic abilities got them out of them.

"Why do people like the smell of country air so much?" David wrinkled his nose.

"Not sure," said Jack. "I think it's because there's less pollution."

"I'm pretty sure that's wrong," David disagreed as he breathed in a lungful of "country" air. "There's just as much pollution. It's just that the pollution in the countryside is organic and of a much more squelchy nature."

Beside the fenced-in area stood an enormous barn and a huge grain silo that looked like an upside-down cider jug. Both were made from red corrugated metal. A long metal wire from one of the electricity pylons in the street was attached to the corner of the barn. Jack noticed that the barn had been placed in exactly the same location where the gargantuan fracking drill had been the previous week. The drill had been used by the queen of Atlantis to try to sink Northern Ireland by making a series of huge holes through the ground. Jack couldn't help wondering how they had managed to fill such an enormous hole so quickly. A model farm, a new barn and grain silo, and more electricity pylons . . . Was it possible they were all connected?

There was a gate in the middle of the fence beside which were a pile of Wellington boots. Jack and David changed out of their school shoes and, with their boots on, pushed open the gate to reveal the model farm. Someone had certainly been busy as much of the ground had been plowed up and neat rows of crops had been planted. There were also several pens containing animals. Jack wasn't very good at country-side lore, but he was fairly sure that he could identify two cows, a small group of pigs, and a donkey.

David looked around nervously.

"What's the matter?" asked Jack.

David pointed at several spots on the ground. "You know that I'm used to falling over. I just don't want to fall over in any of that." They were surrounded by steaming brown piles of you-know-what. Jack saw his point.

It was then that a strange figure jumped out in front of them and David rather predictably fell over.

ANIMAL "WASTE"
POTENTIAL USES

It is worth noting that what we consider "waste products" of animals don't necessarily need to be so. Pig "doings" can be used to produce methane, which can in turn be used to power cars and engines. If pigs actually taught themselves to drive, we can't be certain what kind of car they would drive. However, given the kind of smell that methane gives off, we can guess that they would probably prefer convertibles.

Cows are also known to produce a substantial amount of methane. If cows bought cars, they would also probably prefer convertibles, but at the very least would require a sunroof to poke their horns out of. Additionally, cows would certainly be very interested to know what the seats inside the vehicle were made of. It would be a major faux pas to buy a car with leather trim on the seats that turned out to be your Uncle Crawford.

Elephants are also known to produce a considerable amount of methane. Scientists have shown that if you harnessed all the methane that came out of an elephant in one day you could drive a car twenty miles. Having said that, it would be extremely difficult to get the elephant to stay on the roof rack for the whole journey.

6

MODEL FARMS AND LESS-THAN-MODEL PUPILS

"You don't want to have fallen in that," said the man who was standing in front of them.

"I was just saying that myself," said David, struggling to his feet and trying to brush stuff off the front of his uniform without actually touching any of it.[23]

Jack turned to pay attention to the strange man and smiled politely. "My name's Jack, and this is David. Can I just check who you are—I'm not supposed to speak to strangers. . . ."

When the man smiled there was a wicked glint in his eye. He had long, straggly white hair and a rather unkempt, thick beard. His eyes were a kind of greeny-blue that seemed to swirl like water. He was wearing a white coat so long that

---

[23] Which as you can imagine is almost impossible to do.

it almost seemed like a gown. If it had been a mere inch longer, it would have dragged in the mud. It was a very impractical kind of thing to wear on a farm.

"I work for the film company. I'm running this farm."

"So, you're a farmer?" asked David.

The man seemed annoyed at being called a farmer. "I'm a scientist," he snapped. "I've specifically bred all these crops and animals to benefit humanity."

Jack couldn't help wondering if the man was capable of creating foods that caused bizarre allergic reactions.

"Perhaps you'd like a tour? This way." The man started walking, and Jack and David followed him through rows of freshly planted crops. "Here we have the arable crops. We have turnips, radishes, potatoes, carrots, peas, leeks. . . ."

David and Jack looked at each other. "I do enjoy a pea," said Jack, smiling.

"I know what you mean; I could really go for a leek," agreed David.

The man looked at them sternly. "Very funny. But on a more serious note, these are very special vegetables. I have genetically engineered them so they won't cause allergic reactions—you must have noticed that these days everyone seems to be allergic to something—but with my specially grown vegetables people won't have to worry about that. My crops will also be bigger and more tasty, and they'll even grow more quickly. Imagine if you could grow parsnips that were twice the size that they currently are."

Jack was pretty impressed, David slightly less so. "I'm not sure my parents would like that."

"Why not?"

"Well, it would just mean that they'd have to throw out the compostable waste a bit more often. I mean they do occasionally buy parsnips, and very occasionally they actually cook them, but generally we just eat around them and then throw them out when they've gone cold."

The farm man looked very angry and then said one of those things that parents normally say. "What would you say to someone who was starving?"

David just stared at him. "Probably—would you like some of this parsnip? Because . . . you know . . . I'm not going to eat it anyway."

As with all adults who tried to deal with David, the man found himself exasperated and unable to answer. Instead he walked on and pointed at the pigpen. "These pigs are specially bred to produce the maximum amount of methane possible. One day we'll use pigs to run cars and warm houses."

Jack thought to himself that although this sounded like a good idea, it would still be worrisome. If all the pigs were busy making electricity, there was a risk that such an approach might cause a sausage shortage. And what was the point in being all nice and cozy, with an efficient but smelly car, if you couldn't have a sausage sandwich for breakfast?

Jack would have stopped to pet one of the pigs, but the man turned his shaggy white head and hurried along.

"You know, you haven't told us what your name is," said Jack.

The man thought for a moment. "I don't suppose that would do a huge amount of harm. You can call me Mr. M."

"M? You're called M?"

"*MISTER* M to you," the man snapped. "Titles are important."

David cocked his head to one side. "Mr. M? Didn't I see you on *Sesame Street*? Weren't you friends with the word *beside* and the number 6?"

Mr. M sighed. "Enough chatter! This way . . . this way."

Mr. M seemed very keen to try to get Jack and David to the other side of the farm for some reason. Jack was suspicious but wasn't sure why. Until he could figure out what was going on he tried to slow things down by asking as many questions as possible. "Is there anything special about these cows?"

Mr. M sighed at having to answer another question. "Everything on this farm is special. I have crossbred these cows with strawberries so they produce strawberry milk. I was also working on agitating the cow so it would produce milkshakes."

"Agitating?" queried Jack.

"We put it on a trampoline," admitted Mr. M, clearly embarrassed that it didn't sound quite as grand as he had pretended.

David was thinking. "It's a nice idea, but I'm not sure I'd fancy drinking a warm milkshake."

"We thought of that," said Mr. M. "We actually tried to refrigerate the cow's udders."

David laughed. "Did that work?"

Mr. M winced slightly as he rolled up one of his sleeves to show them a bruise in the shape of a hoof. "As it turns out, although cows quite like playing on trampolines, they really don't like their udders being refrigerated."

"Important safety tip there," said Jack. "I thought that this would have been a waste of time, but I'm learning things about the countryside already. This is great. Mind you, strawberry milk doesn't sound like health food."

David agreed with Jack about this. "If strawberry milk-shake is a health food then I have been grossly misinformed about the kind of foods that are good for you."

"Of course strawberry milk can be healthy. We take it straight from the cow. Unlike the kind of milkshakes you normally have, there are no added chemicals. In fact we actually make it even more healthy by adding vitamins and extra iron."

They were approaching the fence at the far side of the farm, which was covered in long green tendrils that snaked up from the soil. There was nothing interesting to see apart from a small pile of stones lying on the ground. "What are these for?" Jack asked.

Mr. M looked at Jack and picked up a few of the smaller stones. "Nothing, they're just stones. These are sandstone, limestone, mudstone. This one is granite. And these are pieces of flint. Just stones."

"Are you trying to grow stones?" asked Jack. "Because while I wouldn't consider myself an expert on farming, I'm not sure that's going to work."

Mr. M sighed. "No, we aren't trying to grow the stones. When we plowed up the land we found these pieces of stone beneath the soil. There's only one stone that I was ever really interested in. . . ." Mr. M seemed to drift into a trance for a minute before he looked up again.

Jack looked at Mr. M and knew that there was something very odd about him. Who got excited about stones? "So, you've set up this farm to teach kids to eat more healthily. And that way they'll look all buff on the film sets. Is that what you expect?"

A small, slightly wry smile that had been playing across Mr. M's lips turned into a full-blown grin. "What do I expect? I expect you to die."

"Sorry?" said Jack. "I think I may have misheard you there."

MINISTRY OF S.U.I.T.S HANDBOOK

COWS
WHY THEY ARE BLACK AND WHITE

You will almost certainly have noticed that cows come in many different colors and shades. However, one of the most "cowlike" varieties is black and white. But this seems strange—after all, cows mostly live in fields that are green. So being black and white doesn't actually act like great camouflage—and given cows' lack of combat ability you would think they would be one of those animals that would have worked on their hiding skills.

Interestingly enough, you may have noticed when armies are patrolling in war zones they frequently wear black, white, and gray patched uniforms meant for hiding in cities. This pattern is called *urban camouflage*.

And this is precisely what cows were designed for—hiding in cities. The obvious truth is that cows were originally bred to look this way by the Vikings.

You will be aware that Vikings used to be famous for invading towns and cities that didn't belong to them and generally making a nuisance of themselves. However, one of the major problems that Vikings encountered during their raiding parties was that, as no one had yet invented the backpack, it was very difficult to carry provisions. Of course, Vikings could bring large lines of wagons filled with food and drink; however, these almost inevitably gave away the element of surprise as you could see them coming from miles away.

It was the great Viking leader King Thomas the Eminently Practical who came up with the idea of breeding a cow covered in urban camouflage that would blend in and become invisible in cities. The cow would be difficult to see (thus preserving the element of surprise), but would also provide a source of drink, food, and even dung for the campfire.

After a Viking attack, the townspeople would eventually capture a few leftover cows, move them to the countryside, and use them for milk. Why did the Vikings leave cows behind? Well, with their excellent "urban camouflage" cows were hard to find in a town after a battle was over. If you were a Viking, it was therefore vitally important to always make a mental note as to where you had parked your cow.

It is interesting to note that this is also the reason people think that Vikings had horns on their helmets. As your history teacher will no doubt have told you, Vikings originally didn't have horns on their helmets. The reason for the confusion is simple—although the cows' bodies were "urban camouflaged" and could not be seen by city dwellers, their horns were not.

Therefore, every time Vikings attacked they were accompanied by strange disembodied horns that seemed to float alongside them, thus starting the horned-helmet rumor.

Some of you may think that you have never seen a black-and-white cow in the middle of a city. This just goes to show you how effective their camouflage really is.

(EDITOR'S NOTE: Ministry operatives interested in learning how human beings can become invisible, please contact the Misery for further training.)

7

THE TENDRILS OF DOOM

"You can't kill me," said David. "We're studying the Trojan War in English and I can't die before I find out how it ends."[24] It was a fairly nonsensical thing to say, but it was in line with David's overall approach to life.

Jack felt slightly less worried than normal. This was his third week working for the Ministry of Strange, Unusual,

---

[24] If you want to know how the Trojan War turns out, you're going to need to read two very long poems called *The Iliad* and *The Odyssey*. If that sounds like an awful lot of work, we can summarize it like this. Two guys fight over a girlfriend. One guy turns up at the other guy's house and creates a bit of a fuss about this. That's *The Iliad*. *The Odyssey* is basically where this guy hides his friends inside a big wooden horse and burns the house down. Then one of the guys heads off to get his dinner and bitterly regrets that he didn't pay to get the optional extra of GPS fitted to his boat.

and Impossible Things and frankly, he was getting used to people attempting to murder him. What made this occasion slightly different was that, unlike previous attempts, he wasn't really sure why Mr. M was attempting Jack-i-cide. "People have tried to kill me before. It hasn't worked—for some reason I'm actually quite murder-resistant. Mind you, on a point of etiquette it's generally considered good villain-type manners to have the courtesy to explain why you're going to bump me off."

"Yes, I'm aware that several attempts have been made on your life. But I'm a little bit more competent and skilled than your previous enemies."

Jack was worried that Mr. M was so calm and relaxed. In his experience, villains had a tendency to get themselves quite worked up about their insane plans to take over the world. But Mr. M seemed to be unperturbed by the whole situation. Jack stared at him. "We could just run away."

"Ha!" laughed Mr. M. "I've researched you, Jack. I've been making my plans for a long time. I know all your weaknesses and I've researched all your friends too. I was hoping it would be Trudy here, but I'm quite happy killing your friend David instead. And I know that he can't run at the best of times, but just to make sure I left out Wellington boots for you. And you can't run in Wellington boots."[25]

Jack looked down at his boots and realized Mr. M was

[25] This is true: No Olympic medals have ever been won by a competitor wearing Wellington boots. Although Usain Bolt probably could do that if he wanted to.

right. Running wasn't an option. But at least he could still fight with The Speed. "Well, if you know all about me then you'll know that I'm an agent for the Ministry of SUITs and able to use The Speed."

"Well, of course, but The Speed is of no use if I have already captured you—why do you think I took you on a tour of the farmyard? I was only doing that to maneuver you into position by this fence. The trap I wanted to put you in can't move—so I made you walk over to the trap."

Jack didn't understand what Mr. M meant and went to take a step forward. Rather disturbingly, his legs didn't move. Jack looked down and saw that both he and David were entangled in a series of long, green plant tendrils and vines, with red leaves sprouting from them. The long vines crept farther and farther up their bodies, squeezing their arms and binding them in a standing position.

"I genetically modified these plants to do my bidding. These plants used to like the taste of flies and insects, but now they're larger and rather partial to a slice of people," Mr. M said coldly. "Now, I clearly can't be here while my plants strangle and eat you. I'm going to have to go and establish an alibi for the time when you'll have gone missing. Enjoy your death."

Jack was struggling to breathe as the vines slowly crushed his chest. "But why are you killing us?"

The man shook his head. "I'm not that type of villain. You see, I learn from the mistakes that others make. And the biggest mistake Blackbeard and the queen of Atlantis made was letting you live long enough to figure out what was going on and how to defeat them. I shan't make that mistake. I'm killing you before you have any idea of who I am or what I'm doing."

Jack had to admit this made sense. So often villains waited until they were nearly caught before they tried to get rid of the hero. It made a lot more sense to get the hero out of the way at the earliest possible opportunity.

Mr. M started walking toward the gate out of the farm.

"Trudy will get you; you don't stand a chance against her," Jack half coughed. His breath was being pressed from his body by the tightening tendrils.

Mr. M stopped and turned. "You really think so, Jack? Haven't you even figured that out yet? Trudy will do whatever I tell her to. I told you I'm a scientist—do you remember a scientist being mentioned recently?"

Something clicked in Jack's mind and he would have gasped if he had had sufficient oxygen. "You're the evil scientist who's holding Trudy's mother for the queen of Atlantis."

"Yes," said Mr. M. "I worked with both Blackbeard and the queen. Of course, unlike them I am going to defeat you. Now, I'm afraid I'm going to have to finish this conversation. After all, you'll be dead shortly—and I find conversations with dead people frightfully dull."[26]

Mr. M walked out of the farm, leaving Jack and David encased by the green tendrils that were slowly crushing

[26] It needs to be said that dead people are astonishingly bad at conversations, and in my experience they never even bother to say thank-you no matter how many flowers you bring them.

them to death. A large Venus flytrap's spiked mouth appeared out of the ground where the tendrils emanated from. The exterior of the pod-mouth was a dark green, but it split open to reveal a scarlet mouth lined with long needle teeth, each dripping a purple fluid. The mouth moved through the air, snapping almost at random, but slowly snaking closer and closer to the two boys. Jack wondered whether the tendrils would suffocate and strangle them before the plant's mouth started to chew chunks out of their bodies.

Jack made a positive decision. He could be frightened later—possibly even have nightmares if that proved necessary—but right now what he needed was a plan. He turned to his friend David.

"Any ideas how we can get out of this?"

David was staring down at his feet. "I think my shoelace is undone."

"That's not desperately helpful."[27]

The plant mouth was hovering in front of them so close

---

[27] Not only was David's statement unhelpful, but it was also nonsensical given that David was wearing Wellington boots. In point of fact, what David was looking at was a very small plant tendril draped over his boot giving the impression of an undone shoelace. However, this is entirely irrelevant to the plot and probably defuses the pace and excitement from an otherwise tense situation. Therefore, my agent will almost certainly make me remove this overly long footnote and she'll probably be right about it as well. However, if you enjoy this footnote and it isn't here in the final book *and* you feel moved to make a complaint about it, please feel free to write to Gemma Cooper.

that Jack could smell the bitter aroma from the rancid purple stuff that was dropping off its needle teeth. If Jack didn't know better, he would have sworn that the mouth was gloating. But then he noticed something about it. It didn't have any eyes.

"David, the plant, it can't see us. It doesn't have eyes."

"What does that have to do with my shoelace?" asked David.

"I can't help feeling that you're focusing on the wrong things at the moment," Jack snapped. He had the start of a plan; now he just needed a way to carry it out. He struggled as hard as he could and managed to work a hand partially free. Now, if only he could get to the pile of stones. He needed to fall over, but how could he manage that while he was cocooned in the tendrils? He needed someone to give him a shove....

"David, can you try and move away from me?"

"Okay, but I'm not sure what good that'll ..."

Inside his tendril cocoon David wriggled. Although he tried to move in the opposite direction he predictably fell the wrong way, clattering into Jack and sending him sprawling onto the pile of stones. Exactly as Jack had hoped. All sorts of stones were sticking into Jack, but as he rolled across them he was looking for a very specific type.

"Is this really the right time to be thinking about your rock collection?" gasped David. His eyes looked misty and unfocused, and his breathing was shallow.

Jack found two pieces of the stone he was looking for. With the very last of his strength he wriggled his right arm a little bit further free. He could move it up to the elbow—and hopefully that would be far enough. He took the first piece of stone and threw it toward the middle of the pigpen.

"Jack, it isn't the pigs' fault. Stop throwing stones at them," David murmured seconds before he passed out from lack of air.

The vines were already beginning to pull Jack's arm back to his side. He had one shot at this. It was a million-to-one chance. But on the bright side if it worked he would seem like the greatest hero ever. And equally if it failed at least no one would have seen how ridiculous his last-ever plan had been.

Jack tried to remember skimming stones across the sea with his father when they vacationed on the coast. He brought his hand back as far as he could manage and then, snapping his arm forward, he threw the stone toward the one already lying at the edge of the pigpen.

It worked. The second stone struck the first, sending out a small shower of sparks. And then . . .

And then there was the enormous fireball.

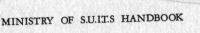

FANTASY DINNER PARTIES
SELECTION OF GUESTS

Occasionally people will ask who you would invite to a fantasy dinner party if you could invite anyone in the world—dead or alive.

If you make this choice, it is strongly advised that you choose to invite only people who are alive. Dead people make very poor guests at dinner parties. They don't speak, don't laugh at your jokes, and almost always overstay their welcome.[28]

And if you want your living guests to enjoy their food you will need to surround your dead guests with a significant number of Glade PlugIn air fresheners.

---

[28] Dead people are also notoriously bad at RSVPing and therefore it's hard to know how much food you need to buy.

SUPER DETECTIVES
How to Deal with Them

The world is filled with super detectives—from Sherlock Holmes to Miss Marple, Hercule Poirot to Columbo, Maigret to Lord Peter Wimsey. Given how many amazing detectives that there are, it is a wonder that anyone ever has the gall to commit a crime.

However, if you absolutely must commit a crime, there is one piece of vital advice that you must heed. Many criminals kill someone and then go back to being a law-abiding person. This is a mistake. Rather, kill your intended victim and then when a great detective shows up—murder them before they get a chance to do any investigating. In fact, murder them before they have a chance to unpack their magnifying glass and fingerprint kit.

If literary fiction has taught us anything, it's that ordinary police officers never actually solve crimes. It's always that one lone genius who manages to vanquish evildoers—and even *they* won't come to a conclusion quickly; rather they'll spend two hundred pages *umming* and *ahhing* before they finally realize the answer was obvious all along.

If criminals actually adopted the approach suggested above, all crime novels and whodunits would finish with the following paragraph:

And so the police officer turned away from Giles and said, "Well, I suppose we'll never find out who killed the vicar. I can't help feeling it might have turned out differently if Jessica Fletcher hadn't fallen down those stairs when she got here. And it was especially unfortunate that she landed on Philip Marlowe. And even then things would have turned out okay, except for the fact that while Jonathan and Jennifer Hart were on their way to the funeral, the brakes in their car failed. And who would have thought that the great Sherlock Holmes would have accidentally cut his own throat three times while shaving. Still, I suppose these little accidents happen."

8

SHAKE THE ROOM

It wasn't the largest explosion that Jack had ever seen, but it was definitely in the top five. Jack and David were tossed backward several feet, causing the tendrils of the plant to loosen their grip. Jack freed himself quickly and then grabbed David by his shirt collar and dragged him out of his tendril cocoon. Once out of the plant's grasp, David recovered consciousness quickly. They both scrambled several feet away from the plant.

"But it's just going to grab us again, isn't it?" David started questioning, but he stopped as he saw the plant's tendrils slowly snaking their way across the farm toward where the pigpen was on fire. Following the explosion, the pigs had sensibly made their way through a gap in the fence to safety.[29]

---

[29] It is interesting to note that the explosive nature of pigs' flatulence is

David looked at Jack. He paused briefly. "Okay, I give up. What's going on? What did you do?"

David would normally never ask this kind of question—he was so seldom interested in Jack's work in the Ministry of SUITs. It made Jack feel inordinately pleased with himself. "Simple. Plants have no eyes.[30] But we know that plants like daisies and sunflowers will turn their heads toward the sun. So that's how plants can tell where things are—they sense heat and move toward it. That's how Mr. M knew the plant would attack us. He just made sure we were standing beside it long enough for it to feel our body heat, and then it attacked."

"But I still don't understand . . ."

"Well, I banked on the fact that an explosion would give us enough time to wriggle free. And then when we were free, the plant would just make its way toward the largest source of heat—which is over there." Jack pointed at the burning pigpen.

David nodded. "That seems to make sense. But how did you know that those were explosive stones?"

---

one of the reasons that you never see them smoking. Very occasionally a really rebellious piglet will ignore its parents' advice that "smoking is *very bad* for your health" and decide to light up. This is where smoked bacon comes from.

It's also worth noting that the fact that pigs can cause such explosions is a fact that had been known for many hundreds of years and is why sausages can sometimes be referred to as *bangers*.

[30] Yes, yes, okay, I know that potatoes have "eyes," but they really aren't those kind of eyes. Frankly, you're just being silly now.

"They weren't explosive stones. Remember—Mr. M said that the pigs were bred to produce methane, so I knew that there were bound to be a few pockets of explosive gas around the pigpen."

"There were," agreed David. "I smelled them when I came in."

"And Mr. M said that when they had plowed the ground they'd found a few pieces of stone, including flint. When you strike two pieces of flint together it causes sparks. And when you cause sparks near a pocket of methane . . ."

"Boom!"[31]

"Precisely," agreed Jack. "Now we'd better get out of here before that fire burns out and the plant starts looking for other sources of heat."

When Jack and David walked out of the gate of the model farm a group of pupils had already gathered. Trudy pushed her way toward them.

"Hey, Trudy," said Jack.

"What are you doing, Jack? Even if you aren't going to help me find my mother, you can't start blowing things up without me. You know how much I enjoy explosions!"

"Sorry, we could certainly have used your help."

"What happened?"

---

[31] Although pigs are probably the animals that are best known for expelling methane gas, a range of other animals have also been found to eject this useful fuel. One of the animals that has been found to give out a substantial amount is the kangaroo. But this is obvious—after all, you didn't really think they were jumping that high just by using their legs.

It was at that point that the headmaster ran over. Sweat was pouring down his forehead. Jack imagined that if you were a headmaster at a school where a pupil had turned into a monster in the morning and then a farm had blown up just before lunchtime, it would make you fret slightly. "What happened here?"

In the background fire engines could be heard with their sirens blaring. Jack knew that there was no point in trying to blame Mr. M for the disaster. After all, he had been elsewhere establishing an alibi. As so frequently happened in his adventures, Jack was going to have to be slightly creative with the truth.

MINISTRY OF S.U.IT.S HANDBOOK

FLINT TOOLS
EARLY INEFFECTIVE TOOLS

As you will know, sparks can be created by striking two pieces of flint together. However, it is also interesting to note that during the Stone Age people often made tools out of flint. The reason for this is that by striking flint against hard objects it can be made to splinter into sharp edges. Flint knives, axes, and arrowheads have all been found.

A Ministry archaeologist has controversially contended that Stone Age man also invented flint salad tongs. Other archaeologists have claimed that this is clearly ridiculous as no one has ever found the remains of flint salad tongs.

However, with even a moment's thought the reason for this is apparent. Given that striking flint together causes fire, every time a Stone Age man tried to lift a lettuce leaf out of the bowl with the flint salad tongs, both edges of the flint would have struck together, causing it to catch fire. The reason that we have never found Stone Age salad tongs is because they were all thrown away shortly after they were invented. Even Stone Age man didn't like burnt lettuce.

Interestingly enough, it is due to the creation of flint scissors that Stone Age arts and crafts classes were the only ones that were never considered a bit dull. Because although cutting out construction-paper people shapes may be unexciting, it's a lot more interesting when they keep catching fire.

9

LOST AND FOUND

It turned out to be relatively simple to explain the explosion at the model farm to the headmaster. He had rather easily accepted that it had merely been an accident involving methane gas generated by the pigs. Jack hadn't even mentioned his involvement with the flint stones. One of the key advantages of being twelve was that everyone assumed you weren't capable of blowing things up. The truth was that Jack and Trudy were remarkably effective at destroying things in this manner. In the past two weeks Jack and Trudy had blown up a steam dinosaur and a soap factory and had smashed an enormous drilling platform to smithereens.

Jack and Trudy had asked the headmaster for the rest of the day off. Although it would not normally have been the kind of thing to which he would have agreed, today was not a normal day. And getting rid of two pupils who frequently seemed to be at the center of mayhem and destruction appealed to the headmaster a great deal.

They had called for a Ministry car and they were now on their way to the headquarters of the Ministry of Strange, Unusual, and Impossible Things. As usual they had invited David along, and as usual he had refused and instead had headed to the library to try and find out once and for all what had happened in the Trojan War.

As they traveled in the car Jack explained to Trudy about the strange Mr. M and how the explosion had been caused. But there was one part of the story he found himself hesitating to tell her because he was slightly scared of how she might react. He was rolling ideas around his head about how to broach the subject when Trudy created what could only have been considered a conversational opening.

"Jack, when we get to the Ministry I don't want you to tell them about Edwyn's allergic reaction or Mr. M and the model farm."

"But those are exactly the kinds of things that we're supposed to investigate in the Ministry."

"I know, but you promised that you'd help me find my mother. That's what we're supposed to be focused on at the moment. If we start on another case we'll never find her. I know you want to find out the truth about everything—but just for once can you try and focus on what I need you to?"

Jack gulped. This was exactly the part of the story he hadn't shared with her yet. He braced himself, unsure of how Trudy would react to the full truth. "About that, Trudy—I was kind of accidentally focusing on what you wanted me to. Mr. M . . . he didn't give much away—but he did say he was a scientist. . . ."

Trudy's brow furrowed with thought, then rebounded in surprise as she realized what Jack was saying. "A scientist? Like the scientist who is supposed to be holding my mother captive?" She grabbed Jack by his blazer lapels and shook him. "What exactly did he say?"

Jack gently removed Trudy's hands from his lapels and tried to remember the number of a TV commercial he had seen that promised to deal with whiplash injuries. "He didn't say a whole lot more than that. He said he was going to kill us before we figured anything out. He'd learned that much from how we'd defeated Blackbeard and the queen of Atlantis. He basically said he was the scientist who worked for the queen of Atlantis—and therefore he was holding your mother."

Trudy leaned forward and rapped on the glass partition that separated them from the driver. "What are you doing?" asked Jack.

"We're going back to the school. We're going to find that scientist and get answers out of him."

Jack slowly shook his head. "That won't work. We need to be smarter than that. There's no way Mr. M will go back to the model farm after it got blown up."

Trudy sat back in her seat. A tear appeared in the corner of her eye. "But . . . but . . . well, we should go back and at least see if there's any evidence."

"Mmm," said Jack, "normally I'd agree with you on that, but you might remember that I sort of accidentally set fire to

69

most of the evidence. There'll probably be lots of firemen around it at this point." Jack never thought he would feel guilty about blowing up a farm, but Trudy looked so sad he couldn't help feeling that his actions may have been slightly irresponsible.

"We need to do something. We need to find my mum."

"That's what we're doing. We know what the scientist looks like now. Maybe we can talk to Grey—he might have an idea who Mr. M actually is. And that might give us enough evidence to find your mother."

Trudy thought for a moment. "Okay—so tell me everything you remember about him."

Jack collected his thoughts in his still slightly rattled head. "Okay. Well, he has long white hair and a beard. Wears a lab coat. . . . Okay, that isn't too helpful. . . . But wait—he's involved in genetic engineering. Plants, crops, even animals. That kind of thing."

Trudy nodded thoughtfully. "And do you think he might have something to do with Edwyn going crazy this morning?"

"Quite possibly. Mr. M said he'd genetically engineered crops so that they didn't cause allergic reactions; maybe he can do the opposite as well. It could have been a genetically engineered peanut that turned Edwyn into a monster!"

Trudy sighed. "But why would he want Edwyn to have such an extreme allergic reaction?" She thumped her fist on the door in annoyance. Jack's shoulder, which was what Trudy normally thumped in annoyance, felt slightly sorry for the car door.

"I think it's all connected," Jack mused. "The film people are providing healthy food. Also a lot of kids and parents will be scared into stopping eating junk food by Edwyn's allergic reaction."

"But why would some kind of villain want us all to eat healthier?"

"It never makes sense at this stage," said Jack. "On the bright side, I've nearly been killed already, and that's normally a sign that we're making progress."

Trudy smiled. "Yes, you were nearly killed. That is good."

"Oh—and there's one other thing. Mr. M said that he had been looking for some kind of boulder or stone. He sort of went into a daydreamy state when he talked about it."

The Ministry headquarters were hidden under the Ulster Museum in the center of Belfast. When they got there, Jack and Trudy ran through the visitor entrance, up the stairs, and into the Mummy Room, where the elaborate sarcophagus of the ancient mummy Takabuti sat. Trudy quickly punched the stone hand that made the glass case and the sarcophagus lift up, letting them run down the stairs that led to the Ministry.

As they reached the bottom of the passage they were greeted by Grey, their erstwhile mentor. Normally Grey was the picture of elegance, with a haircut that was calibrated to the last inch and an immaculately tailored Savile Row suit. However, on this occasion Grey did not look like his normal self. His hair was mussed, his jacket was flapping open, and his shirt was covered in rips and tears.

"We need to get to somewhere safe," he barked at Jack and Trudy.

"Is the Ministry under attack?" Trudy asked.

"I wish it were that simple. . . ." Grey turned and glanced down the corridor. "Look, I'll explain later—in the meantime we should run."

Trudy and Jack peered at what Grey was looking at. There was a thundering sound as a crowd of figures ran toward them. Although they were moving quickly, Jack made out a stone giant, a fluffy teddy bear, a half-lizard-half-chicken creature, a cyclops, a large floating sheet, and a horse with an enormous pair of wings.

"Oh," Jack said, "there's a name for a horse with wings, isn't there?"[32]

The crowd continued running toward them with no sign of stopping. Trudy grabbed Jack by his shirt cuff and pulled him. "Jack, if you stay here any longer you won't be worrying about what the name for a winged horse is. You'll be worrying about what the name is for a boy who has hoof-marks all over his back."

Jack realized Trudy had a very good point and bolted down the corridor following Trudy and Grey. They avoided being trampled by ducking down a side passage. Jack tried to catch his breath and hoped that nothing else dramatic would happen.

"DOWN!" Grey leapt forward and pushed Trudy and Jack

---

[32] Jack is right. All horses with wings have names. This one was called Ivor.

to the ground. Three javelins sailed mere inches over their heads and thunked into the floor.

"If the Ministry isn't under attack, what's happening?" Trudy asked.

Jack looked at the javelins. He had an idea. "Sports day?"

Grey smiled, impressed at Jack's deductive ability. "Precisely, Jack. It's the annual Ministry Sports and Training Day."

Trudy frowned. "Sports days can't be that bad."

"Normally I'd agree with you, Trudy, but unfortunately the Minister himself organizes the events and he really doesn't know that much about sports."

Trudy pulled one of the javelins out of the ground and felt its tip. "These are deadly sharp."

Grey nodded. "They're for the javelin catching contest."

"Javelin catching?" Trudy's eyes widened.

"There's a really nice medal for it if you win." Grey paused for a second. "Of course, no one who has ever won the competition has managed to stay alive for long enough to collect their medal. Come to think of it, they'd probably be better giving the winner bandages and an antiseptic instead."

"Are all the activities on sports day this dangerous?" Jack asked.

"Oh no." Grey shook his head. "The Minister's idea was to create a Sports and Training Day that would enhance Ministry staff skills. Some of the events are quite safe indeed."

"For instance?" asked Trudy.

"Well, there was a disguise competition earlier today— there were hardly any injuries in that."

"And did the winner get a medal?"

"Sadly, no," admitted Grey. "We aren't sure who won it. The winner was wearing a *really good* disguise." Grey pushed Trudy and Jack flat against the wall as a massive ball of blubber and tentacles rolled down the corridor past them. "I think that was the wrestling competition—but it's hard to tell."

"Look, Grey, can we find somewhere quiet to talk? I think we might have the first clues to finding my mother," said Trudy.

Grey's face shone with excitement—he used to work with Trudy's mother and was keen to find her. "Well, I can think of one room in the Ministry where people don't generally go."

It took a long time for Grey to lead them to the room. They found themselves walking back and forth, going around corners, climbing up ladders, and running down stairs. Jack began to suspect that Grey didn't really know where he was going.

Just as Jack was giving up hope of ever getting to the room, Grey turned to the wall at random and opened a door that seemingly appeared out of nowhere. Grey quickly ushered Jack and Trudy inside.

Jack had been in some strange rooms in the Ministry, but this one was definitely amongst the oddest. This was partly because the term *room* didn't really seem to properly apply to it. As far as Jack could see, there wasn't a floor, there weren't any walls, and there certainly wasn't a ceiling. Jack was fairly certain that there had been a door. . . . He could remember that because they'd used it to walk through. But the minute they had gotten inside, the door had snapped shut, sealed itself, and then winked out of existence.

And now they were hanging in the air surrounded by nothing. But at least it was a bright, white nothing—which was a lot more cheery than those kind of black and sinister nothings that you occasionally came across.

As if the room itself wasn't weird enough, they were surrounded by objects that seemed to be randomly floating in the air—just like they were themselves. Jack looked around and could see pairs of glasses, odd socks, umbrellas, wallets, marbles. . . . "Um, where are we, exactly? And is it safe to just be hanging in the air like this? Surely we should be over a net or wearing some kind of safety harness?"

"We're lost," said Grey.

"How can we be lost? Didn't we just come in here?" asked Trudy as she floated in a rather leisurely and nonchalant manner. It annoyed Jack that she even seemed to float more gracefully than he did.

"We're lost because this is the Lost and Found room. It's a bit strange and disorienting, so people don't generally come here. But it's a good place for a quiet chat for that very reason."

A green golf umbrella that had been hanging beside Jack's head suddenly winked out of existence. "What happened there?" Jack said, startled. "Can that happen to us? Are we at risk of disappearing?"

"We're perfectly safe. Look, it works like this. Things can be both lost and found—right?"

"Okay, that seems sensible," said Trudy.

"And you'd also agree that something can't be both lost and found at the same time, right? Because if it was lost then it wouldn't be found. And if you found it, it couldn't be lost?"

"That seems more confusing than it needs to be," said Jack, "but let's just say that we understand so far. . . ."

"That's the problem. It doesn't make any sense. Logically 'lost' and 'found' have to be two different places. Because they're very different things. But having said that, when you find something, it's in the same place that you lost it."

"You're being deliberately confusing here; don't think that we don't know that," grumbled Jack.

Trudy disagreed. "No, it makes sense. Lost and found are two completely different things. Therefore, they couldn't be in the same place. In the same way that light and dark can't be in the same place. If a place is light then it can't be dark. And if it's dark it can't be light. It makes sense for lost and found to be the same as well."

"Exactly," said Grey. A set of car keys appeared right in front of his face, seemingly out of nowhere. He pushed them out of the way. "So that's what this room does. This is the 'lost' dimension." Grey waved his hands, signaling the white space around them. "When you 'lose' something it goes to the 'lost' dimension. Then when you 'find' it, it winks out of existence here and reappears back in the actual world. That way it stops 'lost and found' from being in the same place."

"So . . . ," said Jack, reluctant to accept this logic, but not seeing any real alternative, "what would happen if this place didn't exist?"

"Then 'lost and found' would be in the same place. It would be like antimatter and matter coming together. No one really knows—the universe might explode. Or . . . we just might not lose as much stuff. One or the other."[33]

"O—kay, let's not try that just in case it's the exploding option," said Jack. "Just out of interest, who built this room anyway?"

Grey shook his head. "No one built it, Jack. This place has always existed as long as people have lost things."

"In that case, why is it here in the Ministry?"

Grey laughed. "Well, it isn't always 'here.' In fact, I don't even know how to get here."

"But you led us here!" Trudy exclaimed.

"Don't you remember how we got here? I just wandered around and around, going in a random direction until I was . . ."

"Lost!" cried Jack. "That's how you find this room! You just get lost and then open the first door you can find!"

Grey nodded. "That's it! Simple, really."

A mobile phone appeared beside Jack's head. "Umm, this phone's a more up-to-date version than mine is. . . . Do you think I could . . . ?"

"Take it? Afraid not. Apart from the moral implications of stealing, mobile phones never stay lost for long. Just wait." Grey paused for a few seconds. The phone started ringing.

---

[33] Some Ministry scientists have suggested that there isn't actually any need for a Lost and Found room and the entire setup is a conspiracy invented by sock manufacturers to keep their profits up.

"This happens a lot. People lose their phone and then they ring it to try to find it. And then . . ." The phone disappeared back into nothing. "They find it again and so it pops back into existence."

"But why are we floating?" asked Jack.

"Ahh, now that is quite interesting. According to Ministry records there used to be gravity in this room right up until 1687."

"What happened then?"

"Sir Isaac Newton discovered gravity. And once gravity had been 'found,' it disappeared from the Lost and Found room. Hence us floating so elegantly."

"This is really fascinating, but I didn't come here just to float and talk about losing and finding *things*. I wanted to talk about finding my mother."

Jack and Trudy updated Grey on what they'd discovered so far. They were slightly disappointed with Grey's answer. "I wish I could be more helpful—but a man with shaggy white hair and a lab coat? That describes about fifty percent of the world's male scientists."

"What about the fact that he was looking for a stone?"

Grey shrugged. "I'm afraid that could be almost anything. Magic stones are a dime a dozen. It could be a rune stone, or perhaps the control stone for a golem. Or something else entirely."

Jack thought hard. "What about Stonehenge? Those are some pretty famous stones."

"They are, Jack, but they're also some pretty large stones. It seems unlikely that someone would have brought them over to Northern Ireland. I'm sure if that had happened we'd have seen something on the news."

Jack looked at Grey sarcastically. "You're right, that seems pretty unlikely. Whereas someone sailing the country off, or sinking it under the sea, those seem like normal things. Don't we deal in things that are unusual?"

Grey laughed. "You're right, Jack. I suppose that could be something, but you'd need some kind of evidence."

"We aren't making any progress on finding my mum," Trudy complained.

Grey disagreed. "You're making brilliant progress, Trudy. Jack nearly getting killed means you're definitely heading in the right direction. If you want to find your mother, locate the most dangerous direction and keep heading that way."

Trudy sighed and looked around the Lost and Found room. "My mother's lost. And yet she isn't in here."

Grey put a hand on Trudy's shoulder. "I'm afraid that isn't the case. Your mother isn't lost. She knows exactly where she is. It's us who don't know where she is."

"We'll find your mother, Trudy," Jack said with a confidence he didn't feel. "We just need to put together the clues and track down this Mr. M. But we aren't going to get any further floating around. Grey, how do we get out of here?"

"Figure it out for yourself!"

Jack thought hard. "Well, we got lost to get in here. And that's how you found the door."

"You're on the right track," Grey encouraged.

"So, we found the door because we were lost. But then it

disappeared from the room because we'd found it. So . . . all we need to do is realize that we don't know where the door is. Because that makes it lost again and then . . ."

The door winked back into existence, floating right in front of them. They opened it and left the Lost and Found room as quickly as they could.

STONEHENGE
Purpose Behind Its Being Built

Many people have suggested different ideas as to what Stonehenge was actually used for. Ministry scientists have not come up with a definitive answer yet, but have confirmed that current suggestions are unlikely to be true.

Some people think it may have been a calendar, but this is unlikely, because if it were a calendar it would have been covered in carved pictures of kittens or ladies in swimsuits or Justin Bieber or even David Hasselhoff.

Another suggestion was that because they found so many people buried around it, Stonehenge might have been a primitive hospital. But quite clearly this is ridiculous. If Stonehenge were actually a hospital, it would have been a *really, really awful* one. A good rule of thumb is that if you are deciding which hospital to visit, it's best to pick the one without lots and lots of dead people outside it.

10

STRANGE FOOD

Jack and Trudy both decided to head to their respective homes after leaving the Ministry. There didn't seem to be much else they could achieve that day, and Jack was feeling quite tired from being attacked by plants and blowing things up.

Jack wandered into the kitchen at home. His dad looked up from where he had been preparing dinner. As always, as Jack's father looked up, his mustache did so also. "Hello, Jack."[34]

"Dad." Jack nodded back.

---

[34] I should be clear here that it was Jack's father saying this and not Jack's father's mustache. The mustache didn't actually say "hello" at all but just kind of nodded in a relaxed and nonchalant way, because that's just how cool Jack's father's mustache was.

Jack's mother walked into the room. "You're home later than usual. Where've you been?"

Jack thought about this for a minute and realized that for once honesty would be the best policy. "Well, I was helping out at school, then I was *lost* for a while—you know, just *hanging around* with Trudy. And then I pretty much came straight home."

Jack plumped himself down at the kitchen table and his mother sat herself down in front of him. "You're seeing an awful lot of this Trudy girl recently. Is there something that you want to tell us?"

Jack thought that the main thing he wanted to tell his parents was to mind their own business. But he was far too well brought up and polite to say such a thing. "There's nothing to tell you, Mum. She's just a friend!"

Jack's mother smiled at him. "That's fine. But you know if you wanted to invite Trudy over here at some stage we'd love to meet her."

The thought of inviting Trudy over sent a cold shiver down Jack's spine. His parents made enough fun of him without Trudy being there to join in as well. "We'll see about that sometime . . . maybe . . . never."

Jack's father came over to the table and put a plate down in front of him. Jack knew something was up because his father's mustache was looking amused. Jack looked down at the plate and realized what the cause of the frivolity was.

"Dad."

"Yes, Jack."

"I'm just looking at this plate." Jack pointed in case his

father was unaware of which particular plate he was referencing. "And there's something about it I don't like."

"And what would that be?" asked Jack's father. Jack's father's mustache was barely trying to conceal its smirk now.

"The food, Dad, the food. If you could call it food."

Jack's father frowned. His eyebrows turned downward, but his mustache was still turned upward, smiling. "What do you mean? This is very nutritious. It contains all the major food groups."

Jack wasn't sure what all the major food groups actually were. What he was sure of was that if they were all represented on the plate he would have starved to death years ago. "What food groups? The sausage food group isn't represented. The potato waffle food group isn't represented. The baked-beans food group isn't represented." Jack was looking sadly at a plate that was filled with what looked like two small burgers, but made out of a sort of greeny, yellowy mush instead of actual meat.

"Dad, what is this? Have you been cleaning out the drains again?"

Jack's mother felt the need to join in the conversation at this stage. In order to give her words more force she held up and waved a printout of an e-mail. "This came from the school today. Apparently you had blood tests."

"I know, and I hadn't even studied."

Jack's mother ignored his joke. "Your school is worried about the increasing number of allergies amongst the children. According to your blood tests, you aren't eating enough of the right foods. You don't have enough vitamins, and you have particularly low levels of iron."

"What?" Jack snapped, grabbing the e-mail and reading it for himself.

"And that's why I cooked these veggie burgers tonight," said Jack's father. "They're a new type—guaranteed not to cause allergies. Fortified with vitamins and iron in particular."

"Yes," his mother agreed. "And there was a story on the Internet about a young boy at your school having some kind of allergic reaction to peanuts or processed food. Therefore, we're going to start eating healthy food from now on."

Jack was only half paying attention to his parents. He was concentrating on the e-mail from the school that confirmed his iron levels were dangerously low. Which was strange, because Jack didn't feel unhealthy. And even if he did, he imagined that eating vitamins and iron probably wouldn't make him feel better anyway.

"Stop reading that and eat your dinner. It'll be good for you." Jack's mother snatched the e-mail from him.

Jack reluctantly took a bite out of one of the veggie burgers. They didn't taste quite as bad as he thought, although they did seem to have a slightly metallic tinge to them.

"Are they as delicious as they claim on the package?" asked Jack's father, waving the box in front of him.

Jack looked up and was shocked to see the face of the straggly white-haired scientist, Mr. M, staring back at him from the box.

Mr. M's Veggie Burgers—Now Fortified with Iron

Jack didn't know what to say. It was bad enough that Mr. M had tried to kill him in the school. Now he was trying to poison him at home. Jack waited until his parents were looking in the opposite direction and slipped the remaining "burger" into his trouser pocket.

"I think I'm going to go to my room. I've got some homework to do and I'm going to get an early night after that."

Jack's mother was surprised. "We'll have to feed you even more of this healthy food. Not only will it make you fitter, it makes you behave better as well."

THE HEALTH BENEFITS OF IRON
Sword Swallowers

Many people think that there's a trick to sword swallowing. Of course, there isn't—it's done using a real iron sword. The sword is actually swallowed and inevitably causes horrific internal injuries.

However, iron in your diet is good for you, helping your blood, brain, and muscles. In fact, if you don't have enough iron in your blood you may suffer from weakness, fatigue, and anemia.

Sword swallowers are continually swallowing iron and therefore are very healthy—with superpowered brains, blood, and muscles. It is this high level of fitness that means that even after lacerating their internal organs, they recover incredibly quickly.

So, it isn't that sword swallowers don't hurt themselves during the act—clearly, that would be impossible—it's just that due to all the iron in their diets they get well really, really quickly.

11

WAKE UP, SLEEPYHEAD
TUESDAY

Jack was surprised when he woke up. He wasn't surprised about waking up. He'd done that many times before; in fact, he had done it almost every day that he could remember. What surprised him was that it wasn't his alarm clock that was waking him up. Rather it was the pain of walking across tiny stones that were sticking into his feet. That and the crunching sound that the gravel made as he walked across it. He tried to look around but found that he couldn't move his head. He looked straight ahead and realized he was walking up the driveway of his house toward the road.

Jack tried to stop himself but it was as if something was pulling his arms and legs along. He fought back against this strange force and found himself slowing slightly, but he couldn't stop the movement entirely. Jack was thankful to look up and see that their gates were locked—at least that would stop whatever was moving him from making him walk into the middle of the road.

The force that was moving him turned him and he found himself walking toward the hedge that ran around the edge of their property. Jack had a horrible feeling about what was going to happen. And he was especially annoyed because he was wearing his favorite Star Wars pajamas. Jack couldn't resist the movement and he found himself pushing his way through the hedge, the branches and leaves scraping at his skin and tearing his pajamas until they were in shreds.

Jack felt relieved once he emerged from the other side of the hedge. At least it couldn't get any worse. Step by step, foot by foot, he edged his way into the center of the road. He struggled to move his head to look both ways as he had been taught in the road safety lessons at his primary school, but something was holding his neck still. Once in the center of the road, Jack stopped dead.

"This is odd," said Jack, wondering if somehow someone had enchanted his pajamas[35] to put him under a spell. With

[35] There are several cases of enchanted pajamas in history, but the most important were those of Sleeping Beauty. Sleeping Beauty's enchanted pajamas meant that during her thousand-year coma she didn't need to eat or undertake any bodily functions. This is vital, as otherwise when Prince Charming showed up to kiss her, he probably would have smelled the room from outside and have gone home without even pulling back the veil.

It is worth noting that enchanted pajamas can't solve all problems created by magical comas, however. After she was woken from her slumber, Sleeping Beauty insisted that her engagement to Prince a great deal of effort Jack managed to rotate his neck slightly and look around. He kept expecting to see Mr. M, but the only odd thing he noticed were the electrical power lines above his head. There were hundreds of birds flying down out of the sky and landing on the cables.

"And now its getting odder."

A few of the birds saw Jack and flew down out of the sky. He would have jumped out of the way or flapped his hands at them, but the strange force was still holding him frozen in place. A dozen more birds flapped down and began roosting on him.

In the distance, Jack heard a motor revving. He strained his eyes to see into the night. At the far end of his road sat a large silver car. Its motor revved again and it moved forward an inch. Jack gulped and waited since there was nothing else he could do. The car began moving, accelerating, barreling down the road toward Jack. It was still a distance off, but moving so quickly that he knew he had little time to get out of the way. He strained his muscles and found that with a great deal of effort he could move slightly, but not fast enough to escape the car's path.

The car had covered half the distance and was getting faster. He had only seconds before it crashed into him, and that would be the end of that. As the car neared, Jack was shocked to realize that there was no one driving it. Both the

---

Charming last for two decades. The reason for such a long delay is simple: She didn't want to get married while she still had blanket creases on her face.

front seats were empty. And yet it clearly knew exactly what it was doing.

Jack waited for his life to flash before his eyes. However, it stubbornly refused to do so. "Great," Jack muttered to himself. "I'm going to die and the special effects aren't even working."

Jack was thinking as hard as he could, yet he couldn't come up with an idea to save himself. This was one time The Speed clearly wouldn't help. After all, he couldn't move, so at best The Speed would just enable him to stay still, very quickly indeed. In fact, the only thing Jack could think of was something incredibly unoriginal. Still, in the absence of a better idea, it was worth a try.

"HEEELLLLLLPPPP!!!!" Jack screamed in a rather high-pitched voice with the car inches away. . . .

Jack looked down as the car passed under him. He could hear the flapping of wings. His soul had clearly left his body, and now he was an angel flying above it. As he looked down he thought that the car must have done a really good job of squishing him, because his body was nowhere to be seen.

And then he realized he had avoided being squished entirely. His high-pitched scream had panicked the birds, which had landed on his arms and shoulders. The birds had flapped their wings, trying to take off, but his Star Wars pajamas had been so badly torn by the hedge that the birds' claws had become entangled in them. As they all flew upward at once, they had lifted Jack with them, saving his life by mere inches. He now hung, hovering, in the air as the birds strained to try and escape from the tangles of his pajama top.

The car screeched to a halt. Jack wondered how much longer the birds could keep him aloft. Maybe it was only a temporary reprieve, after all. Then he noticed from the corner of his eye a light going on in his house and his father leaning out of the window. Another light across the road went on, and the door of a house farther down the street opened. The silver car revved its engine twice and then drove off into the night.

The birds that were attached to Jack's pajamas began tiring of flapping their wings and slowly lowered him to the ground. Jack suddenly found that he could move his arms again and used them to release the birds from his pajamas one by one. As he let the last one go, Jack's father and mother walked out into the middle of the street.

"What are you doing out here?" his mother asked.

"Umm," Jack stammered, "I think I might have been sleepwalking."

"I heard a young girl scream and looked out the window . . . ," said Jack's father.

Jack frowned but didn't say anything.

" . . . but I couldn't see anything other than a silver car."

Jack considered saying that the reason his father might have missed him was because he had been flying in the air at the time. However, he rightly surmised that this may have led to other more difficult questions.

"Let's get you to bed before the whole neighborhood gets up," said Jack's mother as she led him back inside.

Jack's father put an arm on his shoulder. "We might need

to throw out those pajamas; they're beginning to look a bit ragged."

Jack fixed his father with a stare. "Dad, we're not throwing out these pajamas. Let me tell you something, they're most definitely my favorites."

MINISTRY OF S.U.IT.S HANDBOOK

SLEEPING
HIBERNATION

Many people have trouble sleeping, and so it must be annoying to them that other animals are not only capable of sleeping but can actually hibernate for three months at a time.

The animal most famous for hibernating is the bear, which, when it gets too cold outside, goes into a hibernation state, sleeping until the summer returns. It is interesting to note that biologists generally claim that the bear is extinct in Ireland. However, another school of thought claims that bears still do exist in Ireland; it's just that it hasn't been warm enough for them to get out of bed lately.

12

DAVID BULKS UP

Even though Jack was still tired the next morning, he was up before his alarm rang because he wanted to get to school and tell Trudy what had happened to him. He ran downstairs to find his father pouring out a bowl of Mr. M's Marvelous Muesli.

"Umm, Dad, as delicious as that looks I was wondering if I could get a bacon sandwich instead. You know, on account of me being scared last night when I was sleepwalking."

Jack's father frowned. "This is health food, Jack; it's good for you."

"I know it's good for me," agreed Jack. "That's why it tastes so awful."

Jack's mother walked into the kitchen and ruffled his hair. "He's young; let him have a bacon sandwich."

"Can I also have a bacon sandwich?" asked Jack's father.

Jack's mother smiled at her husband. "You aren't young. So, no."

"There's something very unfair about all of this," grumbled Jack's father as he put a couple of rashers under the grill.[36]

––––––––––––

Jack couldn't help noticing something slightly strange when he sat down next to his friend David on the schoolbus. David was munching on yet another muesli snack that resembled a bar of sawdust. However, Jack was rather more distracted by the fact that David had to stop eating several times to brush the crumbs out of his beard. Jack was pretty certain that David hadn't had a beard yesterday.

Jack strongly suspected that it was a false beard, not only because of the difference in color from David's normal hair, but also because although occasionally some of their classmates went through growth spurts, there was generally a limit to how much facial hair one could grow overnight.

"Have you suddenly gone through some kind of growth spurt?"

"Don't be ridiculous," said David. "It's a false beard. I've stuck it on with extra-strong spirit gum. It's what actors use—means it doesn't come off even if you sweat a lot under film studio lights."

"That spirit gum must be sticky stuff," observed Jack.

[36] It should be noted that Jack's father's mustache thought it was even *more* unfair. The mustache didn't get a bacon sandwich either, and it was younger than Jack's father by about twenty-one years.

"You aren't kidding," agreed David as he held up his hands, which were covered in strands of black beard. "I probably should have been more careful when I was applying it."

Jack felt that the conversation was rather dancing around the point that he was trying to get to, and so he asked a direct question. "Why have you stuck an enormous black beard to your face?"

David raised a quizzical eyebrow. "I told you yesterday— they're holding auditions for extras in that fantasy film."

"I'm still not entirely clear what the beard's about," observed Jack.

"Have you ever seen a fantasy film? Most of the cast have beards. I assume because they used all their metal making armor and swords and shields and then didn't have enough left over for razors. I thought bringing along my own beard might give me an edge during the auditions."

"When are the auditions?"

"First thing this morning. Will you and Trudy come along and support me? Apparently, they're going to have lots of cool effects and things. There's going to be an animatronic giant and a dragon as well."

"Of course we'll come!" Jack suspected there was more to these auditions than David realized.

David crunched some more on his sawdust bar.

"Are you actually enjoying eating that?" Jack asked.

Little bits of the dry and dusty bar fell out of the corners of David's mouth as he munched. "Not so much, but at the end of school yesterday they were giving them out to everyone who signed up for the auditions. They said we'd only be selected if we ate healthily and kept our strength up so we all look like warriors." David thrust the bar under Jack's nose.

Jack poked the bar with an experimental finger—he knew there was something very wrong with it, he just wasn't sure what. Bits of the snack crumbled into dust and fell to the ground.

David nodded. "That's the problem with these kinds of snack bars. They tend to be dry and crunchy. Without toffee and nougat, they don't have a great deal of structural integrity. Which means the carpet[37] in the school is definitely becoming a lot more crunchy than it was previously." David took another bite of the snack. "It doesn't taste too bad."

"Snacks aren't supposed to taste 'not bad,'" complained Jack. "They're supposed to taste fantastic. If all snacks do is taste 'not too bad,' then why wouldn't we just wait until mealtimes instead of spoiling our appetites?"

⸻

Once at school Jack found Trudy waiting for him in the foyer.

David looked at his watch. "All right, I'm going to go and line up for my audition. They're starting at nine o'clock. You guys make sure you're there to see me." He wandered off toward the assembly hall.

[37] Not many schools have carpet in the corridors and classrooms precisely for the reasons that David and Jack are now discussing. However, Jack and David's school had had carpet installed because of pirates. If this doesn't make sense to you, I'd suggest reading the first book— partially because I don't have enough space here to explain fully, but mainly because I get royalties for every book sold.

Before Jack could explain to Trudy that they were going to have to watch David trying to act, she thrust a health bar under his nose. "Have you seen these?"

"Yeah, David was just eating one."

Trudy shoved the wrapper of the bar right into Jack's face so he couldn't help focusing on the brand name. It read *Mr. M's Marvelous Munchies*. Jack's jaw dropped.

"Ughh ughh guhh," Jack said. Then he realized that it was very difficult to speak coherently with a dropped jaw. He pulled his jaw back up and tried again. "Of course! That makes perfect sense. My parents tried to feed me Mr. M's Veggie Burgers last night and his cereal this morning. And if Mr. M's involved in the film, he'd want to persuade the kids at the school to eat his food too."

"Exactly," said Trudy as an enormous grin split her face.

Jack frowned. "Um, Trudy, you do realize that Mr. M might be trying to poison the entire country—including our school?"

"Isn't it great?"

Jack suspected that Trudy's and his definitions of what was "great" might substantially differ. "What's great about it?"

"Think! If Mr. M's trying to poison the entire school, then we're definitely onto something. And if we're onto something, then we're closer to finding my mother."

If it had been anyone else, Jack might have pointed out that the value of rescuing one person might be slightly outweighed if the entire school had to be poisoned, but he knew how much Trudy was missing her mother. He also knew how good Trudy was at punching. A thought struck Jack. "Wait a minute, David's been eating some of these things. He might be . . ."

Trudy shook her head. "Realistically, it isn't as simple as the snacks being poisoned. Look around you." Jack did. Other children were walking up and down the corridors, some of them merrily chewing on Mr. M's nutritious bars. None of them seemed to be jumping up and down, breaking out in strange skin conditions, or frothing at the mouth.[38]

"Okay, but I still think we should go and stop David from eating any more snacks."

"You can explain to him later," said Trudy. "I want to go back to the model farm and see what's going on there."

"But didn't I just blow that place up?"

"The red barn and the grain silo are still standing. I think there's something about them that we're missing." Trudy grabbed Jack by the sleeve and hauled him toward the playing fields.

Jack dug his feet into the ground, thus managing to slow Trudy slightly and annoy her immensely. "What are you doing?"

"We can go to the red barn later; I promised David we'd go and watch him audition." Jack explained to Trudy about David's sudden interest in becoming a film star.

Trudy grimaced. "Do we have to? We're trying to find my mum—don't you think that's more important?"

Jack sighed. "But think, Trudy—Mr. M said he was involved in making the film."

---

[38] Or at least they didn't seem to be doing any of these things any more than they normally did.

"Do you think he might be at the auditions?" asked Trudy.

"I doubt he'd be that foolhardy—but there might be some other clues."

As they walked toward the assembly hall, Jack did his best to explain to Trudy what had happened to him last night. Trudy listened carefully before she spoke. "Do you think Mr. M was controlling you by using the food?"

"I wondered about that—but you can't control people's minds with food. It doesn't make a lot of sense."

"What about the birds then? Were they part of Mr. M's plan?"

"I think they definitely have something to do with it. Why were they sitting on the power lines? And then why did they fly to me? If we can figure that out, I think we'll have solved a large part of the problem."

"And the driverless car?"

Jack shrugged. "Might well have just been a driverless car. Lots of people seem to be making those these days."

"Well, at least you got away safely."

"You say that, but my favorite pajamas were ruined. Mum says she'll try to wash them and then see if she can sew them back together—but I suspect that by the time they go through the spin cycle there'll be more holes than pajamas—so I'd look pretty silly wearing them."

Just as they were speaking of looking silly because of the clothes one wore, Jack and Trudy were coincidentally passing Static's concession stand, where he was still doing a booming trade in selling his superhero merchandise.

"He seems to be doing rather well."

Trudy tutted noisily. "Apparently he's been going around telling everyone he saved Edwyn's life."

"Well he did . . . kind of," said Jack.

Trudy ground her teeth. "We've saved Northern Ireland twice this month and no one's buying any of our merchandise."

Jack considered pointing out that part of the reason for this was that they hadn't actually designed any merchandise yet. Possibly because they were spending too much of their time saving Northern Ireland.

MINISTRY OF S.U.I.T.S HANDBOOK

WASHING MACHINES
PRIOR TO THEIR INVENTION

A long time before washing machines were invented, people had to use different ways to clean their clothes. As with all great inventions they tried all sorts of experiments before they came across a method that worked. They tried shouting at the clothes, dragging them along the ground, and even throwing them into the air. Naturally, none of these approaches worked.

Eventually, one individual suggested that they try beating the clothes against rocks in the river. Stone Age people were astonished to find that this approach worked. (Basically Stone Age washing machines were just large rocks. On the downside, they were quite labor-intensive to operate, but on the upside they did come with very long warranties.)

One of the Stone Age people then suggested that since that had worked so well for washing clothes, maybe they should also try washing their faces that way. This second experiment took slightly longer, largely because they had to wait until the Stone Age man who tried it recovered from his severe concussion before he chiseled up his report.

What we can learn from this story is that it is vitally important to remember that different cleaning methods should be used for different objects. It can also help us understand the difference between a mistake and a disaster. If you accidentally put some clothes into the dishwasher, this can be considered a mistake. If, however, you put some dishes into the washing machine, this is almost certainly a disaster.

13

AUDITION

The assembly hall was packed with children who all wanted to audition for a part in the upcoming fantasy film. Jack tried standing on his tiptoes to see over the sea of faces and spot where David was.

Trudy was less interested in the children and instead was scanning the adults who were trying to get them to stand in neat lines. "There seem to be a lot of people working on this film. Are any of them Mr. M?"

Jack looked around the room. There were half a dozen adults dressed all in black and carrying clipboards. None of them had the distinctive shaggy white hair and beard that Mr. M possessed. "Sorry, Trudy. No luck."

Trudy sighed. "It looks like they're really planning on making a film. They've even got animatronics." Trudy pointed to a series of robotic goblin warriors that stood in one corner. A special-effects woman was pressing buttons on a control panel that made the goblins bang their swords against their shields.

David was standing with a group of other children who were looking at a table covered in props for use in the film. There were armor, face masks, and a range of weapons. Jack tugged urgently on Trudy's sleeve. "Look at David. He's playing with a weapon. This is going to end badly."

Trudy snorted at Jack. "Don't be ridiculous—those are all rubber weapons. Even David can't cause chaos with those." Jack had a feeling that Trudy was underestimating just quite how clumsy David was.

David had picked up a rubber flail—a long pole with a spiked ball attached to its end. He idly began whirling it around his head. For a second it almost appeared as if he was coordinated. Despite the fact that he was surrounded by dozens of other children, he managed to miss all of them. But then, rather predictably, the flail slipped out of his hand and smacked into the head of one of the media executives who was standing across the table. The man stumbled backward, then forward before finally collapsing on the props table.

The table immediately seesawed upward, launching dozens of rubber weapons into the air. In line with the law of gravity, they arched and then began falling down on the children below them, cracking them on their heads and shoulders. David looked sheepish and began walking away, whistling innocently. The other children started scrambling, trying to get out of the way of the falling weapons, and crashed into each other. The room was so packed it was like having a human domino rally made out of children.[39] Suddenly people were swarming back and forth and running into each other.

"Do you think we should help?" Jack asked.

"What would we do? You can't fight a stampede,"[40] Trudy said. "Anyway, at least David has the sense to move away from the props table. It can't get any worse now."

They watched as David moved away from the chaos he had caused. He looked around trying to find somewhere he could sit down and stay out of trouble. Although David's motivation was good, his execution was relatively poor as he sat on the control panel for the animatronic warrior goblins.

The minute that David plopped himself down on the control panel, the robot goblins began moving round the room, waving their swords and brandishing their shields. Children were running, ducking, and crashing into one another trying to avoid the deadly animatronics. It was

[39] Before anyone else tries it: The government won't let you try to create a domino rally out of actual children. I learned that the hard way. What really annoys me was that I was pretty sure I had enough children-dominos lined up to get me into the Guinness Book of World Records.

[40] *Stampede* is a strange word that can almost be regarded as magical—because it's almost impossible to say it at the wrong time. If you notice a stampede and shout out to warn people, then you said it at the right time. However, even when there isn't actually a stampede, if you shout out "STAMPEDE!" you tend to cause one to happen—so it turns out you were right anyway.

hard to tell which was louder, the shouting and screaming or the thundering sounds of feet as people desperately ran to safety.

"Maybe we should help now?" Jack suggested.

"I think the way we can help best is by getting David out of this place before he somehow causes the entire hall to collapse."

Luckily David had already reached the conclusion that he probably wasn't welcome at the audition anymore and was marching rapidly toward the exit. One of the media executives was following and caught up with David just as he reached Trudy and Jack.

"What on earth were you doing, young man? You see the chaos you've caused?"

"I might have sat on the control panel thing by accident," David admitted.

The media executive shook her head. "But that's insane—it takes months of training to operate that thing. How did you manage to turn the robots on just by sitting on it?"

"It might be that he just has a very talented bottom," observed Jack.

"I always suspected it was special," said David. "But it's nice to have it officially confirmed."

The media executive lifted a clipboard. "Well, we don't need that kind of chaos around here. You won't be getting called back to any more auditions. Now what is your name?"

"David Sacher."

The woman looked down at her clipboard and found David's name. Then she frowned. "Actually, maybe you have talent after all. We'll want you to come back to further auditions."

The woman gave David a sheet of paper telling him when he was to audition next.

"That was odd," Jack observed. "I mean, why would they want you back . . . don't you think that's odd?"

David waved the piece of paper in front of Jack's face. "Clearly they recognize talent. Some of us just have a special something."

"You certainly have something special, David." Trudy looked past David and into the hall. The media executives had finally managed to switch off the animatronic goblins and stop the children from stampeding. Someone had found a first aid kit and minor injuries were being treated. "How do you manage to cause that kind of carnage and yet come out without even a scratch on you?'

"It's strange for sure," David admitted. "But generally it's what happens. I put it down to the fact that I know how much of a disaster I am, so when something like this happens I have the good sense to stay out of my own way."

"David, we're going to go and look at the red barn. You go straight to class, all right? And try not to start any further battles."

David turned and walked down the corridor. "I'm not making any promises."

STAMPEDES
Causes

Although stampedes are frequently associated with cattle, almost any animal, including a human, can stampede.

Of course, the danger of stampedes varies enormously from animal to animal. If a herd of cows are stampeding toward you, it's best to get out of the way. If a swarm of mice is approaching you, you're probably safe enough standing your ground (although it is advisable to empty your pockets of any cheese that you are carrying). If you ever find yourself stampeded by tortoises, it's probably best to get out of the way, as they can give you a nasty nip—but at the same time, you don't exactly have to hurry—you probably have time to read to the end of the chapter.

Humans stampede for various reasons, but generally the most common cause is a 50 percent off plasma screen television sale two weeks before Christmas.

14

GRAIN SILO

"Do we really have to do this?" Jack asked as Trudy remorselessly dragged him by the sleeve across the playing fields toward the smoldering farm, red barn, and grain silo.

"Mr. M tried to kill you here. That makes me suspect that there's something he was hiding."

"I'm really not sure I want to go back there. That plant nearly killed me last time."

"It only *almost* killed you," Trudy said.

"Well, yes," agreed Jack, "but what if it's been practicing between now and then?" Trudy ignored him and Jack was compelled to follow his sleeve.

What had been the school model farm had been almost completely decimated by the explosion and subsequent fire. Trudy was walking through the cinders, occasionally kicking at something that caught her eye.

The large grain silo and red barn remained almost completely undamaged. Jack walked over to the grain silo, which looked like a cider jug that had been turned upside down. "What exactly is this?"

"It's a grain container. I've got an uncle with a farm and he has them."

"Well, what's it for?" Jack asked.

Trudy stared at Jack. "Containing grain," she paused. "The clue's kind of in the name."

"Well, sorry," said Jack. "I'm afraid I'm not very familiar with agricultural life. But why do you think they've set it up here?"

"I think they're going to manufacture even more of Mr. M's health-food bars. That's what the grain's for. There were commercials for them on TV last night. They're trying to get the entire country eating them."

Jack scratched his head and wandered around the huge structure. It was an enormous container supported by three thick metal legs. The main body was twenty feet up in the air.

Trudy stood back and looked at it. By the way Trudy was looking at the legs of the container, Jack knew she was sizing it up for climbing. She looked at it in the same way mountaineers look at Everest.

Jack wandered under the structure itself and stood in the middle looking straight up. Right above his head was a large nozzle that he assumed could be opened to allow the contents to pour out.

"There must be enough inside that to make thousands of

health-food bars," he said quietly to himself. "I wouldn't like to be standing here when . . ."

There was a click and the nozzle opened, spraying out tons of corn kernels. He heard Trudy shout at him seconds before he was buried. Trudy threw herself on the ground and began digging furiously into the fifteen-foot-high pile.

Jack's head popped up out of the center of the pile. "What are you doing?"

Trudy fell back, shocked. "I thought you were crushed! Dead!"

Jack smiled and disappeared back under the corn for a minute. Then suddenly he exploded out like a dolphin leaping out of water. "Not dead, no." He disappeared back under the sea of corn kernels. Two seconds later he appeared out of the corn right beside where Trudy was.

"You should have been crushed!"

"Thankfully not." Jack stepped out of the pile entirely and began clearing some of the corn kernels out of his hair and pockets. "I imagine it was another attempt to kill me, but it was never going to work."

"But there must have been tons . . ."

Jack nodded. "It would almost certainly have killed an adult, but I'm still a kid. And up until a few years ago my favorite part of the adventure playground was the ball pool. When the corn fell on me it was like being in the world's biggest ball pool. The key is to move with the balls and not against them." Jack dived back into the corn and frolicked about. "This is a lot of fun. Reminds me of being an eight-year-old again. I practically had a black belt in ball pools."

Trudy was staring into the distance.

"Are you even paying attention to me?" Jack asked.

"I think we're about to have some problems." Trudy pointed to an enormous black cloud that was moving toward them.

Jack squinted into the distance. "Wait a minute, that's not a cloud . . . those are . . ."

"Birds." Trudy took a step backward. "They must have come off the electricity pylons when they saw the corn."

Jack and Trudy half scrambled and half ran away from the huge pile of corn that was being descended on by the cloud of birds. A few chased after Jack and pecked at him, trying to get the last few kernels out of his hair. He tried to shoo them away and after a few moments they left.

The strange white-and-black bird with the red splotch on its head that Jack had seen on Monday was amongst them. It flew right up to Trudy and dropped a small piece of branch it had been carrying in its beak. The bird started hammering at the twig with its beak. It seemed to be trying to tell them something.

"What do you think it's doing?" asked Jack.

Jack and Trudy looked at each other and smiled—they both had the same thought. "Morse code!"

They stood silently as the bird hammered and hammered at the wood. After a while they cocked their ears sideways so they could listen more closely. And then finally they looked at each other again.

"I don't know any Morse code," Trudy admitted.

"Yeah, I know SOS—but . . . that's about it, really."

"But this could be a clue!"

"Possibly, but seeing as we don't know any Morse code we aren't going to be able to figure it out. I'll look up Morse code on the Internet tonight and then hopefully our bird friend here will come back tomorrow."

"Okay," said Trudy with a sigh. "Let's try looking inside the barn."

Jack and Trudy walked away, leaving a very frustrated-looking bird behind them.

MINISTRY OF S.U.IT.S HANDBOOK

MOUNTAINEERS
"BECAUSE IT'S THERE"

People often ask mountaineers why they go to all the trouble of climbing mountains. The answer that is often given is "Because they're there." When this answer is heard, people often assume that it is a deep and meaningful thing to say.

It isn't. It really, really isn't. And it is important to remember that in almost every other area of life it will not be considered a wise answer:

> *"Why did you steal that gold?"*
> *"Because it was there."*
> *"Why did you drink that poison?"*
> *"Because it was there."*
> *"Why did you throw a tomato at that politician?"*
> *"Because he was there."*

From the above examples we can see that the answer "Because it was there" only works one out of three times.

Interestingly enough, a much better answer to the question of why you climbed a mountain is as follows:

> *"Because I had this flag and wasn't really sure what to do with it. And the moon seems an awfully long way away."*

15

THE RED BARN

Jack suddenly had a thought. "Mr. M said that he'd been working with Blackbeard and the queen of Atlantis. And both their plans involved digging."

Trudy realized what Jack was saying. "The barn's right over where the queen of Atlantis was drilling the huge hole to sink Northern Ireland. Do you think . . . ?"

Jack nodded. "Exactly. I think Mr. M was helping them dig not because he cared about what they were doing. He was looking for something that was buried underground— some kind of stone. And maybe that barn is just there to hide where the hole still is."

Trudy walked over to the door of the red barn and tried to pull it open. "There's no way we're getting through this. It's solid metal." She rattled the padlock on the door in frustration.

"We don't have to go through the door," Jack observed. "The ground's kind of muddy and soft." Jack dropped to his knees and started scrabbling in the mud under the door. He noticed Trudy wasn't helping him. "Aren't you going to join in?"

Trudy wrinkled her nose. "I don't want to get dirty."

Jack carried on digging and muttered to himself. "Oh, fine, I don't want to come here because I was almost murdered, but apparently if you don't want to get dirty you don't have to help. . . ."

The ground was soft and it took Jack only fifteen minutes to make a small trench. There was enough space between the bottom of the door and the ground for them both to squeeze under and into the darkness of the barn inside. Jack took enormous solace in the fact that this process meant that Trudy had to get dirty anyway.

It was pitch black inside the barn. Jack stood up and felt his way along the wall. A few moments of searching yielded the discovery of a switch that turned on the lights.

"Wow!" Trudy said. "I don't think I've ever seen this many health-food bars." One corner of the barn was absolutely filled with health-food bars, popcorn snack bags, and Mr. M's Ready Meals, all promising to help people increase their vitamin and iron levels.

Jack was looking in the other direction and was rather glad he had waited until they found the light switch before either of them had taken a step. In the center of the barn was an enormous hole—the hole the queen of Atlantis had drilled when trying to sink Northern Ireland, just as deep and possibly even wider than before.

Huge metal girders had been set across the top of the pit, creating a series of walkways across it. A long line reached from the top corner of the barn, ran down the wall, and then into the enormous hole. "That must be from the pylon outside."

"But what would you need electricity for halfway down a pit?" Trudy asked.

Jack edged his way closer to the pit and looked down. He had a horrible feeling what was coming next. Trudy walked up to him. "We're going to have to climb down."

Jack felt his heart fall through the bottom of his stomach. "Do we really have to?"

"Yes," said Trudy. "Maybe that electricity line is powering a light down there. It could be where Mr. M is holding my mother."

Jack looked over the edge of the pit and felt his stomach apologize and tell everyone it had been a lovely evening but it was feeling a bit sick now and therefore would have to leave the party early. It wasn't falling that Jack was afraid of; it was the horrific fact that gravity dictated that he would eventually reach the bottom.

"Come on, it's perfectly safe." Trudy had found a length of rope that had been lying against the wall of the barn and was tying it to one of the girders that crisscrossed the pit.

"Really? Perfectly safe? I'm not sure how you define perfectly safe. But if your definition of perfectly safe includes standing on the edge of a huge pit that has been dug by an enemy of ours, and who definitely wants us to die, then I'm going to suggest that we're going to need to get you extra English classes."

Trudy just stared at Jack. It was a stare that didn't require any explanation. He carefully took a teetering step onto one of the metal girders and began to wonder exactly how he would swing off it and clamber down the line.

Jack thought he couldn't be more scared. And then the door of the barn slowly scraped open and he realized that he had been wrong.

MINISTRY OF S.U.IT.S HANDBOOK

GRAVITY
RULES OF ATTRACTION

Everyone knows what gravity is, sort of. Of course, it's a lot more complicated than people think. The law of gravity basically states that two objects will attract each other. The closer the two objects are together the more they will be attracted. Which explains why boys are always falling in love with "the girl next door."

It also explains why long-distance relationships almost never work.

Interestingly, scientists consider gravity the weakest force in the universe.[41] And they are right—gravity is certainly a lot weaker than electromagnetism, for example. And both of them are certainly many hundreds of times weaker than love.

[41] People think that gravity's strong because it keeps us from flying off the planet. But the truth is that gravity on Earth only seems strong because the Earth is so big. It's like this. When you see an ant lift a leaf, you tend to think it's strong. But you wouldn't think the same about an elephant that lifted a leaf.

It's also good in many ways that objects have to be enormous before they exert a significant gravitational force. The Earth is huge and round, and we stick to the side of it. But if a football exhibited the same kind of effect, then it would be pretty much impossible to have a sensible game of football. . . .

16

MECHANICAL GIANTS

Jack was amazed at how easily the enormous barn door swung open until he saw what was behind it.

"Well, there's something you don't see every day," Jack observed.

Mr. M entered the barn and smiled. "Yes, do you like my robotic bodyguard?" A frighteningly realistic animatronic giant was standing behind Mr. M. It was thirty feet tall and was wearing what looked like fake animal skins. Its face was swollen and distorted and sported a false beard that was even more impressive than David's.

Jack looked at Mr. M. "Well, at least we know for sure that you're behind the supposed health foods and the fantasy movie—what's it called? *The Once-Forgotten King*?"

"Yeah," Trudy snarled. "Jack's got the whole thing figured out. You may as well give up now, M!"

Mr. M's face contorted in anger. "It's Mr. M. *Mister.* Titles are important. But if you know my whole plan, why don't you tell me, Jack?"

Jack briefly shot an annoyed glance at Trudy. "Well, clearly you've been creating health scares around the country. That's why so many children these days are allergic to things. And it's all to sell your branded health food. . . . And, um, to be honest that's as far as I've gotten."

Mr. M's face was calm again. "You really haven't figured out much, have you? Still, unlike other villains I refuse to discuss my plans. Therefore—quite enough talk—now I'm going to have my animatronic giant crush you into dust."

Mr. M took a small control device from his pocket and punched its screen rapidly. The giant began walking toward Jack and Trudy. Trudy took a step forward and bunched her fists. Jack pulled her back. "What are you doing, Jack? We can use The Speed to fight."

Jack nodded. "Which would be brilliant, but it's an animatronic giant that is probably made of metal and doesn't feel pain. So first we'd break our fists and then second—it'd stomp us into the ground."

"Do you have a better idea?"

Jack looked at Trudy, dumbfounded. "Well, if your idea involves being smashed into the floor, then yes, I have a better idea. Pretty much any idea would be better than that."

The giant was rapidly approaching them.

"I'm waiting."

Jack nodded. "That thing has size-fifty shoes and I bet it weighs a couple of tons."

"And?"

"I'm betting the girder walkways that crisscross this pit won't hold its weight."

Trudy smiled as she realized what Jack meant. "Great idea!"

Trudy darted across the girders nimbly until she was standing where two crossed the center of the pit. Jack achieved the same thing, except considerably more slowly, while realizing that maybe his idea hadn't been quite as brilliant for him as it had been for Trudy. As he inched toward Trudy his foot slipped and he nearly fell. Trudy dashed over and caught him by the sleeve.

The mechanical giant stopped at the edge of the pit, unable to walk any farther. Mr. M followed behind it. Jack was worried that he didn't look even vaguely frustrated.

"So, what are you going to do now?" sneered Trudy. "Are you brave enough to walk out here and fight us yourself?"

Mr. M shook his head. "Bravery is hugely overrated, my dear. I have no intention of walking out over the girders and absolutely no intention of fighting you. You see, I'm a genius, and geniuses never do their own fighting."

"But the giant can't get across the girders."

"Yes," admitted Mr. M. "But you can't escape, can you? You're trapped."

Jack smiled pleasantly at Mr. M. "Perhaps we could discuss this. I'm sure that no one needs to get hurt and we could work something out."

Trudy frowned at Jack. "You see, when you say things

like that, Jack, that's why people call you annoying. He's kidnapped my mother and you're still trying to negotiate."

"Well, if we die we're not going to be able to rescue her, are we?"

Mr. M spoke slowly. "You do realize that you're standing precariously over a bottomless pit,[42] don't you? Now are you going to surrender?"

Jack shook his head. "That doesn't even make any sense. How can you even dig a bottomless pit?"

It was Mr. M's turn to sigh. "Easily. You just dig halfway at a time."

Jack was trying to figure out if this would work when Mr. M raised the giant's control device and punched its screen. "It's fitting you should both die this way. It's very similar to how all my enemies will perish shortly."

The giant lifted one enormous foot and slammed it down on the ground. The girders started to shake. Jack and Trudy grabbed each other, trying to steady themselves. The giant slammed its foot again and again into the dirt. The girders

---

[42] It is interesting to note that bottomless pits are rather problematic things. The most important thing to remember is to have them aligned properly. A pit without a bottom will allow you to fall forever if it's vertical. However, if it's horizontal, it just means that there's a hole at both ends, and that isn't a bottomless pit—it's just a tunnel. However, evil villains do tend to use the phrase *bottomless pit* no matter how it's aligned, because telling someone that they were going to throw you into a *tunnel* isn't as scary.

trembled and shook. Jack and Trudy realized what was going to happen. "This isn't going to end well," Jack observed.

The giant's foot slammed into the ground once more and the girders jumped and bucked. Jack and Trudy fell off the girder and into the bottomless pit.

MINISTRY OF S.U.IT.S HANDBOOK

BOTTOMLESS PITS
SURVIVAL TECHNIQUES

It is incredibly hard to dig a bottomless pit, because it's difficult to tell when you're actually finished. By their very nature bottomless pits have to be infinitely deep. And obviously it's impossible to dig a hole that is infinitely deep. But the solution is simple. You just dig two holes that are only half an infinity deep and then join them up in the middle.

However, even though bottomless pits do exist, they aren't as scary as you might think. Because they're bottomless you won't actually ever hit the ground and so will just continue falling forever. Of course, some people worry that if you are falling forever you will eventually starve. The solution to this is to make sure that you have your mouth open as you fall. This way you will be kept fed by occasionally swallowing a fly during your descent.

It will also be fairly boring; therefore, if you're preparing for this fate, it's probably advisable to pack some kind of travel games compendium.[43]

[43] In point of fact, if you were falling down a bottomless pit, you could actually be falling for such a long time you'd be able to complete a proper game of Monopoly without anyone having to resort to cheating.

17

FALLING FOR YOU

Jack felt his stomach lurch upward as he fell from the girder. There was a high-pitched, screaming kind of noise, which Jack was slightly disturbed to find was coming from himself. Trudy was falling through the air beside him. Even as they tumbled through the black void she still made time to look at him disparagingly.

Jack stopped screaming. They were still falling, but they were no longer tumbling topsy-turvy. Jack had managed to right himself so that he was spread-eagled and facing what he assumed to be downward. They could see the walls of the tunnel on either side of them, but beneath them was just blackness. There seemed to be no bottom whatsoever in sight.

Jack started screaming again, more for something to do than out of any actual sense of fear. Trudy managed to maneuver herself as they fell, reached out, and punched Jack in the shoulder.

Jack stopped screaming. "Oww. Was that really necessary?"

"Was the screaming really necessary?" Trudy asked.

Jack shrugged.[44] "I just couldn't think of anything better to do."

They were silent for a few minutes before Trudy spoke again. "We're going to die when we hit the bottom, aren't we?"

"Hopefully, because otherwise we're going to be in a lot of pain." Jack paused. "Do you think we could use that trick the quartermaster taught you to survive?"[45]

"I don't think so. I think that even if we tried, this fall is far too long. We must have fallen thousands of feet by now."

Jack and Trudy were both silent as they fell for several minutes. There was still no sign of the bottom of the pit. "Do you think Mr. M was really telling the truth? Do you think this really is a bottomless pit?"

"I'm beginning to suspect it might be," Jack admitted. "But then we aren't actually going to die, are we?"

"Not from a fall," agreed Trudy. "But eventually we're going to starve to death."

---

[44] Which isn't as easy to do as you think it is when you're falling down an impossibly deep hole.

[45] During Jack and Trudy's first adventure together, Trudy had learned that although it wasn't possibly to survive a fall of ten thousand feet, it was possible to survive five thousand falls of two feet. Therefore, if you fall off something, it's vitally important that you try and divide your fall into a series of manageable chunks.

Jack frowned. It wasn't a pleasant prospect. "I hate gravity," said Jack. And then he realized something. "Trudy, grab my hand."

Trudy looked at Jack with disdain. "Jack, even if we are going to die I don't want to start holding hands. People would talk."

Jack ignored her and grabbed hold of her hand. "Right, now let's try to pull together. I want to try something that might save us. We'll need to hug."

Trudy sighed and gave in.

"All right, now I want you to concentrate on what I'm saying."

"I'm listening."

"Think about gravity. What do you know about it?"

"Well, it's when things are attracted to each other."

"Exactly," said Jack. "So, when the apple fell out of the tree onto Isaac Newton's head, what was it trying to do? What was its motivation?"

"I don't think apples actually have a motivation, Jack."

"Humor me!"

"I suppose it was trying to get to the ground."[46]

"That's my point. Exactly."

---

[46] Interestingly enough, some people believe that this was not the apple's motivation. Rather they believe that the apple gallantly gave its life in order to spark a scientific and cultural revolution that would change the world. Rather ironically, the people who believe this kind of thing normally have fairly severe thinking problems often after having something heavy fall on their heads.

"What?" Trudy was getting frustrated and she really didn't enjoy hugging.

"Think about it, Trudy—we're falling down a bottomless pit. Which means there is no ground below us—it's bottomless. And if there is no ground, then there's nothing for gravity to pull us toward. Which means . . ."

Trudy gasped as she realized what Jack meant. Jack and Trudy stopped falling and hung in the air. Trudy pushed Jack away from her and they hung motionless.

"This is amazing!"

Jack smiled. "Yes, I suspected that we were just falling out of habit more than anything else. This must really be a bottomless pit, which means that there's no ground. And if there's no ground, then gravity doesn't have anything to pull us toward."

Trudy grimaced. "What was all the hugging about, then?"

"I just wanted us to be holding on to each other so we stopped at the same time. If you hadn't realized what I was saying, you might have fallen farther than me and then we'd have gotten separated."

Trudy and Jack hung in the air for a while longer. Jack looked around him. "It's at times like this that I wish I'd brought a packed lunch with me."

"Well, what do we do next?" asked Trudy. "Gravity might not be affecting us, but we can't just hang here forever."

"Mmm, my planning hadn't quite gotten that far," Jack admitted.

"Idiot," Trudy sneered.

Jack felt slightly put out. After all, he had just come up

with a brilliant solution to their problem and felt that he deserved some credit. He was about to raise this point with Trudy when she started windmilling her arms.

"Umm, what are you doing?"

Trudy continued windmilling her arms and kicking her legs. "Swimming." Trudy's movements were slowly propelling her up the tunnel, as she pushed the air behind her. It wasn't as quick as swimming in water, but she was gradually picking up pace and momentum.

"Swimming without having to get your hair wet," Jack mumbled to himself. "What's not to like?"

It was clearly going to take them substantially more time to make their way back up the tunnel than it had falling down. Falling was a much more efficient form of travel compared to air-swimming.

"I'm . . . glad . . . we've . . . learned . . . this," Jack puffed as he kicked his feet. "It . . . means . . . that . . . we . . . can . . . survive . . . bottomless pits." [47]

As usual Trudy wasn't even breathing heavily, just scything through the air like an Olympic athlete. "I can't imagine it'll be a great deal of use to us. Remember, it only works with bottomless pits. Any pit with a bottom we'd just fall into and die." [48]

---

[47] Many people will tell you that swimming is excellent exercise and burns a lot of calories. Although personally I suspect that this isn't true; otherwise, why are whales so fat?

[48] Mr. M has just made a classic supervillain mistake. It's important that you don't try and overdo things. An ordinary pit with a bottom is

"Point . . . taken," Jack agreed.

Out of the corner of his eye Jack noticed that there was a hole in the wall. The electric cable from the barn above ran down the wall and disappeared into the hole. Rather than panting out any words, Jack pointed to it.

Trudy thought for a minute. "Do you think my mother might be in there?" she asked in a very small voice.

"Or it . . . might . . . be . . . a . . . clue," Jack said, although to be honest he didn't really care if it was a clue or not. He just wanted to sit down for five minutes and catch his breath. Jack and Trudy stopped swimming upward and moved horizontally toward the hole in the wall.

---

obviously a lot more effective than a bottomless one. If you absolutely have to do something more with a pit, just put some spikes at the bottom of it. This should be the first lesson that they teach at supervillain school.

Lesson two should be, if you are trying to take over the world—do it in manageable chunks. All at once is never going to work.

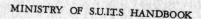

PERSONAL FITNESS
Advised Activities

Given the strains and stresses of working for the Ministry, it is a good idea for all operatives to undertake some level of fitness training. Road running can be a good sport to undertake but is not recommended for Ministry operatives in Iceland and Northern Ireland, where the risk of hypothermia is clearly too high.

Swimming is an alternative exercise you can undertake; however, Ministry agents in Australia are warned to be careful because there is a risk that you may be eaten by a shark or crocodile. Therefore, if you are swimming in Australia it is vital that you undertake some basic precautions. Like bringing along a friend, preferably one who looks tastier than you do.

18

GOING UNDERGROUND

The hole in the wall opened up into a large tunnel. Because the horizontal passageway had a floor, gravity reasserted itself and they both tumbled to the ground. It was difficult to see since they were only relying on the limited amount of light that was shining down from the red barn thousands of feet overhead. The wire from the pylon was pinned to the top of the tunnel, leading off into darkness. "I don't think we're going to find anything desperately interesting in here, given that we can't actually see anything," Jack said.

Trudy was squinting into the darkness. "I think someone was already here and figured out that problem." Trudy had found a wooden board on the wall that had several flashlights hanging off it. She took one, switched it on, and then handed it to Jack. "If there are flashlights then they clearly aren't using the wire from the pylon for light . . . but what would they need electricity for this deep underground?"

The passage was small and Jack and Trudy had to crouch as they moved along it. They waved their flashlights, but nothing seemed to be up ahead. As they went farther the passage seemed to get smaller and tighter, but Jack wasn't sure if that was just in his imagination.

With every step Jack expected to be attacked. In fact, it was more than that. He was sure that he was going to be attacked. It was just a matter of time. The suspense was killing him. He wondered what it would be that attacked him. He'd met giant moles underground before and didn't relish the prospect of having to battle one again. Especially since the last time they had, it couldn't really have been considered an unqualified victory.

Eventually the tunnel opened up into a large cavern. Jack stood up straight and brushed some of the dirt off his school uniform. Trudy was looking around the cavern, amazed at what she saw. Jack felt that she was right to be amazed. He wasn't sure what he had been expecting to see, but it certainly wasn't this.

The cavern they had walked into was the size of a church hall. All around the walls were suits of ancient armor. They were so old that many of them were little more than small pieces of rust held together by other small pieces of rust. One or two of them had clearly been well oiled before they had been left down here and were slightly more well preserved. However, that wasn't the really interesting thing. What was really unusual[49] was sitting in the center of the room. Unusual and yet very familiar at the same time.

There was a large boulder about the size of a sofa. It was brownish-black in color and although it clearly wasn't metal it seemed to glimmer. However, what made the stone especially unusual was that a sword was stuck right into the middle of it. The long metal cable from the pylon outside snaked down and was attached to the handle of the sword.

Jack had read enough stories about kings and queens to be able to have a good guess as to what he was looking at. He turned to Trudy. She seemed as amazed as he was.

"Are you thinking what I'm thinking?" Jack asked.

---

[49] *Unusual* is nothing more than a state of mind. Ironically, *unusual* is not that unusual a word to use. Out of the top 60,000 words, some people claim that in terms of usage it is number 2,048 on the list. Therefore, although the word *unusual* is the word *unusual*, it isn't *that* unusual. Different people use the word *unusual* with differing frequencies depending on how unusual their lives have been. Over the past three weeks, Jack initially found himself using the word *unusual* a lot more; however, the longer he worked for the Ministry, the less he used it. The Ministry operative Grey, after everything that he has seen, uses it very infrequently indeed, as for him the unusual has become the usual. The Minister in charge of the Ministry hardly ever uses the word *unusual* at all anymore. As far as anyone is aware, the evil interdimensional being Cthulhu, who runs the Ministry's filing system, has never been known to use the word *unusual* at all.

Trudy responded slowly. "Possibly. Are you thinking that's not just a sword in a stone. That's THE sword in THE stone?"

"Excalibur," said Jack as he nodded. "That means it's the sword that belonged to King Arthur."

When he was younger, Jack had loved hearing stories about King Arthur and his knights. How they had ridden around the country on massive white horses, hitting baddies with swords, helping the poor, and generally being good eggs. Although he couldn't remember the details about all the stories, there was one that shouldered its way to the forefront of his mind. Arthur had been made the king after he completed the feat of pulling the sword Excalibur out of a stone. And now here it was right in front of them.

"Why do you think they have the electrical line running into it?" Trudy asked.

Jack screwed his eyes up tight and then did one of those things that children are advised to never do without supervision of an adult (and probably not even then). He quickly touched the blade of the sword and then jumped back. "Nothing—it isn't electrified."

"Which means that the pylons maybe aren't carrying electricity, then? Or at least not all of the time."

Neither Jack nor Trudy moved. "Try and pull the sword out of the stone," Jack suggested to Trudy.

"Why me?" Trudy was irked and punched Jack in the shoulder.

Jack scowled at her. "Well, I think it should be you because I'm nursing a fairly serious shoulder injury here—I suspect you may just have bruised my rotator cuff.[50] But quite apart from that I'm the one who is supposed to do the weird thinking. You're the one who does the physical stuff."

Trudy shook her head. "You aren't getting me like that. If I pull that sword out of the stone, I might become queen."

Jack arched an eyebrow. He knew why he didn't want to pull the sword out of the stone and potentially become king, but wondered what Trudy's reasons were. "And that would be bad because . . . ?"

"Because queens have to be well behaved and shake people's hands and go on visits to countries whose names they can't pronounce. And they aren't allowed to fight, say bad words, or throw rocks."

Jack nodded. He'd been thinking along similar lines. "Yes, and they have to wear very heavy, silly hats."

"Let's take a closer look at it at least." Trudy clambered up onto the stone and Jack followed her.

The sword was truly beautiful. It was hard to tell exactly how big it was because the tip was buried deep into the stone, but Jack thought it was maybe two yards long. As they shone their flashlights on the blade it seemed to reflect different colors: purple, blue, dark green. It looked the way oil spilled on water did. The hilt[51] of the sword seemed unusually thick

---

[50] Jack had recently started looking up the component parts of the shoulder on the Internet in the evenings. That way he could describe to Trudy exactly where it hurt when she punched him.

[51] *Hilt* basically means handle of the sword. I'm only explaining this here because I've noticed increasingly in schools they aren't teaching

and broad, but that may have been because it was covered in pink-and-white mother-of-pearl. The pommel on the sword was made of a large, shiny emerald.

"This is the most beautiful sword I've ever seen," Jack said.

"Well, that's pretty impressive," said Trudy, "especially with your extensive experience of appraising swords."

"You know there is such a thing as being too sarcastic, Trudy." Jack pouted. "Anyway, if you're so smart, what now?"

"Well, I really, really don't want to be queen, so I say we just leave it."

Jack thought about this. "I don't think we can do that."

"Why not?"

"Mr. M pushed us down this pit expecting us to die. But he must have dug this pit looking for the sword. And there must be some reason that it's connected to the electricity pylons."

"So what?"

"Well, if Mr. M wants this sword, then I *don't* want him to have it."

Trudy thought about this. "But at the end of the day it's just a sword. A very pretty sword—but he must have hundreds of them if he's producing that new fantasy movie that David's auditioning for."

---

sword fighting. Personally, if you ask me it's health and safety gone mad. When I was at school we were always being taught sword fighting. It's something I reminisce about with my old school friends occasionally. It never did us any harm. And if you don't believe me you can ask them, good old "Lefty" McGraw, "Stumpy" Henderson, and "One-Eye" Lahey.

Jack contemplated the sword. "But this isn't just any sword. This is a sword that turns people into kings. And kings control people. So maybe this sword will give Mr. M some kind of magical powers that allow him to control people's minds. . . ." Jack realized something. "Maybe that's what happened to me the other night! And if he can do that we could never stop him."

"Okay, so we take the sword with us." Trudy folded her arms. "Now pull the sword out of the stone."

Jack was slightly miffed that he was going to have to be the one to try. He didn't want to be king. But on the other hand he also thought that he probably didn't want Trudy to be queen either. She'd become absolutely insufferable if he had to bow to her all the time and call her ma'am. "Right, get off the stone, then. Give me some space."

Trudy jumped down off the stone and Jack looked at the sword again. If he was going to be turned into a king, he needed to adopt a heroic stance. He put his feet shoulder-width apart. Then he decided to be even more heroic and placed them slightly farther apart. Then he decided that if he was going to be heroic, he may as well go whole hog and placed his feet as far apart as he could. At which stage he rather predictably[52] slipped and fell off the stone.

Trudy helped him up. "What were you doing?"

[52] Interestingly enough, this was only the second-most-predictable thing that would happen to Jack and Trudy in the underground chamber. You're probably already aware of what the most predictable thing is. And you're right, but it happens at the very end of this chapter.

"Sorry," Jack groaned. "Just trying to look as heroic as I could. I may have overdone it slightly." Jack scrambled back up on the stone. He approached the sword again and placed his feet a sensible distance apart. He looked at his hands and spat on them.

"Now what are you doing?"[53]

"Not sure," admitted Jack. "I've seen people doing this in movies before they try to perform feats of strength."

"And do you feel any stronger?" inquired Trudy.

"Not really, I . . . I just feel like I have spit on my hands." Jack decided he didn't want to get slobber all over the beautiful sword and so wiped his hands on his trousers. Then without further ado he gripped the sword and pulled with all of his might.

Rather unsurprisingly, nothing happened.

"Try harder," Trudy encouraged him.

"I can't," Jack said. "That was literally all of my might."

Trudy looked unimpressed. Following a very brief moment's hesitation she leapt up on top of the stone and shoved Jack off. "When I am queen I'm going to make your life miserable, you know that?"

Jack nodded silently. Trudy grabbed the handle and pulled, her biceps bulging. She pulled and pulled again. The sword didn't budge as much as an inch.

"HA!" laughed Jack. "That'll teach you! I knew it wasn't that easy. . . ."

Trudy glowered at him from her position on the stone.

[53] Which was only a very slight variation on her most recent sentence.

"You do realize that I don't need a sword or a crown to make your life miserable and filled with bruises."

Jack stopped laughing immediately and put on his serious face. "Point taken. Maybe you should give it another try? I mean, you are fairly awesome."

Trudy tried again but with no luck. For a moment Jack thought she might actually move it, but her hands, sweaty with the strain, slipped from the handle. She fell backward and crashed into Jack, sending them both tumbling to the floor.

Trudy sprang back to her feet, but Jack remained motionless. "Aren't you getting up?"

From his position on the floor Jack had noticed something on the ceiling. "There's a camera up there. Someone's watching us."

Trudy shrugged. "Let them watch. There's nothing they can do to stop us."

"Yeah, that's the thing—I rather suspect that the camera's there precisely so they can watch us and then do something to stop us."

"Like what?"

There was a slow, screeching, grinding sound. Jack and Trudy looked behind them. "We really should have been expecting this from the start."

LEGENDARY KNIGHTS
The Pink Knight

You will have heard stories of legendary knights and how they defeated all their foes in battle. However, few people have heard of the greatest of them all—the Pink Knight.

Generally speaking, as knights got older they got more experienced and therefore became more effective at fighting. However, the problem was that their suits of armor also got older and began to get more and more rusty. Their shoulder and knee joints began to seize up at bad moments, meaning that they could miss a crucial sword thrust or vital dodge during combat. Therefore, eventually even the most experienced knights died, thwarted by rusty and stiff armor.

Of course, after a knight died, the bards and troubadours would immediately begin writing songs about all the heroic deeds that they had done.

But there was one very clever knight who figured out how to deal with the problem of rusty armor. He realized that if he wanted to be the best knight ever he needed to ensure that his armor would be kept as good as new. From observing how metal decayed he realized that rusting occurred due to the effects of both air and water combined. Therefore, if he protected his armor from the air and rain with a coat of paint, it would remain good as new. After making this realization, he took an afternoon off jousting practice one day and painted his entire suit from top to toe in a particularly garish shade of pink.

As his armor never rusted, he was able to move more quickly than the other knights. Every year that went past allowed him to learn more about fighting techniques and so he quickly became the best knight in the land, vanquishing armies, saving maidens, and explaining to dragons that their services were not needed in this particular kingdom and requesting that they move on immediately.

You may ask why no one has ever heard of the Pink Knight, and the answer is simple. Although he was the bravest and best of knights, bards refused to write songs about people in the Middle Ages until *after they were dead.* This was partly because they didn't want to give a knight a swollen head, but also because the laws surrounding "image" and merchandising rights in the Middle Ages were very tough——and bards didn't want to have to pay royalties and image licensing fees to the people they were writing about.

In the end, the Pink Knight got so good at fighting that even when he came back to the castle after a battle there wasn't so much as a scratch on him. This made the other knights in the castle suspicious and they began to believe that the Pink Knight was just making up stories and wasn't really fighting people at all.

Interestingly enough, this is not only the reason why you have never heard of the Pink Knight but also why people began to consider pink to one of the less "manly" colors. Anyone who knows the true story of the Pink Knight knows that it is the bravest color of all.

19

THE UNEXPECTED EXPECTED

The suits of armor that were standing around the walls had started shuffling, their metal joints making creaking and squeaking noises as they did so. Trudy jumped down from the boulder and stood beside Jack. "Any thoughts on what's going to happen next?" she asked.

"Currently I'm just hoping that they're friendly," said Jack, showing that sometimes optimism could triumph over experience.

"Well, there's a first time for everything, I suppose."[54]

---

[54] Trudy is right about this. There is a first time for everything. Interestingly sometimes there is more than one first time. For example, there's the first time you do something for the second time, which makes it the first time for that. But to be honest, that's too confusing to think about.

"Of course, we could always run away preemptively."

Trudy scanned the approaching suits of armor. "Okay— let's try that; I suspect we weren't going to get the sword out of the stone anyway."

Jack and Trudy started heading for the tunnel out of the room, but one of the suits of armor quickly blocked it.

"Is there another exit?"

Jack looked around the room. "I don't think so. We're trapped."

Trudy took up a fighting stance. "Well, I'm not going down without a fight. Time for The Speed."

Jack sighed. He had only been in the Ministry for two weeks and was still very far away from mastering The Speed. He could think of sad thoughts and was even able to move impossibly fast. The problem was, even when he moved fast he wasn't as nimble or agile as Trudy was. So being able to move fast frequently meant that he just lost fights in a shorter period of time than it would have taken otherwise.

Nonetheless, he didn't really have any other options. And so Jack thought of a sad thought. He remembered a childhood holiday in Portrush on the North Coast of Ireland. He'd always loved it there with the amusement arcades[55] and the

---

[55] People often complain about the types of machines they have in sea-side amusement arcades. Especially the machines that have claws in them to try and pick up teddy bears. The complaints are largely because the claws never actually pick up the teddy bears but merely *stroke* them. People say that this is unfair and that you never win a teddy bear. Of course, the mistake they are making is thinking the machines

beautiful views over the sea. But most of all he'd loved the ice cream on hot summer days. He remembered one time he had persuaded his parents to buy him a three-scoop raspberry ice cream with Belgian chocolate chunks and mini marshmallows. He had wanted one for ages, but his parents had always said it was too much and would make him sick. Finally, they had agreed and he had taken his ice cream outside to eat it. At the last minute, his arm had been jogged by a passerby and both his ice cream and his culinary daydreams had fallen to the ground. Even now, remembering it made him want to cry.

Jack looked up. "What on earth are you doing?" shouted Trudy. She was surrounded by the suits of armor, which were clumsily swinging at her with their metal fists. She ducked down and grabbed the foot of one of the suits and pulled it off. There was nothing inside the suit—no flesh, no foot, no mechanical innards—nothing but pure air. Trudy threw the empty boot at another suit. There was a loud *clang* as the empty helmet came off the second suit, but it didn't stop moving. Instead it punched out at Trudy, catching her on the back and sending her sprawling to the ground.

"Sorry!" yelped Jack. "I got a bit too involved with my sad thought." Jack made a mental note to try and only think of short sad thoughts in the future.

---

are actually supposed to allow you to win teddy bears. These machines are in fact "virtual reality" machines that accurately replicate the experience a pirate has when stroking a cat or other fluffy mammal. These machines are almost always to be found in seaside resorts— obviously because this is where most pirates used to live.

Jack ran into action, ducking under a punch that one of the suits of armor aimed at his head. He grabbed Trudy by the arm and hauled her up, pulling both of them away toward safety. The suits of armor started jangling and clanking toward them.

"Okay, well, at least you've knocked one of their heads off."

"Yes, but that's the problem. Even when I pull them apart they seem to come back together again."

"Well, maybe we should try harder," suggested Jack.

"We? We? I didn't notice you trying *at all* so far." Before Jack could respond, Trudy had rushed back toward the metal shells and was swinging her fists at them. Their iron gauntlets lashed out at her, but she nimbly dodged under and jumped over them. She kicked one so hard in its rusty chest that it rang out like a gong before shuddering, falling apart, and crashing to the ground.

As usual Jack did his slightly inept best. He ran at one of the suits of armor at full speed and jumped into it, curling himself up like a cannonball. When Jack hit the rusty breastplate it cracked and split neatly into two pieces. Before he could move again one of the suits had grabbed his wrist with a viselike grip. "Not good," Jack muttered. He levered himself up and pressed his feet against the chest of the armor. He pushed with all his might and felt the grip weakening very slightly. A second later he found himself falling away. The gauntlet was still stuck to his wrist, but it had become detached from the suit. Jack banged it against the ground until it let go and then scrambled backward toward the wall of the cavern.

Trudy, meanwhile, was doing much better. Instead of

lashing out indeterminately, she was striking carefully. As each suit of armor came toward her she would circle it for a moment, making her decision, then with lightning speed and pinpoint accuracy she would strike out. Her fist or foot would crash against the knee or elbow of each suit, and half an arm or leg would drop off. While this wouldn't stop the armor entirely, it did render the suits either less dangerous or less maneuverable. "Go for the joints!" Trudy yelled. "We can't hurt metal, and there's nothing inside the suits to defeat, but we can break the armor into smaller parts."

Jack stood up again and rushed to Trudy's side, determined to play his part. They lashed, whirled, and struck at the armor together, Trudy's tactics proving to be quite effective. Soon there were only two complete suits left and they stood stock-still, guarding the exit from the chamber.

"That was a lot easier than I thought it would be," Jack said, sweat pouring down his brow.

Trudy turned to him. "I can't believe you. You know what happens when you say things like that!"

Jack gulped and realized what he'd done. Anytime you said something seemed to be too easy, it always ended up being a lot harder than you could possibly have imagined. Very predictably, the individual pieces of armor started rocking back and forth. Gradually they started moving toward one another. "Not this!" shouted Trudy.

The armor didn't pay her any attention. Slowly but surely the pieces of armor were coming back together and joining themselves up again. Jack gulped. The reconstituted suits of armor started moving toward them. Jack looked down at his fists—they were already bruised and battered from breaking the armor apart the first time. He found himself wondering what was powering the armor; they clearly weren't robots—they weren't clockwork or mechanical—they just seemed to move as if by magic. . . . Maybe Mr. M was a wizard. . . .

Jack was shaken out of his thoughts by seeing Trudy adopting her familiar fighting stance. He was pretty sure that he didn't have the strength to do battle all over again. Even Trudy couldn't keep fighting forever.

"I don't care about myself," said Trudy. "I just wanted to rescue my mother—and now we're probably going to get killed by empty suits of armor. . . ."

The suits had surrounded Jack and Trudy and were slowly forcing them back toward the wall. It would all be over soon and they would have failed. Jack shook his head in annoyance. It looked like he was going to be captured. Normally he didn't get captured until Thursday or Friday at least. This was Tuesday; he was clearly getting worse and worse at being a Ministry agent. Who said practice makes perfect?[56]

Trudy, on the other hand, wasn't used to getting captured. She seemed to be taking it much harder than he was.

---

[56] It is worthwhile noting that this statement is not very wise. In some cases, practice by itself will not make perfect. A better quotation about the importance of practice comes from Steve Langston, the world's greatest tightrope walker. "Practice makes perfect, but it's important to remember the safety net as well. Otherwise practice just makes flatter."

"I can't believe this, Jack. If we get captured like my mother, then we're . . . we're completely hopeless and lost."

Jack's eyes widened. Trudy had given him an idea. But did they have enough time? Their backs were against the wall. He grabbed Trudy by the shoulders and turned her to look directly into his eyes. "Say that again!"

"What? We're completely hopeless and lost?"

"Just the second part."

"We're lost!"

Jack nodded vigorously. "That's it: Say it again and believe it! *Really believe it.*"

Trudy's brow furrowed. "I do believe it. We're lost. We're lost. . . ."

Jack joined in. As they both agreed they were lost, a dozen grasping metal hands reached out for them. . . .

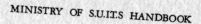

ICE CREAM
WHY ICE CREAM EXPLAINS VIKINGS RAIDING DIFFERENT COUNTRIES

Many people are aware of the Vikings and how they used cows as mobile pantries for their attacks on other countries. What most people don't realize is cows are also the reason that the Vikings behaved so differently from other invading hordes. Generally, when people invaded or explored they sent out armies who were looking for somewhere new to live and settle.

The invaders then set up home in the new country. But Vikings just attacked, filled their boats with pillage, and then went home again. The reason for this is simple and once more heavily bound up with cows. It can be summed up in two words—ice cream.

Vikings and their cows lived in Scandinavia (consisting of Denmark, Norway, Finland, and Sweden). Much of Scandinavia is very cold indeed, and this meant that any cows they had were producing very, very cold milk. Unsurprisingly, the Scandinavians became quite brilliant at producing ice cream.[57] Even to this day Scandinavian nations are still some of the biggest consumers of this freezing deliciousness.

But even the ice cream—loving Vikings eventually had their fill of ice cream. Unfortunately, their cows were too cold to produce anything else. And so the Vikings set off to find warmer places to raid. You can actually track where the Vikings attacked based on the type of food they were hankering after.

They attacked England with its wide pastures and temperate climate when they wanted to drink milk. When they wanted something a bit more rich, they went to Ireland and Dublin.

---

[57] If you don't believe me, just try some Scandinavian vanilla ice cream. Your taste buds will send you a thank-you card.

With high rainfall and lots of lush green grass, cows in Ireland made lots of lovely cream and butter.[58] When they craved something a bit more savory the Vikings packed up their cows and headed to Normandy in France, where the warm weather helped their cheese ripen.

Therefore, the reason the Vikings never actually settled in one location was that they always wanted to travel on after they got bored by a particular type of food. And in the end, the raids always finished when they went back to Scandinavia. Because as we all know—milk, cheese, cream, and butter are all very well. But you're always going to want ice cream for dessert.

[58] I'm pretty sure that because of this ringing endorsement of Irish products, the Ireland dairy product marketing board will send me a lifetime supply of cream and butter. Of course, a lifetime supply won't fit in my fridge. So, if you're ever around at my house and there's a smell of slightly off milk, now you'll know the reason why.

20

THE UPSIDE TO
BEING LOST

Jack was still holding on to Trudy's shoulders and staring into her eyes. But he was also smiling so widely his face almost split in two. Trudy's head spun around trying to get her bearings. "Are we . . . ?" Jack pushed Trudy backward, allowing her to float away from him. "What is . . . ?" And then a wave of realization spread across Trudy's face. "We're in the Lost and Found room at the Ministry!"

Jack nodded. "You gave me the idea when you said we were lost. Grey told us that anything that gets lost pops into existence in this place. So, if everything was hopeless for us and we were 'lost,' then we'd suddenly appear here."

"But that's insane," complained Trudy. "I didn't even mean *really lost*, I just meant lost in the sense of 'hopeless.'"

"But you know that sometimes words and phrases mean *real* things. Remember when the Misery taught us that if you were really surprised and something 'took your breath away,' then you didn't need to actually breathe for a while."

Trudy looked around her. The Lost and Found room was still a huge empty white space filled with keys, wallets, and favorite pencils and pens all winking into and out of existence around them. She looked back at Jack, floated slightly nearer to him, and gave him a hug. "Sometimes you're brilliant."

"Sometimes?"

"Don't push it. Now can you see where the door out of the place is?"

Jack looked around. "No, can't see it anywhere; we seem to have lost it. . . ." And as soon as Jack said those words, the door flashed into existence right in front of them.

"Great. Let's go and find Grey and tell him what we've discovered."

After asking around, Jack and Trudy eventually found Grey in the Ministry cafeteria. It was the first time Jack had seen the café and he felt a bit put out. "You never told me this place had somewhere we can eat."

"Yeah," Trudy agreed. "You could at least have bought us a sandwich at some stage."

Grey laughed. "Haven't you learned anything from your time in the Ministry? Don't you think that there's a reason that I haven't brought you here?"

Jack remembered how incompetent the Ministry's medical teams were and realized that maybe the cafeteria wasn't as safe a place to eat as he initially thought. He looked around the café and noticed that, like all places in the Ministry, it was very strange indeed.

Probably the most unusual thing was that there was a food fight going on. Behind the plastic food guard, a tray of mashed potatoes had started rising up and was shaping itself into humanoid form. Then it began striding across the metal containers, heading for a tray of what looked to be sausage rolls. In response, the sausage rolls had hauled themselves into an angled position, like a pastry cannon, and were firing their meat insides toward the mashed-potato creature. One scored a direct hit, creating a hole right through the mashed-potato creature's stomach. It fell to the ground, but the hole quickly healed up, and it rose to its feet before striding on.

Jack pointed this out to Grey. "That's the craziest thing I have ever seen."

"I agree." Grey nodded. "If the potato creature doesn't get some allies, he's going to find himself outflanked by the broccoli in a minute."

Jack frowned. "That isn't what I meant. . . ."

"But then again what do you expect?" Grey interrupted. "Mashed potato has never been known for its tactical thinking."

Apart from the vagaries of the food on offer, the clientele in the café was also far from normal. Although many of the people standing in line were (largely) human, there were also a number of considerably stranger-looking creatures. There was a floating, rotating cube of what seemed to be a pinkish stone. Beside it there was a life-size, wooden painted puppet held up on strings that vanished into a swirling yellow vortex that hovered a foot above its head.

Three places in front of them was a long brown hooded cloak that reached down to the ground. When the head of the cloak turned there wasn't a face under the hood, but rather a strange reddish-brown mass of tiny objects that seethed and moved. Jack leaned forward and squinted to get a better look. He realized it wasn't a single "person" but rather a mass of ants.

Jack pulled at Grey's sleeve. "That man has ants all over his face. Shouldn't someone tell him?"

Grey shook his head. "Don't be ridiculous. That man doesn't have ants over his face."

"Am I hallucinating, then?"

"Well, you might be, Jack. I really can't be held responsible for the state of any misfiring neurons you may have in your brain. But that 'man,' as you call him, is actually just a mass of ants."

Trudy snorted. "What? You can't be serious!"

Grey nodded. "I very much am. We aren't sure whether she's a mass of ants pretending to be a woman, or a woman pretending to be a mass of ants. But it's one or the other."

"And he's a she?" Jack asked.

"We don't really know. But we call her 'Auntie,' so 'she' seems to be most appropriate. You see, ants work together as a colony, all working for one another and acting in each other's best interests. We think that 'Auntie' came from a colony that decided there was more to life than just eating leaves and finding the odd sugar cube and decided to seek meaningful employment."

"If she wanted meaningful employment then why did she join the Ministry?" Jack smirked.

"Ha ha," said Grey. "But when you're made up primarily of ants there are a limited number of job openings available to you. Prejudice against people made of ants is, quite frankly, frighteningly prevalent in our society. That and the fact she has no qualifications makes it hard to find work." Grey paused and then added an afterthought. "Stay in school, kids."

"What kind of a job does a writhing mass of ants undertake in the Ministry?" asked Trudy.

"Cleaner, obviously," said Grey.

"You're telling me that . . . Auntie operates a vacuum cleaner and a duster?" Jack asked incredulously.

"I'm telling you nothing of the sort," Grey replied. "As you can imagine, a vacuum cleaner would be incredibly dangerous for Auntie to operate. Point it in the wrong direction and she'd lose half her arm. Vacuum cleaners are incredibly dangerous, Jack; remember that.[59] Auntie refuses to go near the Ministry vacuum cleaner."

"Then how does she clean anything?" asked Trudy.

A mischievous smile appeared on Grey's face. "Well, I really shouldn't do this, but . . ." Grey looked around the cafeteria for a minute before he focused on a strange creature

---

[59] Jack would not appreciate how true this was until Chapter 34 of this book.

shaped like a long, coiled metal spring with red and black balls threaded through it. Between two of the coils of its spring it held a tray on which there was a large portion of trifle. As the creature slowly walked[60] past them, Grey pretended to be looking in the opposite direction and whistled nonchalantly. Then at the last minute he carefully stuck out a foot. The spring creature collided with Grey's foot and its tray shot up in the air, launching the trifle all over the floor. Grey then turned in the direction of Auntie and yelled "Spill!"

Auntie turned quickly and looked at the mound of trifle on the floor. Suddenly it appeared as if Auntie melted into the ground, as millions of ants ran out of the bottom of the cloak and toward the spill. Jack had never seen anything quite like it. It was like a tide of brown-red water washing across the floor, devouring the trifle, and then sweeping backward before re-forming as a human shape. The floor was completely clean again after mere seconds.

"That's amazing," Jack said.

"Yes, and yet people still think that robot vacuum cleaners are pretty cool things. The interesting thing about this world is that it's a lot more in balance than people realize. There are animals that are supposed to eat our crumbs and keep our houses clean, but because we find them icky we kill them and then have to buy ourselves robot vacuum cleaners. And the great thing about Auntie is that she doesn't scare your pets or need plugging into an outlet."

---

[60] I say walked, but to be honest, creatures that are mostly spring don't really walk; they more sort of *undulate*.

The spring creature got up and glared at Grey.[61] Grey smiled a "sorry" and moved up the line slightly. "All right, I'm getting a cup of tea and a sandwich. Do either of you two want anything?"

Trudy selected a small slice of millionaire's shortbread and a glass of milk.

"What about you, Jack?"

Jack thought for a minute. "I might have some of this Jell-O over here." Jack picked up a scoop from the counter and was about to help himself to some.

"DON'T!" Grey snapped at him.

Jack dropped the scoop into the Jell-O, which swallowed it immediately. He was amazed as the plastic scoop started to fizz around the edges and then dissolve. The Jell-O shaped itself into the form of a vaguely human face. "Do you mind? I was just resting here." The Jell-O started to slime its way across the counter, moving toward the exit.

"What on earth was that?" Jack asked.

"That's the problem with the Ministry cafeteria. Sometimes it's hard to tell the difference between the food and the customers. That was Malcolm; he's actually one of the best agents we have in the Ministry. Brings a lot of bad guys in."

Jack thought. "What? Because he can shape-shift and sneak into places through cracks and holes?"

"Maybe," said Grey with a sigh, "although I also suspect

---

[61] Or at least it glared at Grey as much as is possible when one is largely made of a long coil of wire with some red and black balls strung through it.

that it has a lot to do with the fact that no one ever expects to be brought to justice by a bowl of Jell-O."

"I can see how that would give you an edge," agreed Jack.

Jack decided that after the incident with Malcolm he wasn't desperately hungry after all. Grey paid for his and Trudy's food and they found a table to sit down at.

Trudy and Jack brought Grey up-to-date with what they'd found. For once even Grey was impressed. "Excalibur. That's . . . that's pretty major."

"Oh, come on," said Trudy, "that's nothing to us; we've fought Blackbeard and the queen of Atlantis."

"Don't underestimate this," Grey said. "Excalibur is legendary. Look, you know that there's truth in most legends and most of the time the people in the Ministry are actually behind the myths. But not this time. I know there really was a King Arthur and an Excalibur—but I don't know how the sword worked and I certainly don't know how to pull it from the stone."

"Well, we aren't going back to get the sword anytime soon. At least not until we figure out how to defeat enemies that pull themselves back together after you break them apart."

Grey thought. "You're up against someone trying to use King Arthur's sword, Excalibur. What do you know about King Arthur?"

"We know King Arthur pulled Excalibur out of a stone to become king," Trudy suggested.

"Yes," agreed Jack. "And his castle was called Camelot. And he had a wizard named Merlin . . . and . . ."

Trudy and Jack turned and looked at each other. "Merlin!"

"Mr. M!"

Jack gulped. "I think we've just put a very big piece of the puzzle in place."

Grey frowned. "Of course, Mr. M is Merlin! If you're right and Merlin is who you're up against then this is going to be trouble."

"But wait," Jack said, "Mr. M claimed that he was a scientist, not a magician."

Grey slowly shook his head. "Jack, science and magic are almost the same thing.[62] And Merlin was rumored to be the most powerful human scientist that ever existed."

Jack's eyes widened. "THE most powerful? I don't like the sound of that. How can we possibly defeat him then?"

"We go and speak to someone with even more power than him," Grey said.

"But didn't you just say he was the most powerful . . ."

"The most powerful human, Jack. Not everyone in the Ministry is human."

"Yeah, stop being so human-centric." Trudy laughed.

---

[62] The difference between science and magic is simply that in science, you tell people how the trick was done. Which, when you think about it, is pretty stupid. This is why David Copperfield lives in a mansion in Las Vegas and most scientists live in small flats and spend their lives writing letters to government organizations begging for funding.

ANTS
RELATIVE STRENGTH

Ants are amongst the most amazing creatures to exist on the Earth. Scientists have noted that an ant can lift up to fifty times its own body weight. So it's vital not to pick a fight with the fat ones, as they're clearly the strongest.

It is interesting to note that ants are the reason that we know that Noah did not load the creatures onto his ark in alphabetical order. Because if that were the case, the ants would have gone on in front of the anteaters. Which, as you can imagine, would have been a disaster waiting to happen.

21

NON-EUCLIDIAN FILING CABINETS

"Welcome to the filing room of Cthulhu,"[63] said Grey. "Now, a couple of safety tips: Don't stray away from the yellow line on the floor; try not to fall into alternate dimensions; and above all, remember where you put your sanity, so you can take it with you when we leave." Grey pushed open a rather ordinary door, to reveal a rather extraordinary room.

It was quite unlike anything Jack had ever seen.

---

[63] Cthulhu was a strange, squid-headed interdimensional creature of pure evil that ran the Ministry's filing department. He didn't like people much. Or things. Or things that weren't people or things. Cthulhu was capable of manifesting himself in several dimensions at once, so you know that when he turns up things are about to get very weird indeed. Jack was quite rightly terrified of him.

Although much of it was colored in murky grays, greens, and blacks, there were also brighter colors—purples, yellows, reds. In fact, there were some colors that Jack had never even seen before—colors that would have made a rainbow seem drab. When Jack tried to describe the colors inside his head it was impossible. They weren't similar to any other colors and so he had nothing to compare them to.[64]

Jack screwed his eyes up as he looked around the room. Even looking at it started his temples throbbing, and it felt as if something was swelling up in the middle of his head. It wasn't so much the contents of the room that made him feel like this. It was more the way those contents seemed to bend, wave, twist, and move. And how some of them were on the floor, others were in the air, and still others seemed to jut out of nothing and expand on into infinity.

"How does anyone ever find anything in here?" Jack asked.

"Generally speaking, they don't," said Grey. "But then again, that is Cthulhu's idea. He's a creature of almost impossible interdimensional evil. He regards filing and bureaucracy as a way to drive people insane, remember?"

Trudy looked around her, while being careful to make

---

[64] Yes, I know that this seems like a rather lousy explanation, but it's the best I can do. People often pretend they have created a new color and say "it was a sort of greenish blue." But that's just turquoise. To describe these colors, I would need to invent a whole new language. And then *you* would have to learn that whole new language. And I'm pretty sure that neither of us is prepared to make that kind of commitment.

sure her feet stayed on the yellow guide line. "Why have you never brought us here before?"

"Mainly because of the high risk of madness or dismemberment. Anyway, a filing system where you can never find anything is of limited use."

"How does this place even work?" asked Jack. He gazed up at a filing cabinet that was thousands of feet in the sky. "I mean, how could you get near that cabinet up there?"

"Simple," said Grey. "The laws of physics don't exist in this room."

"Why?"

Grey grimaced. "We rather suspect that the laws of physics are scared of Cthulhu."

Jack thought back to his own encounters with the squid-headed, evil, multidimensional Cthulhu. "Well, that makes sense, I suppose."

"So what if Cthulhu scared off the laws of physics? That still doesn't explain how you could reach a filing cabinet miles in the sky," Trudy said.

"Ahh, well, without the laws of physics to take control, strange things can happen. For instance, would you agree that the quickest way between two points is a straight line?"

Jack and Trudy agreed that this was something they had heard in their math classes.

"Well, clearly that's just nonsense." Grey took a pen and a notepad from his pocket and drew a short, straight line on it. "Now use this to get to America."

"What?" Trudy wrinkled up her face. "We can't use this to get to America."

"Exactly," said Grey, "because the quickest way between two points isn't a straight line. It's an airplane. Now, watch this...." Grey looked at the space around his head as if trying to pinpoint an exact location. Suddenly they saw a tiny shimmer in the air. Grey reached his hand toward the shimmer. When he touched it, his arm seemed to extend, impossibly stretching miles into the air. With his elongated arm he tapped the side of the filing cabinet that was hanging so far above them. "See?" he said, before retracting his arm, which shrank back to normal size. "When you suspend the laws of physics, it's amazing what you can achieve." Jack thought about trying it himself but was too scared that his arm wouldn't shrink back to normal size. Long arms might be useful sometimes, but the downside would be that he would only be able to go out in the summer, as you'd never find a long-sleeved shirt that would fit.

Grey led Jack and Trudy through the maze of cabinets and piles of paper. Occasionally they seemed to be walking up the walls, or on the ceiling, but it was hard to tell, because even when they took a step onto a different plane, it always felt as if they were the right way up.

Eventually they saw Cthulhu sitting behind an enormous green desk, which seemed to be fashioned out of decaying skulls and bones. As usual he was wearing his dark-blue monk's robe. The large leather chair he was sitting on had been split in two to allow his enormous bat-like wings to stick through the back of it. His gray-colored head looked squid-like and unhealthy with green pustules bursting on its surface. Cthulhu appeared to be deep in conversation with the man sitting opposite him.

Just looking at the man Cthulhu was talking to sent a chill down Jack's spine, although he wasn't sure why. He was a tall, bony angular figure, draped in a series of yellow rags and bandages that rustled back and forth despite the fact that there was no wind in the room. The rags were torn, and some had small spatters of blood on them. The man's face was hooded, yet even when he leaned forward into the light, there was nothing but blackness visible.

Jack felt his insides shrink. "They look busy; maybe we should come back later."

"Nonsense. Actually Cthulhu's in remarkably good form these days."

"And who's that he's with?" asked Jack.

"That's the King in Yellow," Grey said.

Even hearing the name spoken out loud made Jack shudder. "And what's a King in Yellow?"

"No one's really sure, but we suspect that he's created through all the fear and despair in the world coagulating into a single physical entity."

"Maybe Jack's right," Trudy said nervously, shifting her feet.

As they were talking, the King in Yellow stood up, bowed elegantly to Cthulhu, and then seemed to dissolve into the air.

"See, now there's nothing to be scared of." Grey smiled and strode over to Cthulhu's desk.

"I can't believe he said that," Jack grumbled as they

followed Grey. "There's clearly a lot to be scared of. It's just that one of the things to be scared of has vanished. Which, if anything, makes it more terrifying because we don't know where it's going to pop up next."

Cthulhu stood up and three tentacles shot out from under his cloak. They ratcheted into the air, twisted, turned, and then shot directly at the three friends. Jack looked stunned; Trudy stumbled backward. Grey, however, merely stuck out an arm and shook "hands" with the tentacle. Jack and Trudy nervously imitated him.

After shaking "hands," two of the tentacles shot into the corners of the room and pulled two chairs out of the darkness for Jack and Trudy to sit on.

Jack nervously lowered himself into his chair, slightly perturbed that it was covered in leather buckles and straps clearly used to restrain people. He would probably have been more worried, but too much of his mind was taken up with wondering why Cthulhu had offered them a seat. The monster he remembered had been much too interested in banishing people to alternate dimensions to be bothered politely receiving guests.

"Good to see you, Cthulhu," Grey said.

Cthulhu made a strange retching noise that sounded like two splintered pieces of metal being dragged against each other. "I see you were being visited by the King in Yellow?" Grey added.

Cthulhu looked serious and nodded. He proceeded to make a series of noises and gesticulated wildly with dozens of tentacles. Grey nodded thoughtfully.

Jack knew it would have been better not to interrupt, but his natural curiosity got the better of him. "What's he saying?" Jack whispered to Grey from the side of his mouth.

Grey translated. "Apparently, Cthulhu's trying to get the filing into order so that it's actually useful. But to do that he's going to need to persuade the laws of physics to come back into the room. That's why the King in Yellow was here. Cthulhu is trying to persuade the king to use his powers and influence to dispel some of the misery and fear from this area."

Jack was puzzled. "Cthulhu, I thought you were generally in favor of increasing despair and torment."

Cthulhu shook his head and the tentacles around his mouth writhed as he spoke. Grey translated. "Cthulhu says that he's struck a deal with the Minister. Apparently since Cthulhu's daughter helped us defeat the queen of Atlantis, the Minister has agreed she can leave Lough Neagh[65] on weekends and go for trips in the sea with her father. They just have to promise to try and avoid disrupting weather patterns and destroying shipping. In return, Cthulhu has agreed to try to make the filing system easier to understand."

Trudy nudged Grey in the ribs. "While it's lovely to hear about interdimensional beings having family picnics, that isn't going to rescue my mother. We're here to ask for help in defeating Merlin. So—ask."

---

[65] Cthulhu's daughter was the Kraken, a giant sea beast that lived in Lough Neagh.

Grey was suitably chastised and asked Cthulhu what he knew of Merlin.

Cthulhu went deadly silent and sat staring at them blankly. His green eyes sparked slightly and caused a halo to glow around his head. Everyone was silent as Cthulhu told them what he knew of Merlin.

Merlin had been considered one of the most powerful people of the ancient world; however, he wasn't generally a very nice individual. And considering that Cthulhu was the one saying this, Jack suspected that Merlin was a very horrible person indeed.

Cthulhu admitted that he did not know the full story of Merlin. He did, however, confirm that for many years Merlin and King Arthur had worked together to bring stability to a kingdom that included most of Wales and England. Apparently, Merlin had a strange power that allowed him to control knights and make them do whatever he wanted. It was this power that made Merlin and King Arthur almost invincible.

It was generally accepted that King Arthur was a remarkably nice man and would forgive his enemies, whereas Merlin always insisted on destroying them absolutely. Eventually King Arthur and Merlin could stand each other's ways no longer. King Arthur had known all along what Merlin's secret method of controlling people was and used this knowledge to banish Merlin.

"That's great!" said Jack. "All we need to know now is what was Merlin's secret for mind control? And how did King Arthur manage to banish him?"

Cthulhu looked straight ahead. Then a tentacle sneaked out from the bottom of his cloak and scratched the center of his squid-shaped head. Cthulhu made a few brief yipping noises of the sort you hear if you accidentally sit on a hamster.

Grey turned to Jack. "Cthulhu says that he can't remember those details, but they should be in the filing system somewhere." Grey indicated the vast room around them that twisted and bent both space and time. "Where exactly is anyone's guess."

Cthulhu made some more small noises.

"He says he'll let us know if the King in Yellow's negotiations go well and the laws of physics return to the room. In the meantime, that's as much as he can tell us."

"Are you sure there aren't any other details he knows about Merlin?" Trudy asked.

Cthulhu thought hard before speaking.

Grey translated. "Just three facts: Apparently Merlin was responsible for building Stonehenge. Secondly, he definitely wasn't a magician—he was just a very clever scientist who figured out not to tell people how he achieved his results. His father was an herbalist and taught Merlin many secrets about plants and crops. He also knew much about advanced science—but no one knows where he got the knowledge from. And finally, Merlin was a fiercely passionate carpenter."

"Carpenter?" asked Jack.

"Well, yes—surely you know the legends about Merlin? He was most famous for building the round table."

FEAR
WHY IT CAN BE A POSITIVE EMOTION

Fear is one of the most interesting emotions that human beings display. People talk about it as if it is a negative thing, but it is, in fact, a very positive emotion. It was developed as a survival mechanism for letting us know when we should run away. Most people are scared of something. Occasionally you will come across a completely fearless person, but generally they don't tend to live very long and rarely if ever find themselves drawing a pension.[66]

---

[66] Work in the Ministry is incredibly dangerous and as a result the accountants who work in the Ministry Pensions Department are in the Guinness Book of World Records as having the longest-known tea breaks in the Western world. No one knows how they put in their days, but it is interesting to note that of the last four Sudoku world champions, three have worked in the Ministry Pensions Department.

For example, if you find someone shouting "Oh, no—there's a lion loose in the city center!" the sensible person will become afraid and run away immediately. However, the fearless person instead says "I'm not afraid. I'll go and catch the lion."

And inevitably the fearless person is eaten.

Some fearless people in history include:

> **Joan of Arc** with "I needed a tan anyway."
> The **captain of the *Titanic*** with "It's only a bit of ice."

And not forgetting . . .

> **Captain Scott** with "A bit of cold never hurt anyone."

The only type of fear that isn't good is irrational fear. Such as fear of small, nonpoisonous spiders. Small spiders can't hurt you at all and therefore there is no point in being frightened of them. This is irrational fear.

Unless of course the spider has a bad attitude and is wielding a switchblade, in which case the fear becomes entirely rational again.

22

HIDING IN PLAIN SIGHT

Jack, Trudy, and Grey walked along the corridors of the Ministry. "This is all beginning to make sense," Trudy said.

"Is it really? Because if so, I certainly hadn't noticed," Jack muttered.

"Think about it. Merlin controlled people's minds somehow to make the knights follow King Arthur. And that's what he's doing now. There's probably some mind-altering ingredient in those health-food bars."

"Okay," Jack agreed. "That makes sense—especially if his father was an herbalist. That's how he gets his expertise with man-eating plants. But what else?"

"That fantasy film they're making—*The Once-Forgotten King*—is giving out his health-food bars, and we know he's behind that as well. But why?"

Jack snapped his fingers. "It makes perfect sense! Think

about it. Merlin's from a time of knights, swords, and wizards. He pretends to be making a film about those things and then if anyone sees suits of armor or swords being used they just assume it's part of the film. Also, it means he can use huge animatronic machines as henchmen. Like the giant."

"Exactly," Trudy agreed. "So he's trying to take people's minds over again and create a new army."

"But why Northern Ireland? Why not back in England and Wales? There are a lot more people over there."

"Remember, he was banished, Jack," interjected Grey.

"But that was ages ago. And King Arthur's dead."

Trudy sighed deeply. "We need to figure this out if we're going to find my mother. Merlin must be hiding her somewhere. We just need to figure out where exactly."

A thought struck Jack. "And that isn't all we have to do. We need to get back to the school."

"Why? I don't think Merlin will be there."

Jack looked into Trudy's eyes. "Not Merlin. David. Think about it. He's eating the health-food bars and auditioning for the films. Merlin knows he's my friend—so he'd make a great hostage. That must be why they didn't throw him out of the auditions despite all the chaos he caused."

"I'll get you a Ministry car immediately," said Grey.

The minute the Ministry car pulled up outside the school Jack and Trudy leapt from it. "Which way?" Trudy asked.

Jack saw a poster attached to the wall that read *THE ONCE-FORGOTTEN KING—REHEARSALS*. An arrow pointed to the school hall.

Jack and Trudy stood in the entranceway of the school hall. The room was teeming with dozens of children who had also been successful in the auditions and were now beginning rehearsals. Standing at the front of the hall on the stage was David, dressed in a suit of knight's armor and holding a sword in each hand.

David was surrounded by five animatronic goblins, all of whom were clutching dangerous-looking spiked clubs.

Jack shuddered. Maybe Merlin wasn't intending to capture David; maybe he'd try and kill him! "We've got to get up there! They'll pretend one of the animatronic goblins went haywire and accidentally killed him."

Trudy immediately started pushing her way through the crowd, but the hall was packed full. Even with Trudy's strength and the general level of fear she inspired in many pupils, they only managed to edge forward slowly.

"We'll never make it," Jack despaired. Then he looked up onstage and noticed something strange—something he'd never seen before. David was holding a sword in his hand. He had been holding it for over a minute, and . . . and yet so far he hadn't dropped it and hurt someone. Something very unusual was going on.

The goblin robots started slowly approaching David. He smiled and twirled one of the swords like a baton. Trudy noticed that something was wrong too. "Jack, did David just spin that sword in his hand?"

"Yes—and yet no one needs stitches. This is very odd indeed."

One animatronic goblin leapt at David and flung its club. David jerked his head to one side and the club flew past him. Behind him the club crashed into another goblin's head and clattered to the floor in a shower of sparks. David spun around and cut the disarmed animatronic goblin's head off. It sank to its knees before totally collapsing.

The remaining three goblins circled David cautiously. Two jumped at him and swung their clubs. David blocked their blows and effortlessly moved past them. The third goblin moved in and struck at David. He used the blade of the sword in his left hand to block and then twisted his elbow so that the club fell from the goblin's hand. Despite the fact that David was still surrounded by three enemies, he paused and smiled into the crowded hall. The other pupils roared their appreciation.

Jack was speechless.

"You know," Trudy said, turning to Jack, "David's actually quite good-looking when he isn't falling over all the time."

Jack gaped at Trudy, who suddenly realized what she had just said. "Although obviously if you ever tell him that I'm going to punch your shoulder so hard that your right hand will become your left."

"Understood," said Jack.

Back onstage David was fending off the goblins with effortless ease. He had even gone as far as kicking the third goblin's club back to him in order to give the crowd a bit more of a show.

The three goblins retreated back slightly and then all charged at once. David yawned and threw both his swords into the air. He ran straight at the goblins, weaving his way through their clumsy strikes. When he was at the far side of the stage he reached into the air and caught his swords as they fell. The goblins turned to face him and raised their clubs. David spun in a circle and decapitated two of them before sticking both swords into the belly of the last one standing. It fizzed slightly, stiffened, and fell to the ground with a metallic clang. David turned to the audience and dramatically flourished one hand in a sign of triumph. The hall exploded into applause, all except Jack and Trudy, who were too confused to do anything other than keep pushing their way through the crowd.

They found David sitting backstage with four assistants around him. One brought him a large Mr. M health-food bar while the others were removing his armor. "Hey Jack, Trudy! Did you see my audition?" David said with a smile.

"How did that happen?" asked Trudy. "Have you been getting secret knight lessons or something?"

David frowned. "What? No, I sleep at night, Trudy. Do I look tired to you?"

"Not that, David! Look, you're normally clumsy and yet you were . . . well, to be honest, you were amazing fighting those goblin robot things," Jack said.

David nodded. "I know I'm clumsy—but just because I'm clumsy it doesn't mean that I'm not good at other things."

"I know you're good at lots of things," Jack said,[67] "but it

[67] Although for the life of him Jack couldn't think of one.

doesn't stop you from being clumsy. So how did you defeat those robots? How did you suddenly stop being clumsy?"

David continued crunching his health-food bar. "I didn't stop being clumsy. But I'm a wonderful actor. And although I'm clumsy, the character I was acting isn't clumsy. So, I can do amazing things because the character I'm playing can do them. That's how good an actor I am."

"I don't think that's the way acting works," Trudy said.

"You just saw what happened onstage—that's clearly exactly the way acting works."

Jack tried to explain to David what was going on. "You've got to stop eating those health-food bars and you can't be in this film. It's a front for something. There's something bad going on."

David put his health-food bar down and stared at Jack. "I've been your friend for years now. And yet you still do this?"

"Do what? Try to save your life?"

"I've found something I'm good at. I'm a great actor. Look at all these film people fussing over me." David pointed at the assistants running around him. "I'm going to get a speaking part in this film. Can't you just be happy for me?"

"David, if any of this was real I'd be over the moon for you. But it isn't. An ancient magician-scientist is behind all this. He's got an evil plan and you're probably part of it."

Trudy agreed with Jack. "He's telling you the truth. There probably isn't even a film."

David's whole body seemed to droop. "Guys, let me be the

hero for once, okay? Just once." He got up from the chair and left, followed by his assistants. He paused and looked over his shoulder. "And if there isn't really a film, tell me what on earth that thing out on the playing fields is?"

Jack and Trudy stood and watched as their friend walked away.

MINISTRY OF S.U.IT.S HANDBOOK

ARMOR
Its Real Invention

If you have ever visited a castle or even a stately home, you may well have seen a full suit of plate-metal armor. Historians will tell you that these were created to help knights fight in battle, but it is perfectly apparent after even the briefest consideration that this isn't true at all.

Fighting people with swords and axes is a very tiring business at the best of times. Trying to do it while totally covered in metal—which weighs you down, makes it difficult to breathe, and makes it almost impossible to see—is very demanding indeed.

So the question is, who really invented armor, and why?

You might think that a knight invented armor because it kept his life safe. You might think that a blacksmith invented it because it would be another product to sell. You might think a king invented it because he wanted to win more battles.

The truth is much more obvious than that. Armor was invented by a man called Artemis who worked in a castle laundry. Battles are smoky, muddy, and bloody places. And the major advantage with armor is that it has a "wipe clean" surface. By inventing armor, Artemis came up with a way of substantially reducing his own workload.

Sadly, Artemis never got the credit for his invention, because after creating it he was stabbed thirty-six times and died. A description of the assailant who killed Artemis was not forthcoming, which is strange, because the thirty-six boys who were in charge of polishing duties at the castle were coincidentally all witnesses to the crime. It was clear they were witnesses as they were all absolutely covered in blood.

Interestingly enough, although Artemis invented armor, he was not responsible for making it popular. That was achieved by a young blacksmith whose name remains unknown.[68]

[68] At least it remains unknown until Chapter 37.

23

THERE BE DRAGONS

Jack stood silently blinking and watching his best friend get smaller and smaller as he walked away. Part of him was angry, but another part of him knew exactly what David meant. Even before Jack had joined the Ministry he'd clearly been the "hero" in their friendship. He'd been the popular one, the one who was better at sports (although he wasn't actually any good at sports—just better than David was), the one who got invited to parties . . . and David was the "sidekick." Jack wondered if he should have thought about this more. Maybe David didn't like being the sidekick.[69]

---

[69] Just to be clear on this, no one likes being the sidekick. And if you're the sidekick for long enough, you're going to end up hating the hero. I'm pretty sure that at this stage Robin only sticks around because he wants to see if the Joker finally gets to kill Batman. After all, if Robin

Jack felt like talking to someone, but Trudy's skills as a sympathetic listener were somewhat limited, and so instead, Jack and Trudy decided to investigate what David had mentioned about the playing fields.

"What do you think it's going to be?" asked Trudy as they walked through the school. "Cameras? Props?"

Jack and Trudy walked out the back door of the school and stopped dead. They didn't need to go any farther to see what was on the playing fields. The enormous giant from the red barn was standing close to a set of rugby goalposts. It was thirty feet tall and yet it looked small compared to what was nearby.

A giant animatronic dragon was slowly prowling across the fields. It stood on four feet and was the length of five school buses. It was covered in blackish-green scales and had golden spines sticking out of its back. It reared up on its two hind legs, and two enormous wings unfolded. Jack blinked and rubbed his eyes with his fists to check that he wasn't seeing things. Strangely, rubbing his eyes didn't seem to help much; they just made his eyes go blurry for a minute.

---

didn't want to see Batman get captured or killed, why would he wear such a bright and gaudy costume to attract the attention of villains?

Of course, Batman is a brilliant detective and already suspects this:

"Merry Christmas, Batman."

"Umm, Robin, I can't help noticing that you got me socks again this year. Are you trying to tell me something?"

"Why no, Batman. Now let's talk about updating your costume again. I'm thinking of something in neon pink, possibly with a 'target' motif."

Apparently, rubbing your eyes didn't help you see better at all—another thing that cartoons had lied to Jack about.

The animatronic dragon let out a piercing shriek, its internal machinery made a loud clicking noise, and then the sky was sprayed with a long, thick, smoky cloud of fire. A second later the dragon collapsed back onto all four feet, sending a shockwave shuddering through the ground.

It turned its long elegant neck and looked at Jack and Trudy, its yellow eyes glittering. Despite the fact that they were over a hundred feet away, the effect was terrifying. Jack and Trudy backed inside the school and closed the door.

"We're going to have to fight that at some stage, aren't we?" asked Trudy.

"I really hope not," said Jack, "because the best plan I can think of is trying to get trapped in its throat, choking it. And I'm not sure that works with animatronic creatures."

"But should we really be that worried about the dragon? I mean, didn't we beat the steam dinosaur?"

Jack thought for a minute. "Yes, but remember that we only beat that because it was made of a set of old bones and a potentially explosive school boiler. That thing out there looks a lot more sturdy. I think Merlin's a lot more professional about this than the pirates ever were."

"I'm going to suggest we leave school today by the front entrance."

"I like your thinking on that."

Jack and Trudy couldn't help feeling dejected as they left school later. They were no closer to finding Trudy's mother,

David wouldn't believe them that he was in danger, and they knew they were up against an incredibly powerful scientist with enormous mechanical machines at his command.

Jack got home and slumped at the table where his mother and father were sitting.

"Hard day?" Jack's father asked.

"You'd better believe it," said Jack.

"This will cheer you up," said his mother as she set a plate down in front of him.

Jack looked at it suspiciously. "Is this more of Mr. M's health food?"

At the prompting of his mustache, Jack's father picked up the package and read from it. "It's a new, even tastier recipe. With more vitamins and iron to keep your body healthy."

Jack pushed the plate away from him. "I don't think I can eat anything tonight. I'm really not feeling well."

Jack's mother came over and put a hand on his forehead. "Are you coming down with something? Early to bed for you tonight."

Jack's father nodded in agreement. "And I'll give you a lift to school in the morning if you still aren't feeling well. But only as a treat. I don't want you getting used to being spoiled."

In his room, Jack put a new pair of unshredded pajamas on. Then, in order to make sure he wouldn't find himself walking out of his room in the middle of the night, he took the belt from around the middle of his bathrobe. He sat on the bed tying one end around his ankle and the other to the bed frame. He then slumped into the bed, hoping that he would be able to get a good night's sleep for once.

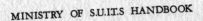

BIRDS AND THEIR ABILITY TO DELIVER MESSAGES
WHY PIGEONS LIKE STATUES SO MUCH

It is interesting to note that pigeons were used to deliver messages during the two world wars. This is why to this day they walk with their chests puffed out, because they still expect someone to pin a medal on them.

It is also this fact that explains why you will so often see pigeons sitting on statues. Walking around any European city, you will notice that most statues are of people who achieved something during one of the world wars. Pigeons recognize these people and go over and land on them in case they want a message delivered.[70]

---

[70] One of the best things about pigeons is that they will carry a message to its destination no matter what the message actually contains. Even if it's a recipe for a tasty pigeon stew. Because pigeons are efficient, but not very intelligent.

The reason pigeons are no longer used to carry messages and packages is that although they are speedy and excellent at delivery, they struggle writing out little cards that say "We're sorry we missed you; your package will not fit through your mail slot."

Scientists have discovered that pigeons navigate their way using sensitive magnetic organs in their brains. This is an absolute miracle, but it does mean that if you try to send someone a present of a fridge magnet via pigeon post, it's almost certainly going to get lost.

24

PUT ON YOUR DANCING SHOES
WEDNESDAY

Jack was woken in the middle of the night by falling on his face. It wasn't a pleasant way to be woken, and Jack decided to try and avoid it in the future. Once more he had been sleepwalking, but fortunately the bathrobe belt had caused him to trip and fall before he left his bedroom.

Jack felt something trying to move his limbs, but by concentrating he was able to force them down. Whatever had controlled him the previous night was much, much weaker this time. Jack had definitely made the right decision about not eating any more of Merlin's "health food"—clearly that must have been how he had been controlled the previous night.

After a few moments the tugging at his limbs seemed to cease entirely. Jack heard a revving outside the house. He untied the bathrobe belt, walked over to the window, and looked out of the curtains. The silver driverless car was sitting right outside his house. Its engine switched off and it sat still. Jack was pretty sure that it was waiting for him. He felt a cold shiver go down his spine.

The next morning Jack's parents were shocked to come down to the kitchen and find their son waiting for them. "You must really be sick, if you're getting up early," Jack's mother observed.

Jack's father's mustache was just about to make an observation when the microwave pinged.

"I've made us all breakfast." Jack smiled as he picked up an oven mitt and took a plate of steaming hot sausage rolls[71] out of the microwave.

Jack's mother and father sat down at the kitchen table in shock. Jack put a sausage roll in front of each of them. "I just thought it would be nice for me to do something for you guys for a change."

Of course, Jack's goal had not been one of altruistic kindness, but rather he wanted to avoid the threat of having to eat any more of Merlin's mind-controlling health food. If that involved him having to take the radical step of cooking, he was prepared to do that.

"Here—sauces," Jack said as he jammed brown and red bottles into his parents' hands.

His parents merrily chomped away on their sausage rolls, while Jack went to the front door and peered outside.

---

[71] Unlike the sausage rolls sold in the Ministry cafeteria, these were not military-grade sausage rolls.

The driverless silver car was still sitting there. Jack felt a little nervous as he wandered back to the kitchen. "Hey, Dad, can I still get that ride to school?"

His father had just finished the sausage roll. His father's mustache was savoring the last of its tomato ketchup. "Certainly, Jack, but only today, mind you—getting the bus is good for you." Jack thought of asking if his father had any empirical[72] evidence that buses were good for you, but decided not to risk it in case that would have meant the withdrawal of the ride altogether.

As Jack's father pulled out of their driveway, the silver car revved up and followed them at a safe distance. Jack's father adjusted his mirror. "Hey, look, Jack—that must be one of those driverless cars you always hear about on the news. It's amazing what they can do today, isn't it?"

"Yeah," Jack said flatly. "Brilliant."

<hr>

When they reached the school, Jack's father pulled up right outside the main gates. "Thanks, Dad," Jack shouted as he bolted out of the door and straight into the school. The driverless silver car revved in annoyance and then drove off.

As Jack tumbled into the school, he crashed into Trudy. "You aren't going to believe what happened again last night."

"If we're going to play a game of 'you aren't going to believe,' then I think I should go first." She pulled Jack by the

[72] *Empirical* is basically a fancy way of saying "evidency." But saying "evidency evidence" sounds a bit silly. So, scientists tend to use the word *empirical* instead.

cuff of his blazer into the school hall. A group of children was standing and clapping in a large circle.

"Is it a fight?" Jack asked. Fights were generally the only reason people at his school would have been in a circle clapping. Jack pushed his way through the circle and was astonished to see David spinning on his back before jumping up, body popping, and doing the robot dance.

Jack didn't need to see any more. "His mind is definitely being controlled."

"No, that's precisely the point. It can't be that. If it was that, he'd still be as clumsy as he was before. You dance with your feet and your legs, not your mind. If you used your mind to dance, then Einstein would have been in a boy band. Merlin must be controlling *his body* somehow."

Jack realized Trudy was right. "The driverless car was waiting outside my house again last night. But this time whatever was controlling me didn't work. I think it was because I didn't eat the health food."

"We should definitely steer clear of anything branded 'Mr. M,'" Trudy agreed. "But none of this is getting us any closer to stopping Merlin or finding where he's keeping my mother."

Jack and Trudy wandered out of the hall and sat on the steps in front of the entrance. The pylons in front of the school were covered with hundreds of birds. Jack noticed the strange black-and-white bird they had seen recently fly down and land in one of the trees that flanked the school entrance. It began hammering away at the tree with its beak. Jack was convinced that it was still trying to give them some sort of a message.

"Rats!" Jack exclaimed. "I'd meant to look up Morse code last night so I could figure out what it was trying to tell us."

Trudy walked over to the bird and watched it closely. It kept drilling its beak into the tree, seemingly undisturbed by Trudy's presence.

"Let's think about this logically," Jack said. "Maybe we've got too many clues—we just need to focus on one. All Merlin's health foods seem to consist of muesli-type bars. So where in a city could you store large amounts of grains, nuts, and seeds without anyone noticing?"

"Jack, stop thinking for a minute. This bird's trying to tell us something. . . ."

"But where in the center of the city could you find a place to store grains, nuts, and seeds . . . except maybe a . . ."

" . . . Zoo!" Jack and Trudy said at once.

Jack smiled at Trudy. "You figured it out at the same time!"

Trudy pointed to the tree where the bird had been hammering with its beak. "The bird wasn't trying to give us a Morse-code clue, Jack. It's a woodpecker. It was carving the answer out for us."

Jack looked at the branch, which had the word *Zoo* clearly carved on it. "Mmm. Sometimes I suspect we make things more difficult for ourselves than we need to. So what do we do next?"

"It makes sense that Merlin would base himself at the zoo. Space to grow genetically modified plants and animals for the model farm he set up, and zoos have lots of space for grain storage—because that's what half the animals eat."

"Agreed, and it also makes sense that's where a woodpecker would come from—I'm pretty sure they're not native to Northern Ireland."

"We're going to the zoo. If Merlin's based there, that might be where he's keeping my mother."

MINISTRY OF S.U.I.T.S HANDBOOK

WOODPECKER
SKILLS AND ABILITIES

Ornithologists will try to tell you that woodpeckers use their drilling-beak ability to dig into trees to eat grubs and insects. This is clearly ridiculous, as woodpeckers live in forests, and if there's one thing that forests are absolutely full of it's insects. Suggesting that woodpeckers would make life difficult for themselves by eating only bugs from trees would be like walking into a KFC and then insisting they lock your food inside a treasure chest before they give it to you.

After the matter is given even a second's consideration, the reason that woodpeckers drill into trees is simple. Birds live in wooden houses. Ornithologists refer to these wooden houses as "nests," and generally they are made of twigs. However, you occasionally see a proper birdhouse that is stuck to the side of a tree and has walls, a little round door, and a roof. Some people say that these are placed there by humans, but after extensive research we have established that no human ever admits to this. Additionally, it is ridiculous to suggest that humans would put up little houses for wild birds when they never do the same for wild rats, wild fish, or even wild insects.

Some people have claimed that they have occasionally seen woodpeckers in the wild measuring up a tree with a tape measure. But this has yet to be verified.

25

HIDE AND SEEK

After school had finished, Trudy called a Ministry car, which sped them both to the zoo in under ten minutes. There was a large, friendly-looking entrance and a nice man behind the counter sold them two tickets.

"This place doesn't seem evil," whispered Jack.

"It doesn't necessarily have to be evil. Maybe Merlin's just made his base here."

Jack and Trudy slowly walked through the zoo looking for anything unusual, but there didn't seem to be anything out of the ordinary. Just normal animals wandering around in spacious exhibits. Jack stopped outside the lion enclosure. "It's strange that lions have beards but not mustaches,"[73] Jack observed. "Makes me suspect that they're up to something."

---

[73] For a full explanation as to why shaving a beard to make it smaller is

Trudy said nothing and walked on.

"There must be a real art to designing a zoo," Jack mused. "I mean, you wouldn't want to put the tasty animals next to the hungry ones. Like if you were a lion you wouldn't want to be in an enclosure next to a nice tasty zebra. It'd be too tempting."

"Focus, Jack! If Merlin's here my mother might be here as well."

"Okay, so we need to find Merlin, then. Let's think about where he might be hiding in a zoo."

As Jack was thinking, a small electric cart went by, pulling a trailer behind it. Trudy suddenly nudged Jack in the ribs. "Ouch! What?"

"Look at the animal feed in the trailer!"

Jack looked. There were large, blue canvas sacks of animal feed. All of them were branded *Mr. M's Delicious Zoo Chow.*

"Okay—Merlin is definitely here somewhere," Trudy said.

Jack nodded. "But that still doesn't help us to figure out where, exactly."

Trudy looked around. "I can't stand it. My mother might be trapped here somewhere and there's nothing we can do to help her. Maybe we should start asking the keepers some questions."

"But for all we know the keepers could be working for Merlin. We need to be careful—we don't want to give the game away!"

---

more sinister than a completely hairy face, see *The Ministry of SUITs* Book 1, Chapter 6.

"I don't care about careful; I want to rescue my mother."

"And what good would it be to your mother if we got caught?"

"I don't care if we get caught. If we get caught at least we'd get locked up with her. Anyway, you're always getting caught and you always manage to escape, don't you?" Trudy paused in thought and then her eyes lit up. "That's what we should do! We should deliberately get caught. Then you could perform one of your legendary escapes. It's a brilliant plan!"

Jack began backing away from Trudy. "Look, while it's true that I am excellent at escaping from things, there's always the chance that I'd mess it up this time."

Trudy turned away from Jack and started shouting. "Merlin! Where are you? We want to be CAPTURED!"

Jack cringed. Other visitors to the zoo were looking at them. If they got caught, could he manage to escape again? After all, Trudy's mother had been a much more experienced Ministry operative than he was and yet *she* hadn't managed to escape.

"Come and GET US!"

Trudy was good at shouting. Jack noticed that one of the lions was looking at her. It was probably wondering whether Trudy could give it roaring tips. Jack thought about the lion. It was the king of the jungle—and yet it hadn't managed to escape from the zoo. What chance would he have?

Jack began thinking about all the animals in the zoo. They all had their own unique skills. The cheetah was superfast; the monkeys could climb anything; the lion was good at roaring; the giraffes would be the ideal lookout. And yet for some reason, with all these skills the animals hadn't managed to escape.

For a few seconds Jack wondered why you never heard about animals teaming up and staging a mass breakout. And then he remembered that a lot of the animals would have eaten the other ones. It's generally hard to work together as a unit when you're always wondering if the people you're cooperating with consider you a real teammate or only a halftime snack.

Jack remembered an old war film his dad made him watch every Christmas. It was about a group of World War II prisoners working together to escape from a prison camp. *The Great Escape*—that was it. They used all sorts of ingenious ways to break out—and then it clicked in Jack's head.

"MERLIN, I'M WAIT . . ."

Trudy was interrupted in mid-shout by Jack's hand clamping over her mouth. "Stop shouting. I've figured out what's wrong with the zoo. . . ."

Trudy's eyes, which had been widening, were now looking down at Jack's hand.

" . . . and if you promise to stop shouting, I'll take you to the place I'm thinking of."

Jack dropped his hand from Trudy's mouth.

"You think you've figured something out?"

"Yes, there's one type of animal that you should never see in a zoo. So that's what we go and look at."

"Thanks, Jack."

"No problem."

Trudy punched Jack hard in the shoulder.

"What was that for?"

"Never, ever put your hand over my mouth again."

Jack felt that being punched in the shoulder was slightly unfair, particularly when you'd just come up with an idea about how to rescue someone's mother.

Trudy then punched Jack in the shoulder again.

"OWWW! And what was *that* for?"

"That was because you really need to start washing your hands more often."

Jack gingerly sniffed the palm of his hand. His nose wrinkled and he decided that the second punch had been justified.

MINISTRY OF S.U.I.T.S HANDBOOK

HANDWASHING
THE IMPORTANCE OF

It is worth noting that having clean hands is a matter that has become of paramount importance to the Ministry over the years. However, it has been brought to our attention that this can be problematic.

When people want to clean their hands because they have germs upon them, they turn on the tap and rub soap on them. Then, after dousing them in water, people generally put the soap back and turn off the tap. The problem with this is clear. Although their hands have been cleaned, afterward they touch the tap to turn it off. The very same tap they touched when their hands were covered in germs. The problem of recontamination is obvious.

The finest Ministry minds were put to trying to solve the problem of how to keep one's hands continually clean. A solution was quickly reached to deal with this problem. However, the Minister himself has indicated that it is important for operatives to learn how to think logically and solve problems themselves. Therefore, we shall not explain how this problem was solved.

We shall merely note that the Ministry is the only organization in the world that owns a laminating machine but doesn't actually have ID cards.

26

MEET THE MEERKATS

Jack and Trudy were standing in front of the meerkat enclosure. The enclosure was surrounded by a ten-foot wall of
clear Plexiglas. It had recently been renovated, and a few old
iron bars from the previous cage lay at their feet. The fact
that the enclosure had been updated recently made Jack
even more sure that he was correct that Merlin was somewhere nearby. Jack looked at the small pile of iron bars—
there were nowhere near enough to have surrounded the
enclosure entirely. He couldn't help wondering what had
happened to the other leftover bars.

Trudy looked unimpressed. "You think my mother is
being guarded by meerkats?"

"Not precisely."

"Then what?" asked Trudy. "They put her in the meerkat

enclosure and she was so taken with how cute they are she decided to never come home again?"

For a brief moment Jack considered pointing out that he really liked meerkats because at least they didn't punch you in the shoulder all the time. However, he quickly realized that this would be a particularly ironic way to get a punch in the shoulder and decided to say something else instead. "What do you know about meerkats?"

Trudy looked into the enclosure. A few meerkats were standing up on their hind legs. Their little scruffy snouts were sniffing the air and their little black eyes looked slightly glazed. They slowly swayed back and forth.

Trudy read the information card outside the enclosure. "They're from the mongoose family. They're carnivorous and they're burrowing animals. So what?"

Jack pointed at them. "And yet they're inside the enclosure, right?"

"Of course they're in the enclosure."

Jack laughed. "There's no 'of course' about it. In fact, it's ridiculous."

Trudy still hadn't realized what Jack meant.

"Look, every Christmas my dad makes me watch films about prisoners of war escaping from military camps. And in every single one of those films the best way to escape is by building a tunnel."

Trudy looked at Jack and then back at the meerkats. "Burrowing!"

"Exactly—if those meerkats were just in a normal

enclosure, they'd have dug a thousand escape tunnels by now and would be roaming free all over Belfast."

"But since they're still here something's keeping them inside the enclosure."

Jack nodded. "And that's probably because Merlin did something to them. If he can control humans, he can probably control meerkats," suggested Jack. "And remember, he was trying to dig to find the stone. What creature would have been better suited to making a cavern around the stone than nimble little meerkats?"

Realization dawned across Trudy's face. "Jack, you're brilliant."

Jack smiled to himself, feeling very brilliant.

"Now we'll just wait until no one is watching and climb into the enclosure," said Trudy.

Jack felt slightly less brilliant. He hadn't realized they'd have to climb into the enclosure. If it had been made of old-style metal bars or chicken wire it might have been possible, but with a modern Plexiglas it was different. Jack was sure that this must have been why Merlin had renovated the enclosure by getting rid of old-style iron bars.[74]

Jack looked at the meerkats. With their black glass-like eyes, little snouts, and tiny sharp teeth they looked a lot less friendly than they were made out to be in wildlife documentaries.

The meerkats were one of the most popular animals at

[74] Jack was sure about this, but he was also wrong about this. . . .

the zoo, and in another country Jack and Trudy might have had to wait for a long time before they could have sneaked in. Luckily, because they lived in Northern Ireland they didn't have to wait long before there was a rain shower. The zoo visitors scurried for cover and headed for the cafeteria to enjoy a Popsicle.[75] Trudy confidently strode toward a tree that was hanging over the edge of the enclosure. She scrambled up it so nimbly that a monkey in the enclosure next door gave her a round of applause. "Come on, Jack, it's easy. You must have climbed trees when you were younger."

Jack hadn't climbed any trees when he was growing up. He liked the look of trees and in many ways admired their work, but that was as close a relationship as he had with them. He scrabbled at the base of the tree briefly. The rain wasn't helping. "I can't help feeling that if trees wanted to be climbed they would grow in the shape of a ladder."

Trudy sighed and then started pointing out a series of footholds and handholds Jack should use. Under this direction he made it to the overhanging branch, barely even breaking his neck once. "All right, so how do we get down?"

"We're going to let gravity take care of that." Trudy smiled.

Jack muttered under his breath again. He really wasn't at all a fan of gravity. It always seemed to be trying to hurt him in some way. He would have much preferred to be

---

[75] People in Northern Ireland seem to enjoy Popsicles no matter what the weather is like. It is almost as if they might have a little ice cream–loving Viking blood in them. They also have a lot of black-and-white cows. You do the math. . . .

falling down a bottomless pit where gravity wasn't such a worry.

One branch hung far over into the enclosure, and Trudy edged her way toward the end of it. As Trudy got farther along the branch, it started bending down more and more. She shimmied farther along and hung herself off the end of the branch so it lowered her to within six feet of the ground. Jack wondered how she was going to make it that final six feet when she suddenly let go. The branch catapulted back up with Jack hanging on for dear life. Trudy landed as nimbly as a cat. She stood up and smiled. "Your turn. It's easy!"

Five minutes later Jack was lying in the grass, rubbing his back and groaning softly. Trudy's face appeared over his. He stopped groaning long enough to speak. "I'm thinking of training for the Olympic gymnastics next year. But I'm not sure I'd look good in a leotard."

The meerkat habitat was rather unremarkable. There were several small grassy hillocks, with occasional sandy hollows. Every now and then Jack almost twisted his ankle by putting his foot in the mouth of a burrow.

"Clearly these meerkats know nothing about being liable for causing trips and falls," Jack complained. "Frankly, their health and safety procedures are shockingly lax."

"These little vermin really do like digging," Trudy agreed. "But there's nothing unusual in that."

Jack was just about to agree with Trudy when he tumbled into a massive hole eight feet across. "I think I may have found an unusual burrow," Jack said. "Either that or we need to start running now. If there's a meerkat big enough to dig this by himself, I worry that we might look too much like a tasty bug to him."

Trudy carefully made her way into the mouth of the enormous tunnel, pulling a flashlight out of her schoolbag.

"Did you steal that from the chamber where Excalibur is hidden?"

"I'm sorry, I didn't have a chance to return it," sneered Trudy. "I was too busy almost being killed by empty suits of armor."

"Just make sure you put it back later. We don't want people going around saying we're thieves."

"Well, I could just leave the flashlight here," said Trudy, switching it off.

Jack looked into the darkness. "No, I don't think that'll be necessary. After all, the only thing worse than having people talk about us would be having people talk about us in the dark when we wouldn't even be able to see who they were."

Trudy clicked the flashlight back on and walked into the tunnel. Jack scurried behind her trying to keep up while pretending to be braver than he really was.

HEALTH AND SAFETY
HORNED VIKING HELMETS

As you will already know, Vikings did not originally wear horns on their helmets. However, after the rumor started that they did, King Hendrick the Caring suggested that it might not be a bad idea.

King Hendrick was a thoughtful and caring king who had noticed that when Vikings poured off their longboats for a raid, frequently there was something of a stampede and many of his warriors were crushed underfoot.

Hendrick decided that it would be a good idea to have a way to warn the warrior in front of you that he needed to get a move on. He therefore got the Viking Health and Safety Executive to fit a set of horns onto all helmets. This meant that when Vikings charged head-down into battle, you knew if you needed to speed up because the Viking behind you would poke you with his horned helmet.

Although people no longer remember that this is how the practice started, it continues to this day—as motorists "sound their horns" in order to tell someone in front of them that they need to get a move on.

27

FAMILY REUNION

Jack talked as they headed down the tunnel. Jack found talking extremely helpful, because if he chattered enough it helped him to forget how scared he actually was. "There's something very odd about this tunnel. We know that the meerkats haven't escaped, so they must be using the tunnel for something else. Also, did you notice the way the meerkats were standing up on their hind legs?"

"Isn't that the way they always look?"

"Maybe, but they were standing bolt upright. It's almost as if something's holding them in place. Maybe they've been affected by the animal feed the way humans are by the health-food bars."

Trudy stopped and turned. "That makes sense."

"Does it?" said Jack, quite pleased. "Because when I was

saying it out loud I was slightly worried that I was losing my marbles."

"And it makes sense that Merlin would base himself at the zoo. Health food mostly looks like animal food anyway—so he can store that kind of stuff here. And there's plenty of space for him to experiment with plants. But then what would be the reason for . . ." Trudy said as she turned the corner.

"Reason for what?" Jack asked. Trudy had stopped dead still. Jack bumped into her back.[76] As usual he was amazed that her back seemed to be very solid despite the fact that his front was quite soft and hurt a lot.

"Trudy, why are you . . . ?"

Jack stopped and saw why Trudy had suddenly frozen. The tunnel had opened up into a large chamber, and lying at the back of it was a woman chained to the wall. Jack didn't need to ask who she was. Trudy dropped her flashlight and ran for her right away. The woman stood up stiffly and opened her arms. Despite the fact that her clothes were dirty and torn, she was still stunningly elegant, with long auburn hair cascading down her back and eyes that sparkled emerald green. Her arms enfolded Trudy as she leapt into them, making her mother fall backward against the wall. Trudy's mother buried her face in the top of her daughter's head. "I've missed you so much," she said

[76] Thus showing the problems that can be encountered if you undertake these kinds of adventures without wearing a health-and-safety-approved horned Viking helmet.

in a muffled voice. Trudy said nothing, but Jack knew from the way her body trembled that she was crying. Jack felt a tear running down his own cheek, but he wiped it away, because no matter how emotional Trudy became he was pretty sure that she'd still be together enough to make fun of him for crying.

Jack felt as if he was intruding on something incredibly private, and so he pretended that he needed an impossibly long time to pick up and clean the flashlight while Trudy and her mother held each other almost silently, except for tiny sobs.

Eventually Trudy's mother pushed her daughter away softly. "Let me look at you."

Trudy's eyes were red but she still grinned. "Dad's missed you too."

Trudy's mother smiled for a second, but then her face snapped into a more serious shape. "I'm sure he has, but we can discuss that later. We need to get out of here first!"

Jack spoke. "Well, that shouldn't be too hard. I mean, this feels like a bit of an anticlimax as a rescue. We were able to just walk in here."

Suddenly Trudy's mother seemed to notice Jack for the first time. "Who is your friend, Trudy?"

"This is Jack. I met him at the Ministry. He's very good at figuring things out."

"So you're both working for the Ministry?"

Jack nodded. "We're practically old hands at this stage."

Trudy's mother snorted. "Then you should realize that we're in a very bad situation."

"But there weren't any traps or anything on the way in."

Trudy's mother sighed. "This is a prison. And prisons aren't about stopping people from getting in. They're about stopping people from getting back out."

"You mean . . . there are traps?"

Trudy's mother nodded. She pointed up to the corners of the cavern. There were two small black boxes in the far corners aimed directly at them.

"What are they?" Trudy asked.

"Motion detectors."

"What do they do?" Jack asked.

"Detect motion," Trudy's mother said. "You actually work for the Ministry? Obviously the Misery hasn't been training people quite as hard as he used to."

"I meant, what do they do when they detect motion?"

"That I don't know. They were set up here when Merlin brought me in. But I suspect we'll find out precisely what they're for if we manage to get this chain off my wrist." Mrs. Emerson rattled the long, rusty chain that fastened her arm to the wall.

Jack picked up a length of the chain and rattled it. "Seems fairly solid. Maybe we could use The Speed."

Mrs. Emerson shook her head. "I've already tried using The Speed to pull it and vibrate it, but it's embedded far too deeply into the wall for that to have any effect."

"Maybe we can find a bolt cutter?" Trudy suggested.

"Whatever we do we'd better do it quickly. Merlin occasionally checks in on me to ensure that I'm here."

Jack thought as hard as he could but there was no easy

solution. He looked at the manacle that secured the chain to Mrs. Emerson's wrist. "I don't suppose Merlin keeps the key nearby? If we could get the key, we'd be able to get you out."

Mrs. Emerson's shoulders sagged. "If that's what we're relying on, we're really in trouble. Merlin thought that someone might come and try to rescue me, so he said that he had mixed the key in with some animal feed. One of the animals will have eaten it and then pooped it out in a random location. There's no way anyone will ever find it. It's just impossible—the key is lost."

A thought struck Jack and he smiled. "What does the key look like?"

"Why?"

"Humor me."

"It was maybe an inch long, made out of a dark gray metal. The top of it was shaped like a crown. But it doesn't matter. You'll never find it. It's lost forever."

Jack laughed. "Maybe Merlin isn't the genius we took him for. He's made a very big mistake." Jack took off his schoolbag and started looking through it to find one of the poetry books from his English class. He handed it to Trudy. "Read some of this to me."

"Is this really the appropriate time for poetry?"

"I don't think there's ever an appropriate time for poetry," said Jack. "Now read!"

Trudy shrugged. She was getting used to Jack behaving like this.

"I will arise and go now, and go to Innisfree,[77]
     And a small cabin build there, of clay and
          wattles made:"

"Clay and wattles," Jack muttered to himself. "What are clay and wattles?"

Trudy carried on reading:

"Nine bean-rows will I have there, a hive for the
     honey-bee;
And live alone in the bee-loud glade."

As Trudy read, Jack carried on with his muttering. "Why would you need a hive for a single bee? Shouldn't that be 'honey-bees'? And if you only had a single bee how loud could it possibly be?"

Trudy read on.

"And I shall have some peace there, for peace
     comes dropping slow,
Dropping from the veils of the morning to
     where the cricket sings;

---

[77] For those of you who are wondering, this is from the poem "The Lake Isle of Innisfree." I've used it because it's a brilliant poem written by W. B. Yeats. Well, to be honest, that's only part of the reason; the other part of the reason is that Yeats died in 1939 and therefore can't sue me for copyright infringement.

There midnight's all a glimmer, and noon a
   purple glow,
And evening full of the linnet's wings."

Jack shook his head in consternation. "Is the poet saying the sky at noon was purple? I've never seen a purple sun before. And what on earth is a linnet?"

Trudy stopped reading. "Jack, why do you want me to read this if you don't understand it?"

"Don't you get it? Anytime I try and understand poetry I always get completely lost. . . ." And after saying that sentence Jack disappeared.

Mrs. Emerson blinked twice as she looked at the empty space where Jack had until recently been. "Maybe there's more promise in that boy than I thought."

Trudy smiled at her mother. "That's how I feel about him as well."

Jack suddenly reappeared where he had been, but he was clutching a key.

"The Lost and Found room?" guessed Trudy.

"Exactly," said Jack. "Merlin had deliberately lost the key, so it had to be in the Lost and Found room. Once I found the key it wasn't lost anymore and so I just popped back into existence with it." Jack held up the key proudly. Then he noticed that it was covered in elephant dung.

Trudy handed him a tissue and Jack thanked her profusely. When the key was moderately cleaner they freed Mrs. Emerson from her chains.

"Now we can get out of here." Trudy smiled.

Mrs. Emerson was looking less cheerful than her daughter. "I suspect that now that the chain is removed we'll find out what the motion sensors are for."

On cue, the motion sensors clicked and turned toward the heroes.

MINISTRY OF S.U.IT.S HANDBOOK

MIND CONTROL
MIND READING

To date, Ministry scientists have discovered that mind control is, for all intents and purposes, impossible. However, this does not mean that all psychic arts are beyond our capabilities.

Indeed, one particularly distinguished psychic within the Ministry, called Sarah the Grand, discovered that with a judicious application of psychology, concentration, and sheer force of will she could hear what people were thinking.

In order to do this she had to stand on one leg, wave her hands in the air, and stare with one eyebrow raised. Using this technique she was able to perfectly understand what someone was thinking.

Unfortunately, using this method, she invariably discovered that what they were thinking was "I wonder why on earth that idiot is staring at me like that."

Therefore, the skill was of somewhat limited use.

28

GETTING THE POINT

Jack, Trudy, and Mrs. Emerson all froze on the spot. The motion detectors stopped moving and the room was silent. Jack tried to speak without moving his lips. "If we move, is that going to set off an alarm?"

"Ha ha," Mrs. Emerson said, clearly worried that really laughing might have set off the motion detectors. "If that was the problem, I'd be walking out of here already. I rather suspect that they're the trigger to some kind of deadly trap."

"Why do so many traps have to be deadly?" Jack grumbled. "Can't we have some mildly inconveniencing traps for once?"

"We can't just stand still forever," Trudy said. "I'm going to try something."

"You will not," Mrs. Emerson said firmly. "I'm the adult, and if anyone is going to . . ."

As Mrs. Emerson spoke Jack saw a frown fall across Trudy's face. It was a sure sign she was going to use The Speed. Trudy's body suddenly jerked and she sped across the cavern. The motion sensors twisted and followed her progress. As they did there were several small eruptions of soil from the walls of the cavern. Three long, metal poles burst from inside of the walls and shot toward Trudy. She turned her head and caught sight of them.

"TRUDY!" Jack and Mrs. Emerson shouted at once—both frozen, not daring to move.

Although she was already moving at an impossible pace, Trudy pushed harder with her legs and dived forward. The three poles missed her by a fraction of an inch and crashed into the wall behind her, sticking with a series of *thonks*.

Trudy rolled and came to a halt, sitting on the ground. She froze instantly.

"Okay," Jack said, "at least we know what the motion detectors do. And I've also just realized what must have happened to the other metal bars that were replaced by the Plexiglas around the meerkat enclosure."

Trudy swiveled her eyes toward where the poles had stuck into the wall. "They seem to have sharpened ends. I think if we get hit by one it'll be fatal."

"Don't you ever do anything as foolhardy as that again, young lady," Mrs. Emerson lectured her daughter.

"Do you think there were only three sharpened poles in the wall?" Jack asked.

Trudy and Mrs. Emerson barely moved their heads and

yet managed to give him withering stares. Jack was sure that if they had been able to move he would have been suffering from two badly bruised shoulders.

"Look, I've already shown that the poles can be outrun. We can all move at once—if we dodge and zigzag we can get out of here."

Jack felt very worried indeed. Trudy had barely managed to avoid being turned into a shish kebab. He knew that he was nowhere near as fast as she was. He was going to say something but Trudy's mother beat him to it. "You two go on. I'll try to follow."

Trudy frowned. "We're all going together."

Mrs. Emerson risked a sigh and a slight sag of her shoulders. "We can't, Trudy; there's no way I'd be fast enough even using The Speed. I've been chained to a wall for almost a year now. I'm not strong enough and my legs are so stiff they're practically boards."

"There's no way we're leaving without you."

"Yeah," Jack agreed, secretly glad that he wasn't going to be skewered.

"Jack, we need an idea how we can get out of here."

"Right. Ummm."

"And hurry up—Merlin could be back at any minute."

Jack concentrated as hard as he could and came up with . . . nothing. The silence in the cavern was deafening until it was broken by Mrs. Emerson speaking. "Trudy, whatever happens I need you to know that I'm proud of you. You tried your best and that's the main thing."

Trudy's face turned red. Jack suspected that she was

emotional at her mother's touching words. "No," Trudy said calmly but firmly. Her voice sounded fierce rather than emotional.

"No?"

Trudy let out a long breath. "Trying your best isn't the main thing. That's what people say to losers. And I am not a loser. I'm going to get us out of here."

"But I can't think of anything," Jack said apologetically. "I don't know how those metal bars are being fired out of the wall—I don't know how to stop them. And the motion sensors are far too high on the cavern roof for us to reach them."

A sparkle appeared in Trudy's eyes. "That's it—you're thinking about this wrong, Jack. We don't need to stop the iron bars. They're the solution—not the problem."

If Jack had had more time he would have been confused by Trudy's statement. However, he didn't get the chance as his confusion was replaced by worry when Trudy bolted across the room, using The Speed. As she moved, small clouds of dirt burst out of the walls of the cavern. And behind each spray of dust a sharpened iron bar followed, zipping toward Trudy at an incredible rate.

The first missed her by more than two feet, the second by a foot and a half. Trudy was running toward where the two motion sensors were mounted high on the wall. Jack wondered how she could climb the wall quickly enough to avoid being pierced by a deadly bar.

As Trudy reached the wall she leapt in the air and then tucked and tumbled back to the ground. A metal bar zoomed over her head and stuck into the wall, vibrating for a second.

"Now the difficult part," Trudy muttered to herself as she leapt back up again. With both hands she grabbed onto the bar above her head and spun herself around like an athlete on the horizontal bars.

"Go, Trudy, go!" Mrs. Emerson yelled.

Trudy spun around like an airplane propeller. Two more long rods slammed into the wall above her, missing her spinning body by a fraction. Trudy let go of the bar she was holding and caught one farther up. As more and more bars thwacked into the wall it was almost as if Trudy was creating her own adventure gym. Jack began to suspect she was showing off.

"Just a few more . . ." Trudy panted as she twirled from one to another.

"Be careful!" Jack shouted. "They're getting closer!"

With each leap Trudy made, the motion sensors seemed to be getting more accurate. What made it worse was that with each successive effort of spinning and leaping between the bars on the wall Trudy was getting slower.

"Trudy, you need to freeze again," Mrs. Emerson shouted. "They're getting too close."

Trudy smiled as she spun. "I want them to get too close." A metal bar shot toward her and the tip caught the edge of her shirt, tearing it.

"Okay, that's probably close enough now!" With those words Trudy spun around one of the bars for the last time then let go, launching herself through the air. Three more poles burst from the wall and fired toward her. Trudy curled herself into a ball and tumbled in a graceful arc. Her body brushed the ceiling and she started falling, right past the part of the wall where the motion sensors were mounted. The three sharpened poles missed Trudy by mere milli-meters and crashed into the wall behind her—right into the motion sensors. There was a sudden fizzing and a shower of sparks as the sensors were smashed into a million pieces.

Trudy tumbled toward the ground. At the last minute, she reached out an arm, spun around a pole, and landed with a neat somersault. She turned and smiled at Jack and her mother, who were safe to move again.

"You're amazing, Trudy." Mrs. Emerson smiled at her.

"That is the general opinion," agreed Jack.

"Now let's get out of here before Merlin arrives."

They quickly made their way along the tunnel and out into the sunshine once more. Once outside, they made their way to the exit of the zoo and phoned for a Ministry car. As they traveled toward the museum, Trudy kept looking at her mother, almost as if to make sure that she was still there.

GYMNASTICS AND ACROBATICS
Origins

Many people assume, based on the abilities
of modern-day gymnasts, that acrobatics were
invented by the most coordinated and capable of
their tribes. And yet this is entirely erroneous.

The truth is that the original acrobats were
actually the most clumsy of their group. People
who were well coordinated generally found life
to be relatively easy, walking from one place to
another. The clumsy people, however, could
never make a journey without tripping or
tumbling—they therefore had to learn how to
fall head over heels without hurting themselves.

And you can see this in modern gymnastics—
because it isn't actually that hard to do a
forward roll; it's just hard to do one without
causing a severe back injury.

29

HOMECOMING QUEEN

Somehow word got back to the Ministry of Mrs. Emerson's rescue, and when they arrived, the corridors of the building were full of people overjoyed to see her. Grey; the Bear; Mike, the intelligent vertical beam of blue light; the tiny quartermaster; and all manner of people and things lined up to greet Mrs. Emerson and shake her hand. Trudy shuffled her feet while this went on, smiling proudly. Jack thought it was strange for a child to be proud of her parent. Normally parents were slightly embarrassing and best kept out of the way at public gatherings.

After a while the frenzy died down and the staff started drifting back to their day jobs. Of all the Ministry staff, only Trudy, Jack, Mrs. Emerson, and the Minister were left. The Minister urged them to follow him back to his office.

"Do you think you're up to a debriefing, Tania?" the Minister asked Mrs. Emerson.[78]

"Fit as a fiddle and ready for active service again."

"You got captured by the queen of Atlantis?"

Mrs. Emerson frowned. "I'm afraid so. I thought I could take on the Atlanteans with The Speed, but their continual use of aquarobics makes them quite fierce opponents."

The Minister nodded. "I believe Trudy and Jack found that out too, but luckily they defeated them in the end with a little help from Cthulhu and the kraken. But that's all very much yesterday's news. Today's problem is Merlin, I believe."

Mrs. Emerson nodded. "That's certainly who was keeping me prisoner—until my daughter and her friend helped me escape."

The Minister turned to Trudy and Jack. "How did you find your mother?"

"There were a few clues—we knew Merlin needed somewhere that he could store grain without anyone noticing, and we thought of the zoo."

"That's right," Jack agreed, "but the major clue was when a woodpecker arrived and spelled out the word *zoo* for us. Originally we thought that it was a message in Morse code."

Trudy's mother wrinkled her face. "Why on earth would you think that?" she asked. "I mean, who would teach a woodpecker Morse code? How would you even do that?"

---

[78] Jack felt slightly awkward upon learning that Mrs. Emerson's first name was Tania. He always believed that adults shouldn't actually have first names. It made them feel a bit less grown-up somehow.

"Yes," agreed Jack. "Thinking back on it now, it was a really stupid idea." Jack began to suspect her mother was the source of Trudy's interpersonal skills.

"When Merlin came to feed me in the cavern, he often brought some woodpeckers with him."

Jack nodded. It made perfect sense that Merlin would befriend the woodpeckers in a zoo. After all, he was the carpenter who had made the round table in the Middle Ages. Back then they wouldn't have had drills or electric saws. Training woodpeckers to undertake intricate carving work would have made the job considerably easier.

Trudy's mother continued. "Over a number of months I gathered up bugs and worms, any kind of insects I could. I used them to feed one of the woodpeckers. Eventually he became friendly."

"And then you told the woodpecker about Trudy? And asked him to take a message?"

Mrs. Emerson looked sternly at Jack. "You have some fairly outlandish ideas, Jack. You can't give instructions like that to a woodpecker. I just showed him this picture of Trudy standing outside her school—it's the picture of her I always keep in my purse. Then I scraped out the word *ZOO* on the ground alongside a rudimentary map. He was an intelligent bird and thankfully he seems to have figured out what I wanted him to do."

"Wait a minute," Trudy said. "That makes perfect sense! Because you were feeding the woodpecker, he would have stopped eating Merlin's food. So, it's definitely something in the health food and animal food that allows him to control people and animals."

"Brilliant, Trudy!" her mother said. "But . . . how would he do that? I mean, you can't control people with food just because it's fortified with iron and vitamins."

The Minister interrupted. "As interesting as your escape is, we need to focus on what Merlin is planning next."

Mrs. Emerson nodded. "He seems to have been working with the queen of Atlantis. From what Trudy and Jack have said I don't think Merlin was actually helping the queen as much as he was using her to further his own ends."

"I think that's right," Jack spoke up. "Both the pirates and the Atlanteans were digging under the ground. We suspect Merlin was looking for Excalibur—King Arthur's sword. It's hidden under our school rugby field for some reason. It also seems to be connected to the electricity network, but we have no idea why."

"Did you bring it back to the Ministry?" The Minister asked.

Trudy shook her head. "We couldn't; it's stuck in the stone and we weren't able to pull it out. Plus, it's protected by suits of armor that can move. They're practically invincible. Even if you knock them to pieces they pull themselves back together."

Mrs. Emerson turned to her daughter. "Trudy Emerson! I won't have that kind of talk. You know that when we put our minds to something and work hard at it we can achieve anything."

"Yes, Mum," said Trudy. Jack was shocked, partially because he'd never seen Trudy so meekly agree with an adult about anything, but mainly because he was amazed that there was someone in the world even more terrifying than Trudy herself.

"What do we do next, then?" asked Jack.

The Minister looked sternly at them all. "You and Trudy will continue with your investigations. Tania, you'll be fully debriefed and have a medical examination."

"Not with the Ministry doctors!" Trudy said quickly.

"No, we'll get her to go to a regular doctor." The Minister smiled.

Mrs. Emerson tutted. "I don't think there's any need for . . ."

The Minister interrupted her. "Tania, you know the rules. Agents are only allowed on active duty if they are completely fit. Agents operating at less than one hundred percent effectiveness risk endangering entire cases."

Mrs. Emerson slammed her fist down on the Minister's desk. "I think you're underestimating the danger we're facing here. This is Merlin. At one stage he was practically ruler of all of England and Wales."

"Tania. The rules are there for a reason. And just because you won't be on a mission, it doesn't mean that we won't be looking into this. Jack and Trudy . . ."

"They're twelve," shouted Mrs. Emerson. "They aren't ready to face potentially the biggest threat that the Ministry has ever dealt with!"

Jack felt slightly put out by this. "Can I just point out that we're more than capable of dealing with Merlin, whatever he's up to. I mean, we weren't the ones that got captured by him." The minute the words were out of Jack's mouth he regretted saying them. Mrs. Emerson turned and glowered at him. Jack noticed that her hands balled into fists the way her daughter's did when she got angry. But at least she wouldn't hit him. Adults weren't allowed to hit children.[79] Mrs. Emerson's eyes narrowed and she turned to look at Trudy. There seemed to be a moment of psychic communication between Trudy and her mother. Then Trudy shrugged, balled one of her own fists, and punched Jack in the shoulder. Mrs. Emerson smiled and turned around to the Minister. Trudy looked slightly sheepish and mouthed "sorry" at Jack.

"They are children. Merlin was reputed to be one of the most powerful scientists of his day. He was so powerful people mistook what he did for magic," Mrs. Emerson said firmly.

The Minister shook his head very slowly. "You're off the case. Go to the doctor and then go home."

Mrs. Emerson stared at the Minister for a few seconds and then turned and stormed toward the door. Trudy followed her. When Mrs. Emerson noticed, she spun on her heel. She glared at her daughter and then her eyes softened. "Trudy, no—you have to stay."

"No way! I've just gotten you back. There's no way I'm leaving you."

Mrs. Emerson hesitated for a second before grabbing Trudy and giving her the longest hug imaginable. Then slowly she pushed Trudy away. "You have to stop Merlin.

---

[79] Technically children aren't allowed to hit children either. But for some reason this is generally regarded as more of a *guideline* than an actual rule.

Freeing me wasn't enough. If Merlin has a plot, you can be sure it's big. He's used to controlling entire countries."

"But you were missing for months and . . ."

Trudy's mother shook her head and then spoke through gritted teeth. "The Minister's right—I spent months chained to a wall underground. I'll need some rest before I'm back in shape. What I need is for you and Jack to try to find out what Merlin's up to. By then hopefully I'll be back in good enough condition to fight him."

Trudy hesitated for a second but then nodded sadly.

"Now, you and Jack stay here with the Minister. I'm going to go home and see your father."

Jack could tell that Trudy was practically bursting to ask her mother if she could go along too. But he also knew that she would never say that out loud. Mrs. Emerson hugged Trudy again. Then she walked toward the door. "I'll see you tonight," she said, smiling at her daughter. Then she turned to the Minister. "You'd better make sure they're okay. If anything happens to my daughter, I'll be coming back after you—and you know I will find you."

Mrs. Emerson walked out the door. The Minister gulped nervously. "Maybe we ought to get you both some extra training. Just so you're fully prepared for whatever happens next."

"What kind of training?" asked Jack.

The Minister thought about what Mrs. Emerson had just said to him. "Learning how to hide effectively is always useful." For just a second the Minister seemed to cheer up, and a mischievous look appeared on his face. "Get the Misery to teach you how to become invisible."

HIDE AND SEEK
WORLD CHAMPIONSHIPS

Given the wide range of skills and abilities that Ministry operatives have, it is unsurprising that many of them become world champions in a variety of areas. One example of this was John Johns, a Ministry operative who was the world's most successful hide-and-seeker. If you ask John Johns about his career in world-championship hide-and-seek, he will proudly take you to his trophy room, throw open the door, and let you see dozens and dozens of empty trophy cabinets.

John Johns does not have a single trophy, ribbon, or medal. And that's how you can tell how amazing John Johns is at hide-and-seek. Because if they can find you in time to present you a medal, well, then you clearly weren't hiding hard enough.

30

HAPPINESS AND SECRETS

Training in the Ministry was overseen by the world's grump-iest teenager. His black, lank hair hung over his eyes and he wore a baggy black sweater with the letter *M* emblazoned on the front. He was rather appropriately called "the Misery." Jack was slightly scared about going to see him. Apart from anything else, it almost certainly meant that he was going to get shouted at. Any training with the Misery involved a level of shouting and humiliation. When Jack had first met the Misery, he assumed that he just enjoyed being mean. But more recently he had realized that he was mistaken— because the Misery didn't really enjoy anything.

Trudy had always been happier about visiting the Misery. She seemed to share a kind of bond with him—inasmuch as anyone could have "fellow feeling" for a perpetually unhappy teenage boy. However, on this occasion she seemed even more happy than normal. If Jack hadn't known better he would have sworn there was actually a skip in her step.

"Why are you so happy?" Jack asked. "I thought you'd be annoyed about having to leave your mother."

Trudy looked at Jack as if he had two heads.[80] "Jack, my mother has been missing for months. Okay, I was annoyed that I couldn't go with her, but for the first time in what feels like forever I know that when I go home my mother will be there waiting for me. And that's the best feeling in the world."

Jack thought about this and reflected on how it was quite possible to have "too much of a good thing." After all, both of his parents would be waiting for him when he went home, and all that they would have for him would be a series of awkward questions. It certainly didn't make him want to skip along the corridor toward the Misery's room.

When they arrived, the Misery was sitting cross-legged on the floor. As usual, although there was some light in the center of the room, it was impossible to see the walls, which were shrouded in a perpetual and nearly impenetrable gloom. Jack wondered if the room was just a physical manifestation of the Misery's mood.

Jack and Trudy peeked around the door. "He looks busy," Jack said. "Maybe we should just leave him alone."

Trudy glared at Jack, knocked on the door once, pushed it fully open, and walked in. The Misery looked up from the floor, peering at Trudy and Jack through his long black bangs.

---

[80] Which he didn't.

"Well, well, it's my two favorite agents. No doubt you're here to improve yourselves at training."

Jack didn't know if there was an infinite amount of sarcasm in the world. But if there wasn't, there was a serious risk that the Misery was going to deplete Ireland's share well before the end of the decade.[81]

The Misery stood up and then did something completely unexpected. A tiny smile appeared on his face. "I hear your mother's back, Trudy."

Trudy smiled back. "Yes."

The Misery stopped smiling almost immediately; apparently he felt you could overdo the touchy-feely stuff. "That's quite enough of the pleasantries. What particular training are you going to be awful at today?"

For a second Jack thought that the Misery was being unkind, but then he remembered their last attempts at training and realized that, statistically, he had a point. From previous experience Jack was likely to be awful at whatever the Misery taught them.

"The Minister suggested you might teach us how to hide properly," Trudy said.

The Misery's face fell instantly. "Exactly what did he say?"

---

[81] Since the invention of Twitter many social scientists have worried that we may have reached "peak sarcasm." (This is mainly a joke for economists. So if you're not an economist please feel free to ignore and read on. If you are an economist, *you're welcome*. Now get back to your day job and make sure you give us a bit more warning the next time the world is about to go into financial meltdown.)

Jack had never seen the Misery look nervous before. It was amusing and yet disconcerting at the same time. "He told us that you'd teach us how to become invisible. But, I mean, that's impossible. I assume it was just a figure of speech."

The Misery's shoulders sagged. If he'd become any more floppy he would have turned into a puddle on the ground. "If he'd asked me to show you anything ... anything else, I'd have done cartwheels[82] ... but he said invisible?"

"Well ... yes."

"Sit down." The Misery indicated the floor in front of him. Jack and Trudy sat down in similar cross-legged poses. "Becoming invisible is the hardest thing any agent can do."

In the past few weeks Jack had learned how to move at almost impossibly fast speeds and also how by shocking yourself you could stop breathing for short periods of time. The first skill had been acquired by being shouted at and the second by being unfairly startled. If becoming invisible was going to be even harder than that, Jack wasn't sure that it was a skill he really needed.

"Is this going to involve a lot of shouting?" Jack inquired.

"Do you think I'd look this unhappy if I was going to be shouting at you?" asked the Misery. "This is going to be the most unpleasant thing I'll ever teach you to do."

"Explain!" Trudy said.

"If you're invisible it basically means that you're transparent. Now, have you ever heard about anyone being completely transparent?"

---

[82] I think we all know this isn't true.

Jack thought. "Well, yes, if a politician or a movie star or a businessperson tells the truth about something. Then the newspapers say they're being transparent."

Trudy nodded. "Yeah, but that's just a phrase, isn't it?"

"How many times do I have to explain this?" The Misery sighed. "People don't just make up phrases. They all have a basis in fact. And it isn't just phrases about being transparent. There are dozens of similar ones. Think about it. When you know the truth about someone, you talk about being able to 'see right through them.'"

"How does that work?" asked Trudy. "I mean, being honest can't make you just disappear, can it?"

"It has to do with the speed at which the molecules in your body vibrate," the Misery said. "You see, molecules are very honest things. In science they always talk about how molecules follow laws. And molecules don't just occasionally follow laws—they follow the laws *all the time*. People are a lot less honest than that and only follow laws occasionally. People breaking laws and lying make the molecules in our bodies confused—and when they are confused they vibrate slowly and sluggishly—because they are trying to stop you from telling lies."

"So that changes when we're honest?" asked Jack.

"Yes, the more honest you are the more excited your molecules get. And if you're completely honest they vibrate so quickly that you begin to blur and then eventually fade from view entirely."

"That doesn't make sense." Jack shook his head as if

trying to clear it. "I'm honest most of the time and I don't disappear."

"You think so?" The Misery laughed.

"Yes!" Jack snapped.

"I never . . . well, hardly ever lie," Trudy agreed.

"You're misunderstanding," the Misery said slowly. "Not lying isn't the same thing as being completely honest." The Misery bit his tongue for a second before continuing. "It's like this. Not lying isn't the same as being a hundred percent truthful. Being a hundred percent truthful means that you have to tell your deepest, darkest secrets—about everything. Look, truth is more than an absence of lies. Truth means telling about everything. Every time you wet the bed when you were young. Every time you did something embarrassing. Who you have a crush on in school. Everything."

Jack and Trudy looked at each other, slightly panicked. "I'm not sure I ever could be that honest," Jack said.

"There'd be a risk of dying of embarrassment," agreed Trudy.

The Misery continued explaining. "You know how when things vibrate they make a humming or a high-pitched noise? That's where the phrase 'ring of truth' comes from. So, if you get this right, there's a slight ping and you just vanish. But it only works if you're one hundred percent honest about something that you never wanted to admit to anyone."

Jack felt slightly awkward. He had a horrible feeling that pretty soon he was going to move from talking about turning invisible to having to tell about the most embarrassing incidents from his life. Which was something that he really, really didn't want to do.

Trudy spoke quietly. "Is this the part where we practice telling the truth and turning invisible?"

"It isn't that kind of training," said the Misery. "The more you do something, the less exciting it gets. And the same is true of your molecules. Although they'll be excited the first time you tell the complete truth, it won't work quite as well the next time. So, this is something you don't practice. And you only use it when you absolutely need to."

"But how do we know that it actually works, then?"

"I knew you were going to ask that. I knew it. . . . I knew it." The Misery broke eye contact with Jack and stared at the floor. There was a very uncomfortable silence. Then the Misery looked back up. "I cried when I read the end of the book *Charlotte's Web*."[83]

The idea that someone as tough as the Misery would have cried at a book made Jack want to laugh out loud. But he didn't, because there was a pinging sound and then suddenly there was no one to laugh at. For a brief second the Misery had blurred at the edges, and then he disappeared

---

[83] It is interesting that the Misery cried at the end of *Charlotte's Web*, because he wasn't similarly affected by all children's books. In fact, he was actually quite callous about some of them. Although he hadn't told anyone that he was currently in talks with a publisher to sign a deal for a children's book sequel he'd written called *Velveteen Rabbit 2 : Velveteen Rabbit Stew*.

entirely. Jack and Trudy looked at each other. In part because there was now no one else to look at.

"I can't believe that the Misery turned invisible," Trudy exclaimed.

"I can't believe that the Misery cried at *Charlotte's Web*," said Jack, laughing.

Jack felt something slap the back of his head and a voice out of nowhere spoke. "Still here, remember? Just invisible."

"Sorry," Jack apologized to the empty space.

"Well, now that you know it works, get out of my room and stop bothering me."

As Jack and Trudy got up, they heard footsteps walking away from them but couldn't see anything. Even once they were outside, Jack couldn't help looking over his shoulder to check that they were alone. "That's kind of freaky. I don't think I'm ever going to be sure I'm completely alone again."

Trudy nodded and then asked a question. "Do you think you'll be able to do that? Be so honest that you'll turn invisible?"

Jack thought for a moment. "Not sure. Hopefully we won't have to. I'm not sure that I ever want to be quite that honest. But maybe it isn't that hard. I mean, confessing to crying at *Charlotte's Web*—that isn't *really* embarrassing, is it?"

"You're missing the point," Trudy argued. "For you it wouldn't be that embarrassing, but the Misery pretends that he never gets emotional about anything. That was a big secret for him."

"I suppose so," Jack agreed, wondering what his own biggest secret was. "So, what do we do now?"

Trudy thought. "Well, hopefully my mother will have finished at the doctors by now. . . . I was thinking maybe we could both go home?"

<hr>

They called a Ministry car to take them home. Jack insisted they drop Trudy off first as she wanted to see her mother and father back together again. It also gave him a chance to think about the clues they had so far.

They knew that they were up against Merlin, the scientist who had helped make Arthur king of the Britons. Merlin was a scientist, skilled in carpentry and herbalism and even able to genetically modify plants. It was obvious that in recent years he had been causing people to have allergic reactions to scare the public into buying "health foods." By making people and animals eat these health foods, Merlin managed to control them somehow—but how?

They had also found Excalibur, but it didn't seem to want to come free from the stone into which it was plunged. Which seemed odd: If a sword was sharp enough to cut its way into a stone, wouldn't it be sharp enough to cut its way back out? On top of that, Jack couldn't help wondering why the stone had been wired up to an electrical line from a pylon. Was Merlin trying to shock the sword out of the stone?

And then, of course, there was also the driverless car that had tried to kill him, and the suits of armor. Jack had wondered if the suits were some kind of animatronic robots like the giant and the dragon, but that didn't make sense, because the armor had been completely empty when they broke it apart—there weren't any mechanical innards.

Possibly the most worrying part of all was the fantasy movie that Merlin was pretending to make. It gave Merlin almost perfect cover. He was literally hiding in the open with a giant, a dragon, and as many suits of armor as he wanted. When Merlin had enough people under control he would no doubt equip them with shields and swords and take over the country.

But Jack suspected it wasn't that simple. There was something more going on, something that he hadn't quite figured out yet. Jack felt nervous that it was Wednesday night already—he really wanted to try to get everything figured out by Friday at the latest. His parents had recently bought him Lego Marvel Super Heroes, and he wanted to spend most of the weekend trying to complete it.

INVISIBILITY GARMENTS[84]
UNSUITABILITY

Although some people do not believe they exist, the world is full of cloaks of invisibility. After all, the cloaks would be incredibly useful, and they are an idea that people have had for many hundreds if not thousands of years. It would be ridiculous to suggest that if an idea had been around for that long, no one would ever have gotten around to inventing it.

You may ask, if this is the case, then why aren't they in more common usage? The reason is

---

[84] Incidentally, if you ever buy an invisibility cloak off eBay, it's essential that you check the user policy on returns. Because sometimes they're selling an invisibility cloak, but sometimes they've just taken a picture of an empty coat hanger in an attempt to fool you. And I refuse to get caught a third time with that particular scam.

simple. Although the idea of an invisibility cloak seems brilliant initially, it is highly impractical. Let us take an example—you use your invisibility cloak to sneak into a party to which you are not invited. It gets you past the person at the door checking the guest list. Then, once inside, you hang up your cloak and start to enjoy the party. At the end of the night you go to the cloakroom to try to find your invisibility cloak. Of course, what with it being invisible, it is basically impossible to find.

Statistical surveys have shown that the most common phrase used by owners of invisibility cloaks is "Now . . . where did I put it?"

Ancient legends are full of people losing their magic swords, magic rings, and even magic lamps. However, the magic item that is most frequently lost, without a doubt, is the invisibility cloak.[85]

[85] One legendary story about invisibility involved the magician Mo the Great. Mo spent much of her life trying to develop an invisibility cloak and astounded her colleagues when she eventually created one. She demonstrated its existence by letting them feel the cloak with their hands—because obviously, they couldn't actually *see* it.

This is why you should never, ever leave your car keys in the pocket of your invisibility cloak. Because if you do, you're going to be cold while you're *walking* home.

Many people were amazed at the cloak and offered to pay several fortunes to own it. However, a young girl witnessing the demonstration pointed out that the cloak was actually of limited use. After all, the cloak was invisible and people could see right through it. Therefore, when you put it on, you didn't actually become invisible. It was *the cloak* that was invisible, *not you*. People saw through the cloak and to what you were wearing underneath. This meant that the sole purpose of the cloak was that when you wore it you were slightly warmer than you *appeared* to be.

Many people have suggested that in the tale "The Emperor's New Clothes," the emperor was not naked at all. He was just wearing an invisibility cloak.

31

BECAUSE SOMETIMES EVEN PARENTS ARE HELPFUL

Jack's parents were sitting at the table eating their dinner. Jack just drank a cup of tea.

"Are you sure you don't want something to eat?"

Jack shook his head. "Thanks, Dad, but we got something to eat at Trudy's after choir practice." Jack wished this had been true. He was literally starving, but looking at the Mr. M's Healthy Meals packages that sat on the kitchen counter made him lose his appetite. For that matter, watching his parents eating didn't really help much either. Jack wondered if they would suddenly find themselves under Merlin's control. And yet he couldn't think of a way to stop them from eating it without explaining his work in the Ministry—and would they even believe that?

"Do you mind if I just go to my room? I have some homework to do," Jack said. And for once he was telling the truth.

When he was in his room, Jack pulled a chair over in front of his mirror and sat down on it. He stared at his reflection in the mirror and thought to himself. The Misery had said not to practice, but being invisible was clearly going to be far too much fun not to try it at least once.

The question was, what embarrassing truth was he going to tell to himself? What did he have to be honest about? What would he hate having to admit, despite the fact that it was true? Jack focused at his own reflection in the mirror and then said something he certainly knew, but wouldn't have admitted out loud. "Trudy's a much better Ministry agent than I am. I'd be lost without her." Jack noticed that his edges seemed to blur slightly.

"Okay, so that was true, but not quite true enough, obviously." Jack thought about things that were both true and hard to admit. Then he realized that the hardest things to be completely honest about were the ones that involved not just saying something, but actually having to change your behavior once you'd admitted it.

Focusing on the mirror once more, he looked sternly at himself. "I take my parents for granted and I should be a lot nicer to them." It was a very honest thing to say, and Jack could almost feel his molecules beginning to vibrate faster and faster. He watched in the mirror as his reflection blurred and then disappeared with a *ping*. Jack leapt up from the chair.[86] "Brilliant! I'm invisible!"

Although Jack felt it was slightly anticlimactic to be

[86] Although he couldn't actually see himself doing that.

invisible by yourself—because no one could actually see that they couldn't see you—it still felt pretty amazing. He ran around the room, feeling smug and singing "I'm not looking at the man in the mirror!"

Which was great fun right up until the moment he ran straight into the mirror and fell over, banging his head on the side of the bed. It hurt a lot and he lay there for a minute feeling sorry for himself. "Okay, important safety tip there—it's incredibly easy to run into a mirror when your reflection isn't there as a warning."

Jack put his hand up to his mouth to see if he was bleeding. Of course, he didn't see any blood, but then again he didn't see his hand either. He sat still and waited. After a few seconds his hand started fading back into view. The effect of telling the truth was wearing off. There was something loose in his mouth. He spat it out. A single tooth lay in the palm of his hand. He felt around in his mouth with his tongue and realized it was one from right at the back. He frowned at his face in the mirror. "Still, it could have been worse, I suppose. At least it isn't one of the front ones."

His mother appeared at the door of his room to find out what the crashing noise had been. He looked up at her from his sitting position and held out the tooth for her to see. His mother suggested they should go to the hospital if he had banged his head that badly, but Jack refused.

"It's okay, Mum. No double vision or anything. I'm fine."

"Well, all right," she said, still not one hundred percent sure, "but if you feel ill or anything, let me know."

Jack promised he would. His mother insisted on tucking

him into bed to ensure that there were no more accidents. Once she had left the room, Jack looked at the tooth lying on top of the bedside cabinet. He got up, walked over to the window, and looked out the curtains. Like the last two nights, the driverless silver car was sitting outside his house again. Revving its engine. It would almost certainly try to get him on his way to the bus the next day. And his father had said that he wouldn't give him another lift.

Jack needed to figure out a way to get to school without getting mowed down by a psychopathic car. He walked back over to his bed and tied his leg to the frame once more. He hadn't eaten any of Mr. M's food, but you couldn't be too safe.

Then Jack had an idea. He reached out with one hand, lifted the loose tooth, and bunched his fist. Then he placed the fist, tooth and all, under his pillow.

ANIMALS THAT ARE GOOD AT HIDING
CHAMELEONS

One of the creatures that is most effective at hiding in the world is the chameleon, which can change color at a moment's notice. It is interesting that chameleons originally didn't develop this ability as a defensive mechanism. If you have ever seen a chameleon, you will have noticed that it has swiveling eyes that can point in different directions. This is because chameleons are incredibly fashion conscious and want to make sure they are following the latest trends. They therefore developed a way to change the color of their skin to ensure that they were on trend and right up to date.

It is also why you will never see two chameleons at a party wearing the same dress.

Some people have asked what would happen if you put a chameleon in a box full of mirrors. The answer is simple. It would turn black, simply because it's the most slimming color.

32

CAR CHASE
THURSDAY

When Jack woke the next morning, his room was bright. Which was surprising, because normally his curtains kept the morning brightness out of the room. In fact, that was the entire point of curtains. Their one job was to keep the brightness out—and yet they seemed to have rather dropped the ball this morning. Jack's eyes opened slightly more; squinting at the light, he sat up and realized that someone had already opened the curtains.

Sitting at the bottom of his bed was an enormous man who would have been more threatening had it not been for the fact that he was wearing a pink tutu, two sizes too small. He had a shaggy brown beard and a scar on one side of his face. "You're holding on to that tooth pretty tight." The Tooth Fairy nodded at Jack's fist, which was still clenched under the pillow.

Most people would have been surprised at this happening; however, Jack had met the Tooth Fairy before. In fact, given everything that had happened recently, Jack would not have been surprised if he had found Little Red Riding Hood, Cinderella, and a dozen other fairy-tale characters hiding in his closet.

Although the Tooth Fairy looked like a dangerous criminal, he was in fact a businessman who sold people's teeth to make the white keys on pianos. Jack pulled his fist out from under the pillow and tossed the tooth to the huge man, who caught it more nimbly than you would expect. "Cheers," the Tooth Fairy said, standing up. "Going rate for these things is two quid." He tossed Jack a silver and gold coin.

"Thanks," said Jack. He completely failed to catch the coin, and it clattered against the wall, rolling under his bedside cabinet. "It used to be fifty pence."

The Tooth Fairy shrugged his impressively hairy shoulders. "Inflation. Exchange rates. You've got to pay the market value." The Tooth Fairy turned to leave and then stopped as if a thought had struck him. He held the tooth Jack had given him up to the light. "This is a second molar. Last of your baby teeth."

Jack's plan was working. . . . "Well, if this is going to be the last time we see each other, perhaps I could ask you a favor."

The Tooth Fairy sneered at Jack. "You gave me the tooth and I gave you the money. That's the deal. I owe you nothing. You are one of the most annoying boys I've ever met."

"I am very annoying," Jack agreed. "So, it's likely that

someone's going to punch me in the mouth at some stage in the future."

"I expect so," grunted the Tooth Fairy.

"Accepting that's going to happen, here's my offer: When someone punches me in later life, if a tooth comes loose I'll leave it under the pillow for you. But in return you do me a favor now."

The Tooth Fairy looked at Jack's face. "It is a *very annoying* face." After a moment's hesitation the Tooth Fairy nodded. "Deal. What's the favor?"

Jack smiled. "Do you still have your black Ford Cortina?"

The Tooth Fairy nodded, then paused before speaking. "Is this going to be something dangerous?"

Jack nodded. "Potentially deadly."

A smile emerged from the middle of the Tooth Fairy's dense beard. "Good."

―――――――――

Jack's parents were both looking rather unexcitedly at bowls of muesli that were in front of them when Jack ran into the room.

"How's the head this morning?" his mother asked.

"Head? What? Oh yeah, great, great," said Jack.

Jack's father stood up and poured a bowl of Mr. M's Nutritious Wheatie Flakes into a bowl. "Right, young man, you'd better have a good breakfast this morning. After all, you didn't have tea last night."

"Can't!" Jack said. "Trudy's father's picking me up this morning for school and I'm already late."

The toaster popped and two slices jumped out the top.

Jack grabbed them and set a new world record for buttering them before disappearing out the front door. His parents followed Jack and watched as he clambered into a black car.

"Is that Trudy's father?" Jack's dad asked. "When he dropped Jack off before I'm sure he wasn't driving a Ford Cortina."

Jack's mother nodded in agreement. "I'm also sure that he wasn't wearing a pink tutu."

<hr />

Jack bundled himself into the seat beside the Tooth Fairy, who shifted the gearstick, stamped on the accelerator, and screeched away from the curb. Jack was pushed backward in his seat and struggled to put on his seatbelt.

As the Tooth Fairy drove, he looked slightly sheepish. "Incidentally, you'll be wanting to tell your father to get his drainpipe replaced."

"Why's that?" Jack asked.

"Umm, well, when I was climbing down it, it may have bent slightly. I put on a few pounds recently."

"Never mind that," Jack said. "You could have ruined all our drainpipes and the guttering as well and you'd still be doing me a huge favor."

"This Ministry business, then?" the Tooth Fairy asked.

Jack nodded. "Someone's trying to kill me."

"Really?" The Tooth Fairy sounded impressed. "Then you must be doing a good job." The Tooth Fairy let out a long sigh. "I remember the days when people tried to kill me. Easter Bunny and I used to have a grudge thing going. But no one even tries to kill me anymore."

"Why not?" asked Jack.

"Turns out I'm what they call 'nearly indestructible.'"

"Nearly?"

"Well, I say 'nearly,' but that's just out of modesty, really. Anyway, who is it that's trying to kill you?"

"Merlin."

The Tooth Fairy let out an impressed whistle. "That's fairly big league."

Jack looked in the rearview mirror. The silver driverless car had pulled up behind them. It sped up and nudged the bumper of the Ford Cortina, causing the Tooth Fairy to briefly swerve before regaining control. The Tooth Fairy made a low growling noise. "That's what's trying to kill you?"

Jack nodded.

"All right then, let's deal with this now." The Tooth Fairy jammed on the brakes and stepped out of the car. The driverless silver car seemed surprised by this move and its wheels screeched as it quickly reversed a hundred meters. The Tooth Fairy flexed his impressive biceps and stood behind the Ford Cortina in the middle of the road.

"Umm, what are you doing?" Jack asked as he craned his neck around to watch.

The Tooth Fairy said nothing but stood stock-still in the middle of the road. The silver car revved. Suddenly its wheels screeched forward again and it barreled down the road toward the Tooth Fairy.

The Tooth Fairy didn't move.

"GET OUT OF THE WAY!" Jack screamed.

The Tooth Fairy turned his head over one hairy shoulder. "Calm yourself." He turned back around and bunched one fist. The car was only meters away from the Tooth Fairy. In one swift movement the Tooth Fairy raised and brought his fist down on the speeding car's hood at exactly the right moment. The entire front end of the car crumpled as if it were an accordion. It flipped into the air and somersaulted over the Ford Cortina before crashing back onto the road, flipping again and again.

The Tooth Fairy blew on his fist before turning, walking around his car, and getting back in. "I told you—nearly indestructible."

Jack couldn't think of anything to say.

The Tooth Fairy started the Ford Cortina up again and began driving at a leisurely pace. After five minutes he nudged Jack in the arm and pointed to the rearview mirror. Jack turned to see what the Tooth Fairy was indicating. There were now two silver driverless cars following them. "Merlin must have a fleet of those things."

Jack looked hopefully at the Tooth Fairy. "But you can smash them as well, can't you?"

The Tooth Fairy rubbed his bristled chin. "Could do, but I'm working on a schedule, see? There's a time for fighting and a time for running. Not from fear, but just because it's the most efficient thing to do. I'm not your chauffeur; I've also got a business to run. Now buckle your seat belt."

Jack had already buckled his seat belt, but found himself wishing he had a second one. The enormous hamlike hand of the Tooth Fairy shifted the gears and his foot hammered down on the accelerator again. The silver cars behind them revved their engines in pursuit.

The Tooth Fairy's Ford Cortina screeched and howled as he threw it around a corner. The silver cars followed, but at a distance. Whereas the Tooth Fairy screeched and smoked his car around every turn, the silver cars moved as if they were on rails, with every move judged to a thousandth of an inch.

"If I push the accelerator any harder, my foot's going to be on the road," the Tooth Fairy observed. "Doesn't seem like I can lose them after all."

Jack sighed. "Look, we aren't that far from my school. Just pull up outside it and I'll try and dive inside before the cars get me."

Horns blared around them as the Tooth Fairy zigged and zagged between traffic. "Nah, I've got an idea. We just need to take a detour—too many pedestrians around here to try it." The Tooth Fairy slammed the brakes, shifted gears, and tore down a side road, pursued by the silver cars. Five minutes later and they were driving down a quieter street running alongside a park. The Tooth Fairy sped to the end of it, threw the steering wheel around, and spun the car 180 degrees.

The silver driverless cars stopped in the middle of the road two hundred feet away. They revved their engines menacingly. Jack turned to the Tooth Fairy. "What are you planning? Can you please bear in mind that those cars are metal. And you're indestructible. But I am neither of those things. I'm pink, surprisingly squishy—and since meeting Trudy, also covered in bruises."

"So?" The Tooth Fairy asked.

"So . . . please don't do what I think you're going to do!"

The silver cars suddenly released their brakes and came barreling toward the Ford Cortina. The Tooth Fairy stamped down and put the pedal to the metal. "TOO LATE!"

Once more Jack would have expected his life to flash before his eyes—but this time unfortunately his eyes were too busy watching the silver cars speeding toward them to see anything else.

At the last second the Tooth Fairy jerked the steering wheel to the left and the Ford Cortina mounted the pavement. The silver cars were almost past them when the Tooth Fairy slammed both feet down on the brake and spun the steering wheel again. The Cortina turned in a circle and its rear bumper nudged the nearest silver car. It was traveling so fast that it crashed into the other car, sending it spinning into an electricity pylon, smashing and crumpling it. The pylon fell to the ground, pulling the wires from both sides with it. The wires smashed to the ground and broke—dozens of birds that had been roosting on the powerlines flapped into the air. And as they did, the second silver car stopped accelerating and glided to a standstill. It stopped moving entirely.

The Tooth Fairy pulled the car over. "Something funny going on here."

"Yeah," Jack agreed. "The second car just stopped when the pylon collapsed."

And then like a flash Jack put it all together.

HANSEL AND GRETEL[87]
THE GINGERBREAD HOUSE

You will have noticed that many fairy tales leave out crucial bits of the narrative, making them seem nonsensical. In an effort to establish the veracity of many of these tales, the Ministry has set up an Evidentiary Folklore section, which has undertaken an investigation into the basis of many of these stories to try to provide more reasonable explanations.

The first story that was investigated was that of Hansel and Gretel. If you are familiar with the story, you will be aware that there are several parts that seem to be far-fetched, to say the least.

---

[87] Personally, I don't know why the whole Hansel and Gretel problem happened at all. I mean, why did the witch want to eat children? It wasn't as if she was short of food—her house was made of gingerbread. *Gingerbread!*

The most obvious part is where Gretel pushes the witch into an oven, which, being part of a gingerbread house, must be made of some kind of foodstuff; yet the witch is unable to escape from it. This is ridiculous, because if you were ever trapped in an oven made of food, you could simply eat yourself free.

However, there is a perfectly logical explanation for this. The witch's oven was made of white bread.[88] Sadly, the witch in Hansel and Gretel suffered from a wheat allergy. If she ate any bread at all, she would come down with the most terrible diarrhea.

[88] Some of you may wonder why the witch chose bread for the oven—but it really was the most obvious choice. Any other food type would burn if used as an oven. However, the bread oven just gradually turned into toast, which the witch was then able to sell on to local cafés.

Many people would ask why the witch would choose to burn to death rather than spend a few days with a rather upset stomach. The reason for this is obvious. Although it may be horrible to burn to death, it still isn't as bad as having to live with diarrhea for several days when your toilet is made out of sticky toffee pudding and the pipes for your plumbing are mainly Pixy Stix. (It should also be noted that sudden and explosive diarrhea in a small, oven-like space would also lead to a considerable risk of the most unpleasant kind of drowning imaginable.)

Some of you will be asking how on earth the witch got official permission for a house made out of gingerbread in the first place. The person at fault is Simon Blenthins, who was the world's most incompetent zoning official. He is famous for waving through the idea of a gingerbread house, but also well-known for approving two applications from Misters Dennis and Roderick Porker for houses made of straw and twigs, respectively.

33

THE PROBLEMS
OF STARDOM

Jack thanked the Tooth Fairy for the lift and ran from the
Ford Cortina through the school's entrance hall. Up ahead of
him, he saw David with a crowd of kids who seemed to be
asking for his autograph. Although Jack had been looking
for Trudy, he decided it made sense to speak to David first.
He ran toward David but hadn't made it more than ten feet
before he tripped and fell head over heels.

Jack briefly panicked. If David had suddenly become
coordinated, had Jack suddenly become clumsy? There was
a whirring noise and Jack turned to see a gleaming black
cylinder the size of a small dog moving toward him—this
was what had tripped him. It seemed to float along the carpet waving seven or eight thick hoses that protruded from
its body. The hoses reached out for Jack, seemingly grabbing
at him. Jack scuttled backward in fear until he bumped into

Dawkins/Static, who was dressed in his full superhero costume.

Static helped Jack to his feet. "Don't worry about that. It's just a robot vacuum cleaner."

Jack looked from Static to the vacuum cleaner, trying to figure out which question he should start with first. Eventually he settled for asking about the vacuum cleaner, since it was poking him annoyingly with its hoses. "So why is the school suddenly full of robot vacuum cleaners?"

Static chomped on a Mr. M health-food bar that he had been holding. Small pieces of the bar fell from the side of his mouth and scattered onto the carpet. The vacuum cleaner darted after them, hungrily sucking the crumbs up through its many hoses. "That's the reason why right there. Mr. M's health-food bars have become so popular everyone's eating them. Apparently, they're the number-one-selling snack in Northern Ireland. But they also leave a terrible mess. Mr. M's company has lent the school these vacuum cleaners."

Jack knocked away the nozzle of a hose that had been ferreting around in one of his pockets. He was sure that the official explanation Static had given wasn't the true reason. However, he had other questions to ask. "Why are you dressed in your superhero outfit?"

"I'm trying to get people interested in my merchandise again"—Static frowned, gesturing over his shoulder—"but your friend David seems to be the flavor of the month."

Jack looked down the corridor—David was still surrounded by autograph hunters. "Yeah, well, everyone gets their fifteen minutes of fame. Sadly, I think David's is going to end fairly soon."

Static didn't seem comforted by this observation. "I'm hoping that if I bulk up on these health-food bars it'll make me look totally ripped like one of those movie superheroes. Then maybe everyone'll pay attention to me again."

"I really wouldn't keep eating those bars. They're not as good for you as everyone thinks. Anyway, I can't stay talking all day—I've got to speak to David."

"Typical," muttered Static. "Everyone wants to speak to David; no one wants to buy a Static hoodie anymore."

Jack pushed his way to the front of the crowd that was surrounding David. David eyed Jack warily. He made no move toward Jack.

Jack found it difficult to look his friend in the eye. "Can we talk?"

"Of course we can," said David.

"In private."

David looked at the crowd of adoring fans and acolytes surrounding them. "That might be more difficult. I have my public to think of."

"Just for five minutes. Please, it's important."

David sighed. "Okay, we'll find somewhere."

Five minutes later Jack and David were crammed into a toilet stall, standing on either side of the bowl.

"This isn't exactly the kind of private location I was thinking of," Jack observed.

"It was the only place I thought that people wouldn't follow us."

"No kidding. Even I didn't want to follow us."

"You wanted to talk?"

Jack hung his head. Then he realized that left him looking directly down into the bowl, and someone hadn't flushed at their last visit. He closed the toilet lid and looked at David instead. "I'm sorry about before. I realize this means a lot to you."

David nodded very slightly before he spoke. "I'm sorry too. I know there's something strange going on."

"You do?" Jack asked.

"Of course I do. There are kids out there who have started a David Sacher fan club. Suddenly, I can do all these amazing stunts—that isn't normal. I'm not stupid. When I do those crazy things it feels like someone else is moving my arms and legs for me."

"Then you realize it isn't just your super acting?" Jack shook his head in disbelief. "But . . . why are you going along with it all? If you know that there's something wrong with it."

"Don't you get it, Jack? I'm the worst in our school at sports. At exams I just about pass them. You're my only real friend. Last week most girls wouldn't even talk to me. And this week everyone loves me. There are winners and losers in life. I've never been a bad loser—but that's only because I've had so much practice at it. Just for once I want to feel like a winner."

"But you know that it's all going to come crashing down at some stage, don't you?"

David laughed. "My entire life is about things crashing down and falling over. But sometimes you can't worry about

266

the crash—you just have to enjoy the ride for a while. Look—tomorrow is the first day of filming. We're going to be shooting the first scene of the film at Carrickfergus Castle and I'm going to be the star."

Jack thought of saying more, warning David what exactly was going on. But he knew it wouldn't change anything. So why spoil his friend's ride? But what he could do was try to get some metaphorical airbags to save him. "I get it, but be careful, okay? You know you and Trudy are my best friends."

David nodded. "I know, Jack, and no matter how good the ride gets, I'm not going to forget that."

Jack and David smiled at each other and hugged. It would have been a beautiful and touching moment except for the fact that they had to lean over a toilet bowl to do it.[89]

––––––––––––––

After they left the bathroom, Jack wandered away, allowing David to be swamped once more by crowds of adoring fans. He wandered the corridors until he found Trudy. She was being swamped too, but instead of fans, it was vacuum cleaners. She angrily batted their nozzles away as they sniffed around her.

"I think I've got this whole thing half figured out."

"Great," Trudy said as she grabbed a nozzle and twisted it. "Let's get away from these vacuum cleaners."

[89] Before they left the stall, Jack leaned over and pulled the flush lever, because that was the kind of socially responsible person he was.

WINNERS AND LOSERS
The Importance of Being a "Good" Winner

All too often in life we are told not to be a bad loser. And that is important—a bad loser is one of the worst things that a person can be.

But only *one* of the worst things.

Because the worst thing that you can be is a bad winner.

Whenever you start gloating about winning you're on a slippery slope. There can only ever be one winner, and a lot more losers. When a winner gloats, there's a very real risk that he'll find himself on the wrong end of an angry mob of so-called losers. And if there's one thing that losers are good at, it's forming angry mobs, complete with pitchforks.

34

PUTTING THE PIECES IN PLACE

Trudy slammed the classroom door behind her, leaving the vacuum cleaners outside. "What's Merlin up to? What does he plan to do?"

"Ahh," said Jack, "well, I don't know that part."

Trudy cocked her head to one side. "It really doesn't sound like you have this figured out as much as you led me to believe."

"Okay, I haven't figured out what he plans to do exactly, but I have figured out *how* he plans to do it."

"It's a start, I suppose."

"It all started with Edwyn having that allergic reaction to a peanut, right? I think that was Merlin's first move. He's been scaring people by genetically altering snack food. That way, when they have extreme reactions people get scared and switch to his health food. The more extreme the reaction the better it works—that's what happened with Edwyn. Think about it—I don't know anyone whose parents have allergies, but almost all children around the world are allergic to something. I think Merlin has been genetically modifying food for years."

"But why?"

"Simple. He wants everyone to start worrying about their health. That way he can sell more and more of his health-food products."

"Merlin's been doing all this in an attempt to sell more muesli bars? Do you think there's some kind of mind-controlling chemical in them?"

"No, it's a lot simpler than that. Think about what else we've been attacked by this week."

"The suits of armor? And the car that was pursuing you? And those sharpened metal spikes that shot at me."

"Yeah, we've been attacked by metal objects." Jack repeated himself slowly. "Metal objects."

"Still not getting it."

"Magnets are the secret to the whole thing."

"I can't help feeling that you're making this more confusing than it needs to be."

Jack sighed. "It all starts with the sword in the stone."

"Excalibur."

"Right, except we were focused on the sword being the powerful part. It isn't—the really important bit is the stone."

"The boulder?"

"It's ridiculous to think that a sword would get stuck in anything that it cut. If it's sharp enough to cut its way in, then it's sharp enough to cut its way out. The sword isn't actually stuck in the stone; it's just that at the center of that boulder is an extremely powerful magnetic source.[90] There's a naturally occurring metallic stone—we studied it in science. It's called lodestone."

"How does that help us?"

"Simple—I think that Merlin is using that lodestone as a power source to control everything. The sword isn't a sword so much as an antenna. It's projecting the power of the lodestone."

Trudy snapped her fingers. "And that's why there was a wire connecting the sword to the electricity pylons!"

"Precisely! We've done this in science; you can use electrical wires to create magnetic fields. Merlin's figured out a way to create shaped magnetic fields that can make things move as if they're his puppets. That explains the driverless cars and the suits of armor that attacked us. It explains how those metal bars shot out of the cavern walls without any kind of mechanism to propel them. Merlin's using magnetic fields to move them."

"Are you sure about this?"

---

[90] There are many enormous magnets in the world. The world's largest electromagnet is the Hadron Super Collider. Not only does this magnet attract metal, but also it draws scientists from all over the world to work at the super collider. All the scientists continually state that it is an honor and a privilege to work there. In fact, the only complaint they have about their work is that they have to eat all their meals using bent cutlery.

"One hundred percent. Think about it. Merlin used to be really powerful when everyone was a knight. But knights don't make any sense. You've seen suits of armor. They're heavy, they make it hard to move, and they rust. If someone attacked you in a suit of armor, you could just run away from them and throw rocks until they fell down. It wouldn't be an effective way to fight a battle at all."

Trudy gasped. "Unless someone could make the suits of armor move all by themselves . . ."

"Exactly. And also, think of electricity pylons. Merlin must have persuaded the first electricity companies to make them. It doesn't make sense to have the wires hanging in the air like that. We bury our water pipes, we bury our gas pipes, we even bury our television cables, and television isn't even dangerous.[91] But we just let electricity hang in the air? It's because Merlin wanted the lines to be above ground so he could use the metal cables to channel the magnetic fields from his lodestone boulder."

"I really hate to have to admit this, but you're making sense."

"That's not all—those wires can't just be carrying electricity—because otherwise birds wouldn't be able to sit on them without being fried."

[91] Television was invented in 1925 by John Logie Baird, a Scotsman. If you'll study the history of science you will soon learn that the Scottish invented more things than almost any other nation. Mostly because if you live in Scotland, it's normally far too cold and wet to go outside and play.

"Of course!" Trudy said. "I've heard it said that pigeons and other birds navigate using the earth's magnetic field—which would explain why they sit on power lines, and when Merlin's using them to control things with magnets it must disorient them—so they sit on the wires until they can get their bearings. Jack, this is amazing!"

"And it's why when I was 'sleepwalking' all the birds landed on me—because I was the center of magnetic waves given off from the nearby pylons." Jack smiled. "And I think Merlin tried this before—remember we were told that he created Stonehenge? What else is Stonehenge but a very early collection of pylons? He probably stopped because without cranes and things like that it would have been very difficult to set up Stonehenges across the country. That's why pylons carry a dozen different wires—because some of them are using magnetism to push things and some of them are using it to pull things. That's how Merlin can control entire objects. He must be using some kind of highly sophisticated control panel to coordinate it all."

"But wait," Trudy said. "There's just one thing that doesn't make sense—your theory explains how Merlin could control metal suits of armor and cars. But not people or animals."

Jack triumphantly took a Mr. M health-food bar out of his pocket and held it in front of Trudy's eyes. He pointed to a line on the nutritional information: *Fortified with vitamins and iron.* "And this brings us back to the start. Merlin's been causing food allergies for years. People get worried about their diet and start eating health food. If you eat enough, then you build up more and more iron in your blood. When it gets to a certain level he can use the magnetized pylon wires to control you. Think about it: I stopped eating his healthy products and the effects wore off on me. He was also feeding the animals at the zoo with iron-fortified products and that's how he controlled the meerkats and got them to dig that cavern where your mother was held."

"And it's also how he controlled the woodpeckers," agreed Trudy. "But when my mother started feeding one with ordinary bugs it lowered the iron in its blood and so it wasn't under his control anymore. Then it could come and find me."

"Exactly!" Jack was feeling very smug. "We've solved it. I think we can afford to take Friday off."

"Really, Jack?" Trudy asked. "I mean you may have figured out how Merlin's controlling people, but you still haven't figured out what his plan is. What's he actually trying to achieve?"

"Oh," said Jack. "Yeah, I'd forgotten about that."

"Well, you'd better start thinking again."

"Apparently, they're starting filming at Carrickfergus Castle tomorrow," Jack said. "Maybe it's something to do with that?"

"Maybe? Is that the best you have? Look, we can't be that much closer to the solution—if we were close to catching him, Merlin would have tried to kill us again."

It was at that minute that the classroom door burst open and a dozen robot vacuum cleaners dashed in, waving their hoses menacingly.

"Oh," said Trudy, "maybe we're closer to the solution than I thought."

ROBOTS
Taking Over the World

Over the years many science-fiction writers have been concerned that one day robots and computers will take over the world. Any sensible person knows that this is not something that we need to worry about. In fact, what we should be worried about is the opposite. The possibility that computer and robots *will not* take over the world.

As you can imagine, running the world is a very stressful and difficult thing to do. This is why leaders of countries always look so tired and stressed all the time.

Computers and robots are much smarter than we are and would do a much better job than we do running the world. However, this is also why they probably won't take over the world, because they are smart enough to realize that being in charge of the world is going to take up a lot of your time and not really be that much fun.[92]

---

[92] Anyone with an ounce of sense can tell that running the world really isn't that much fun. Just watch a politician try to smile. It looks as if someone has attached fishing wire to their mouths and is pulling their lips apart.

Interestingly enough, this is the reason computer games were invented. Originally computers were only meant for doing sums and writing novels. However, it was quickly realized that if only we could fool computers into thinking that the real world was a lot more fun than it actually was, maybe one day we could fool them into taking over.

Therefore, fun virtual games were invented to convince computers that our lives were a lot more fun than they really were. These games involved only the fun parts of life and not the dull aspects. Racing cars—but never filling them with gas or cleaning them. Flying in planes—but never having to wait an hour to get your luggage back. Playing sports—but not having to spend weeks in the gym training to become stronger and faster.

It is hoped that one day computers and robots will be taken in by these games enough for them to start thinking that they want to rule the world. Then finally human beings can let them get on with it while we get to lie around and relax for a while.

This is also the reason people are encouraged to post only positive messages on their social media. That way the computers will think we're all having a lot more fun than we really are.

35

THIS SUCKS

"Okay, so do we have a plan?" Jack asked as the robot vacuum cleaners advanced.

Trudy ducked as a vacuum hose flailed over her head. "I'm not sure how you defeat vacuum cleaners."

"Time for The Speed?" Jack suggested.

"It's as good an idea as any other." Trudy's face fell as she summoned a sad thought. Jack noticed it took her longer than normal. Perhaps now that Trudy's mother was back she was finding it harder to become sad at will. Which was both a good thing and a bad thing at the same time.

Trudy caught one of the vacuum cleaner's hoses, swung it around in a circle, and threw it crashing into two others. As usual Jack was doing far too much thinking and not enough acting. A vacuum-cleaner hose had gripped him around the ankle. It jerked suddenly and he fell to the ground. A dozen cleaners surrounded him and lashed him with their hoses. "Help!" he shouted as he was mercilessly beaten.

Trudy darted over to Jack in a flash, grabbed him by the hand, and dragged him clear. Jack smiled his thanks at her. "How are we going to defeat these things?"

Trudy pushed Jack out of the way of a vacuum cleaner that had charged at them. She kicked out at one with a foot. It tumbled and landed on its back. Then it made a high-pitched squeaking noise, beeped twice, and then went silent. "Jack—that's it!"

"What?"

"Flip them upside down. They seem to have some sort of 'off' switch that operates if they end up on their back."

Something about this didn't seem right to Jack, but it had worked. He dived at the nearest vacuum cleaner, slipped his fingers under it, and flipped it over. It tumbled and landed on its back. It flailed its hoses briefly, but then beeped and switched off. A hose hit Jack across the base of his spine and he turned quickly. A robot cleaner wrapped its hose around his wrist. Jack threw his arm quickly in the air and the effect rippled along the hose—another cleaner was on its back.

Trudy was having even more success. She ran from one cleaner to another using The Speed. She dodged under their hoses and then with a simple flick of her wrist knocked them onto their backs. Less than five minutes later the last vacuum beeped and went dead.

Trudy and Jack looked around them at their vanquished foes. Trudy smiled briefly but then frowned.

"What are you thinking?" Jack asked.

"Too easy," said Trudy. "Far too easy."

"Yeah, I kinda felt that myself."

"Well, we can't leave them here. I'll call Grey and get them to send someone from the Ministry to take them away."

Less than half an hour later Grey, Trudy, and Jack were in the Ministry. Jack and Trudy had explained to Grey what they had figured out about how Merlin was controlling people. They were standing around the deactivated vacuum cleaners, considering them.

"You're right to be suspicious," Grey agreed. "Anything that seems too easy to be true is . . ."

" . . . too easy to be true," Jack and Trudy joined in.

They stood and stared at the motionless machines for a while longer.

Trudy broke the silence. "But we aren't going to come up with any answers just standing here. We need to figure out what Merlin is going to try to do when filming at Carrickfergus Castle tomorrow."

Grey smiled. "Good news on that front. The King in Yellow has been speaking to the laws of physics on behalf of Cthulhu. The laws of physics have agreed to return to the filing room. Therefore, we can find things in it again. Hopefully there's some documentation in there that will tell us of any weaknesses Merlin has."

"That's good news," Trudy said.

Suddenly around them there were dozens of beeping noises.

Jack shuddered. "I suspect that beeping isn't good news."

The vacuum cleaners sprang back to life. Using their

hoses, they flipped themselves the right way up. Jack, Grey, and Trudy pushed against each other back to back, forming a fighting perimeter. Trudy held up her fists. "Here we go again."

The vacuum cleaners formed themselves into a line and shot down the corridor in the opposite direction.

"Oh," said Jack. "It's a pity there isn't someone here who wants to know what the definition of an anticlimax is—because that was pretty much a textbook case."

Trudy was thinking. "This means we never actually defeated the vacuum cleaners in the first place, did we? They just let us think we did so they could get inside the Ministry."

"But why would they do that?" Jack asked.

A look of shock spread across Trudy's face. "Merlin didn't assign them to attack us at all. He knows we're closing in on him. The vacuum cleaners are going to try to destroy any information the Ministry has on him so we can't figure out what his plan is."

Grey slapped himself on the forehead. "And I just told them exactly where that information was being held."

VACUUM CLEANERS
Their Invention

There is much debate as to who invented the first vacuum cleaner. Early vacuum cleaners consisted of a large and bulky body attached to a long hose that could suck things up. While Ministry researchers have not been able to definitively say who came up with this design, they have said that they suspect elephants could be making a fortune in royalties if only they had hired themselves a patent lawyer soon enough.

36

THIS *REALLY* SUCKS

Jack, Trudy, and Grey hurtled down the corridors of the Ministry in pursuit of the vacuum cleaners. However, the cleaners ran far too efficiently on their little wheels to be caught. Their cornering was exceptional, unlike Jack's, which involved a considerable amount of skidding and occasionally a little bit of clattering into walls.

When they arrived at the file room Jack braced himself to see once again the strange colors, the bent shapes, and the impossibly tall filing cabinets. And yet when he stepped inside the room he was shocked. The laws of physics had clearly been busy. The room was still enormous, but now it looked like a perfectly ordinary filing room, with row upon straight row of perfectly ordinary filing cabinets.

Jack was even more shocked by Cthulhu's appearance as

he walked up to the cabinets. He still had the terrifying squid head and glowing green eyes, but he was wearing a black shirt and suit and had a gray tie with a tentacle pattern. He looked like an office worker. An office worker of potentially unlimited power with a tendency toward interdimensional manifestation. But an office worker nonetheless.

Cthulhu gargled furiously at Grey.

"Yes, I'm sorry, Cthulhu. I rather fear we may have been responsible for bringing them here."

Cthulhu rasped and his maw tentacles writhed.

"We think they're being controlled by Merlin. They're probably trying to destroy any information on him. I imagine they're heading for the *M* section. And now that the laws of physics have returned to your filing room, that'll be easy to find!"

At the thought of files being destroyed, Cthulhu screamed and screeched at the top of his voice, making noises that left Jack's vocal cords feeling positively inadequate. Cthulhu's eyes widened into beaming green searchlights.

Jack shuddered. "What's he saying now?"

"Difficult to translate . . . ," Grey admitted, " . . . without using a lot of swear words and turning my head inside out."

"Can you give us the gist?" Trudy asked.

"Basically, Cthulhu is saying that although it's okay to misplace, lose, fold, spindle, or mutilate files, he refuses to let them be destroyed."

"Is he going to do something?" As Jack was speaking, Cthulhu suddenly soared into the air, borne aloft on a green cloud of energy. He didn't even bother to unfold his giant bat wings—which Jack thought was rather a waste. Cthulhu scanned the room and then darted forward at an incredible rate.

On the ground, Jack, Trudy, and Grey followed as best they could, dodging in and out of rows of filing cabinets. Now that the laws of physics were back in the room it was considerably easier to move than it had been before. Apart from anything else there was something reassuring about being able to walk along a floor without worrying it might turn into a wall at a moment's notice.

Cthulhu was hurling balls of green energy at the vacuum cleaners, which tossed them back and forth. The vacuum cleaners dodged and wove, frantically trying to avoid the explosions.

One robot cleaner had found a filing cabinet marked *Merlin* and pulled the bottom drawer open. "We have to stop it," Jack shouted, and pointed.

Trudy turned Jack to face her. "You know, Jack, a lot of the time you shout things that we already know. It's unnecessary and a little distracting."

"Sorry."

"Just think before you shout."

Jack and Trudy dashed toward the filing cabinet. Grey was fending off a robot vacuum cleaner that lashed and prodded at him with its multiple hoses.

Trudy ducked as a vacuum cleaner was thrown over her head by one of Cthulhu's exploding green bolts. Jack ran past her and grabbed hold of the robot cleaner that was attacking the filing cabinet. As he pulled at it, it plunged a hose into the drawer and sucked up the paper inside. One of its other hoses shot straight up in the air and showered them with shredded paper. Jack collapsed on the floor.

"We . . . were . . . too . . . late," panted Jack.

"You see, Jack, this is exactly the kind of thing I was talking about when I said you said things that were unnecessary," Trudy complained.

Grey was being driven back by the vacuum cleaner striking at him. "A little less talk—we're still in a battle here!"

Trudy and Jack backed up against the filing cabinet. "I think we're in some fairly serious trouble," Jack said.

"Stop stating the obvious! We need a plan for how to get out of this."

"I don't think we can." Jack gulped. "It's the suits of armor all over again. Even if we smash them, Merlin could use his magnetic powers to pull them back together."

"Think harder, Jack"—Trudy swatted a probing hose away from her head—"I don't want my gravestone to read 'Trudy Emerson—killed by vacuum cleaners.'"

Jack racked his brains, desperately trying to think of a plan. Cthulhu let out a mind-numbing screech and fell from the sky, landing on the ground in the middle of the battle. The business-suited Cthulhu then spun on one leg while tentacles appeared from his collar, cuffs, and trouser legs. They shot out and pushed and shoved at the vacuum cleaners, rocking and rattling them.

The robot cleaner that had been attacking Grey turned and sped toward Cthulhu. Similarly, Jack and Trudy found themselves free from attack, as Cthulhu was surrounded.

Jack and Trudy quickly ran to Grey. "Even Cthulhu can't possibly defeat that many vacuum cleaners."

Grey stared at Jack. "Really, Jack? Is that what you think? That an interdimensional monster of nearly unlimited power is going to be killed by some rogue vacuum cleaners?"

"Well, I was just . . ."

"We might have had difficulty—but we're only human. I'm sure Cthulhu knows what he's doing."

All the vacuum cleaners had formed a circle around Cthulhu now. They zipped forward, lashed at him with a hose, and then rolled back out of reach. Cthulhu didn't seem too worried. He fended off their attacks with his writhing tentacles and occasionally gestured with a clawed hand, creating a small vacuum-cleaner-deflecting force field.

After a short while the vacuum cleaners seemed to realize that their attacks were having limited effect. They all drove back a few feet and stopped. Jack squinted. He was sure he could see Cthulhu's maw smiling under his facial tentacles. The vacuum cleaners all charged Cthulhu at once, flailing with their hoses.

In the blink of an eye Cthulhu split the back of his jacket with his enormous bat wings and sprang into the air. As he flew upward, he withdrew his tentacles back under his suit and shirt. The vacuum cleaners didn't manage to stop themselves and crashed into one another. Their flailing hoses twisted around together in the carnage. When they tried to pull back, the vacuum cleaners found themselves hopelessly tangled. They pulled and strained, but it only made the tangle worse.

Cthulhu flapped his great bat wings twice and landed beside Trudy, Grey, and Jack. "Well done, Cthulhu," Grey said.

Cthulhu barely nodded. He then gestured with a clawlike hand, and a dark-green bubble surrounded the mass of vacuum cleaners. The bubble expanded, shimmered for a second, and then burst. The vacuum cleaners disappeared with it.

"Are they destroyed?" Jack asked.

Grey shook his head. "Sent to another dimension. I've seen Cthulhu do this type of thing before."

"Couldn't he have done it a bit sooner?" asked Trudy.

"It's kind of a last resort—I mean, he doesn't want to always have to ruin a perfectly good jacket." Grey nodded to where Cthulhu was looking forlornly at the suit jacket, which had been torn apart when he had unleashed his wings. Cthulhu groaned quietly.

Trudy walked over to a pile of shredded paper on the ground. "But Merlin's achieved his purpose. He shredded his file—it'd take us forever to put this back into order."

Jack picked up a piece of paper that had the word *Merlin* written on it. "This looks like the world's most difficult jigsaw."

"A million-piece jigsaw." Grey kicked at a pile of the shredded paper. "We'll never get this put back together before Merlin puts his plan into action."

"If only this was like a little kid's jigsaw," Jack said. "You know, the ones that have large pieces that are easy to put together."

"Maybe that's what we need to do. Is there some way of making the individual pieces of paper bigger?" asked Trudy.

Then an idea hit Jack. "We don't need to make the pieces of paper bigger—we just need to use smaller hands."

MINISTRY OF S.U.IT.S HANDBOOK

CTHULHU
How to Make Sure That You Don't Annoy Him

Stop existing.[93]

---

[93] And to be clear, that means in all dimensions. Being a multidimensional creature, Cthulhu's going to be wise to people who merely stop existing on one plane of existence. And apart from anything else, trying to trick him like that is going to make him *really mad*.

37

THE HISTORY OF
A SCIENTIST

Following Jack's instructions, Grey had sent a message for Auntie to come to the filing room. The robe, filled with the teeming mass of ants, arrived quickly.

"Do you really think this will work?" Trudy asked.

"I'm sure of it," Jack said. "After all—you know that puzzles with large pieces are easy to put together. To the ants, this paper will seem like the world's largest puzzle pieces. And on top of that, they'll be using hundreds of hands to put them together."

"Hands?" Trudy queried.

"Well, legs and feelers and mandibles—you know what I mean."

Grey had finished explaining to Auntie what they wanted her to do. As had happened in the café, her cloak collapsed and a wave of ants ran out the bottom and toward the shredded paper. Each ant picked up a single piece of the "puzzle" and scurried around comparing it with its friends. Slowly but surely the ants were putting the paper file back together again.

As the ants finished each page of the file, Grey followed after them and pressed a sheet of transparent sticky-backed plastic on top to hold it in place.

"Why didn't you just get the ants to rearrange the paper on top of the sticky-backed plastic?" Jack asked.

Grey raised an eyebrow. "Really, Jack? Ants on sticky-backed plastic? Are you trying to cause a tragedy?"

"Oh, yeah, hadn't thought about that."

The ants had finished reconstructing the paper and quickly re-formed themselves under the robe that made Auntie. Grey gathered up the files, and after thanking both Cthulhu and Auntie, he took Jack and Trudy to a quiet room with a table and several chairs.

Trudy and Jack sat impatiently while Grey scanned the files. Eventually he looked up. "I still don't know what Merlin is planning, but some of this might be helpful. . . ."

Grey read to them from the reconstructed files. Much of the story was the same as the legends both Jack and Trudy were familiar with—but some sections were very different indeed.

MERLIN
How He Almost Became King

Merlin was born in Wales many centuries ago. Initially he made his living as a carpenter. He traveled from town to town doing all those things that carpenters do, making tools, designing furniture, and generally carrying out freelance activities related to wood.

One day, Merlin went to the forest to cut down a tree to make a new cupboard for a family of blacksmiths. He raised his ax above his head and swung it with all his might. However, he was surprised to find that instead of biting into the bark of the tree, the ax was suddenly ripped from his hands. It was propelled across the clearing, eventually driving itself deep into the soil. Merlin followed the path of the ax, and after digging in the dirt for several minutes was shocked to realize that his ax-head was fastened to a strange buried boulder.

Merlin realized the boulder could be a source of enormous power. After years of working for other people, he liked the idea of becoming powerful.

But how could he use this magnetic stone? How could he even move it? After much thought, he could not come up with a single idea of how to use the stone, and so he sighed to himself and went back to the village to borrow another ax.

The family of blacksmiths for whom he was making the cupboard made him promise that he wasn't going to lose the ax and he agreed, deciding that he would have to find another oak to cut down. Preferably far away from the strange buried stone.

As he was about to trudge back into the forest, Merlin couldn't help noticing that the blacksmith's youngest son was playing with a bow and arrow. The reason that Merlin couldn't help noticing this was that the young boy had accidentally shot an arrow straight through Merlin's shin.

Merlin fell to the ground, swearing loudly. The father of the family came running out of the forge and shouted at his son. "Arthur! What on earth are you doing playing with that bow again? I've told you, you're far too clumsy to be doing such things."

Merlin looked over at the boy. Although Arthur was only fourteen, he was an enormous, hulking brute. His father had been a blacksmith; his grandfather had been a blacksmith; his great grandfather had been a blacksmith. His great, great . . . But you get the idea. Each generation had grown up bigger and stronger than the last, with enormous biceps, good for hammering metal; enormous legs, good for lifting the anvil; and enormous hands, good for powering the bellows. However, it is entirely possible to have too much of a good thing, and after so many generations, Arthur had been born with a set of hands so large and powerful that he was incapable of any actions that required fine manual dexterity.

Merlin cursed his luck to have strayed across such a clumsy and incapable boy. And then he found himself wishing that the arrow had been fired near that strange stone he had found that morning. If only that had happened, then the arrow would have gone off course and struck the stone instead of him. . . . And then, just before the blood loss from his shin made him pass out, Merlin had a quite tremendous idea.

When he came around again, Merlin threatened to have young Arthur arrested for attempted murder. Arthur's father was terrified and offered Merlin as many free swords and spears as he wanted if only Merlin would agree to forget Arthur's clumsy mistake.

Merlin pretended to consider this offer for a moment. "Perhaps we can come to some arrangement. I won't be able to walk for quite some time, so you must give me a horse." The blacksmith agreed without a second's hesitation. Merlin pretended to need a further moment to think before adding, "And I will need help getting on and off the horse. Therefore, your son must become my servant for a year."

At first the blacksmith was taken aback. Arthur was his son—he didn't want to send him away . . . but then, on further reflection, the blacksmith realized that this might be good for Arthur. Clearly the clumsy boy did not have a future as a blacksmith. Apart from anything else, his mistakes around the forge meant that almost all the swords they had made in the past three weeks were horribly bent. And they couldn't keep trying to pass them off as "Arabian cutlasses," because, frankly, people weren't buying that.[94] The blacksmith agreed that Arthur would serve as Merlin's servant for a period of one year while his shin healed.

[94] Or the Arabian cutlasses, for that matter.

It took Merlin a week to build himself a cart for the horse to pull. It took Arthur three days to dig up the enormous boulder from the forest, and another three days between them to load it safely onto the cart. Yet in less than a fortnight Merlin was ready to put his plan into action.

Arthur had wondered if Merlin was planning to start a rock collection, but Merlin's idea was much more sinister than mere geology.

At first Merlin's plans were relatively modest. He would travel the country looking for battles.[95]

---

[95] It is worthwhile noting that back in the Middle Ages there were an awful lot of battles. Mainly because there was nothing else to do and, frankly, a battle was a good way to spend the evening. Your choices of entertainment in those days were either going out and getting involved in a battle or staying at home and waiting to see who caught leprosy first.

(If you don't believe that entertainment works this way, please consider this fact: Before we invented the Internet we had two world wars; afterward, none. If we do have a future world war at some stage, they'll have to make battlefields Wi-Fi hotspots; otherwise no one will go. Which would be good . . .)

And even if we had to have a world war, these days it would probably be delayed so long that we'd forget what we were all fighting about before it even started. "France, are you coming? We're going to start invading now!" "I'll be there in a minute. I just need to update my

When he located one, he spoke to a general and offered to park his cart with the stone in it to the side of the general's armies. Its magnetic powers meant that any arrows aimed at that army would be pulled harmlessly off course, creating a kind of medieval force field.

Later on, Merlin realized that he could achieve an even better result by offering to drive his stone to the far side of an opposing army. This meant that the other army's metal arrowheads would be attracted to it like heat-seeking missiles zooming through the air—slicing through any soldiers standing in between. Occasionally someone in the army Merlin had parked behind would ask what he was doing, but Merlin always had an innocent and completely plausible explanation ready. "Me? No, nothing to do with the battle! Just taking my boulder for a walk."

It wasn't long before Merlin had amassed a fortune from his appearances at battles. But Merlin was a greedy and vain man, and mere riches were never going to be enough for him. At every battle there

—————————

status to 'participating in conflict.' And then I need to tweet my followers with the hashtag 'deathtotheenemy.' And then I need to decide what pattern camouflage jacket I'm going to wear from the choices on Pinterest. . . ."

were always kings, lords, and dukes surrounded by their riches and fawning servants. Although they needed Merlin, they saw him only as a servant—a carpenter—and refused to give him a title or even call him "Mister."

Merlin wanted revenge for this shabby treatment, so he schemed and plotted to become a king himself. He promised himself that one day he would not take a single step unless it was on a fluffy red carpet.

Merlin told his servant Arthur what he wished to do. Between the two of them they came up with a brilliant scheme. If they could coat men from head to toe in metal, and figure out some way of *directing* the magnetic waves the stone gave out, then they would have an invincible army that could defeat anyone. A soldier that could be controlled by magnetism could keep fighting even if he was unconscious . . . perhaps even if he was dead.

They were left with two problems to solve. First, how on earth could they coat a man in metal? Second, how could they ensure that the magnetic waves were directed accurately enough to be able to control entire armies of people? Arthur easily solved the first problem. His father was a blacksmith and his mother was a seamstress. He went back to his home village and persuaded his parents to work together to create a "suit of armor," a tight-fitting covering of metal that a soldier could wear.[96]

This left Merlin to solve the other problem of directing "magnetic waves." Sadly, this was the Middle Ages and there were very few civilizations with the technology to undertake such a feat. Luckily Merlin had built many boats during his time as a carpenter and was well aware of the existence of the scientifically advanced people of Atlantis. Merlin promised the queen of Atlantis that if she helped him, he would return any favor she (or her descendants) requested in the future. The queen agreed to have her scientists build Merlin an antenna and a control panel that would direct the magnetic waves, thereby turning metal-clad soldiers into puppets. During the building of the control panel Merlin studied everything the Atlanteans could teach him, thus becoming a scientist himself.

The antenna that was created looked, for all intents and purposes, like a sword. Merlin took delivery of it when the queen of Atlantis walked

[96] Arthur would later admit, in a slightly guilty way, that this wasn't actually a completely original idea. He was close friends with a man called Artemis, who worked in the castle laundry and he might have mentioned a similar idea to Arthur at some stage (see Chapter 22)....

out of the water one day and threw it at his feet, thus starting the myth of the "Lady of the Lake."

Once the antenna was given to Merlin, he got Arthur, using his enormous brawny hands, to drive it deep into the center of the stone, and his supreme weapon was complete. Once thrust into the center of the stone, the sword stuck fast, as its tip pierced the very heart of the magnetic field.

Slowly Merlin began to build an army of metal-clad warriors. Using Excalibur, the antenna, and the control panel that the "Lady of the Lake" had built for him, he marched across the country defeating enemies in battle and forcing warlords to swear loyalty to him. Arthur had served the year as Merlin's servant, but decided to remain with him. While Merlin wanted power and riches, Arthur realized that by uniting warring tribes they could bring peace to the land and improve the lives of their fellow countrymen.

Soon there were no more warlords to defeat. Merlin at last thought he was to be king. But he made the fatal mistake of overconfidence. He stood before his army thinking that they loved him and asked them to choose their king. With one voice they shouted their decision. "ARTHUR—ARTHUR—ARTHUR!"

Merlin cursed under his breath. It wasn't that Arthur was more lovable or more intelligent than Merlin. It was simply that, being the son of generations of blacksmiths, he had absolutely enormous hands—and people really wanted their king to have big hands.[97]

What followed was a period of great calm. Arthur ruled the country kindly and thoughtfully. Under Arthur's reign, rampaging dragons went down by 15 percent, evil goblins were forced to see the error of their ways, and although damsels were occasionally locked in towers, King Arthur introduced a new class of male damsel to ensure that there was at least equality for all.

In fact, it would have been a perfect period in history had it not been for Merlin, who was becoming more and more bitter. Although Arthur had appointed Merlin as his chief adviser, Merlin continually found himself relegated back to his old role of a carpenter. The final straw was when Arthur asked Merlin to make him a round table for the knights to sit at. Merlin was infuriated. He should have been king—not a mere craftsman.

---

[97] Remember? All the way back in the first chapter— since people bought their goods measured in the king's hands and feet, they really, really liked kings to have large hands—so they could get more for their money.

In the dead of night Merlin sneaked into the basement of Camelot to where the boulder and antenna, Excalibur, were kept. He planned to steal them and rebel against Arthur. However, Arthur had learned of Merlin's plan and was there to confront him.

"The sword and the stone are mine," Merlin had hissed at Arthur in the dark basement where the stone was stored.

King Arthur was a remarkably fair man, which makes life very difficult sometimes. "Aye, Merlin, the stone is yours. But I can't let you use it to control my knights. Your magnetic waves are too powerful."

"You deny me what is mine, then?"

"No, for that would not be fair. However, you may not remain in Camelot any longer. I will banish you to Ireland. You may take your control panel with you. And I will arrange for the stone to be shipped there too."

"You know I will merely raise an army of metal-clad warriors there and return to defeat you. How can you be so foolish?"

King Arthur smiled sadly at his old master. "I don't think so. You know how rainy Ireland is. Any metal army you create in Ireland would rust long before you could build the boats to invade. And to make sure you do not return anytime soon, although I will transport the stone and the sword to Ireland, they will be hidden from you, Merlin. My royal archaeologist will bury them in a secret place where you shall not find them."

"I will have my revenge on you, Arthur, even if it takes a thousand years," Merlin had snarled.

"If it takes a thousand years, that's fine. Just make sure you put all the pieces of my skeleton back where you found them after you've finished."

"Maybe my revenge will not be on you, but on your people. I swear revenge on the people who rejected me as king. I will destroy you, Arthur; I will destroy your country. Perhaps with magnetic waves, or perhaps with a different sort of wave altogether . . ."

Of course, to this point Merlin hasn't tried anything, so we're probably all safe. . . .

38

COUNTERPLOTTING

Grey, Jack, and Trudy sat and considered what they had learned from the files.

"So, Merlin was banished from Wales and England to live in Ireland," Jack said thoughtfully. "But before he left he swore revenge on Arthur's kingdom."

Grey nodded. "And that's what he's probably trying to achieve now."

"At least no one's trying to destroy Northern Ireland for once," Trudy said. "So that's a positive."

"It seems much more likely that Merlin is planning an invasion of England and Wales with people he will control using the magnetic stone and the iron in their blood," Grey suggested. "Think about it: Tomorrow is a big day of filming at Carrickfergus Castle—right on the coast. It's an ideal place to gather an army and launch an invasion."

"Brilliant, Grey!" Trudy agreed.

Jack said nothing. He was staring down at his feet.

Trudy looked at Jack with a worried expression. "You think we're wrong, don't you?"

"I think so. I mean, an invasion's a nice idea, but I think Merlin's planning something much worse than that. Much worse. There was something about his last words to Arthur that make me suspect he's planning to try to destroy England and Wales."

"So how do we stop him?"

"We need a plan and a lot of luck."

"Luck?"

"Yes," said Jack. "Half the country are eating Mr. M's health-food bars—so he can control an army of hundreds of thousands if he wants—and they'll all be going to Carrickfergus to watch the fake film he's pretending to make. And on top of that he's got an animatronic giant and an animatronic dragon if he needs them."

"I have confidence in you," Trudy said.

"You do?" asked Jack. "In that case you really haven't been paying attention. And I've only got half a plan this time."

Trudy laughed. "As long as it's the important half we'll be okay."

Jack smiled and turned to Grey. "Now, I'm going to need you to speak to Cthulhu. First you need to get him to go to the red barn. . . ." Jack slowly laid out the parts of his plan he had managed to figure out so far.

Jack was tired when he went home that evening. But instead of going to his room early, he decided to sit and watch a little television with his parents. Deep down he was worried that if he wasn't very lucky tomorrow this might be the last time he saw them. Merlin had already shown that his motto was "Kill the good guys early, ask questions later."

"I was in David's parents' corner shop today," Jack's mother said. "I hear David's become quite the star."

"He's appearing as an extra in that new fantasy film they're making," Jack agreed.

"We thought we might come down to Carrickfergus Castle tomorrow and see them filming," Jack's father said. "Half the country's going to be there."

Jack sat bolt upright. He didn't want his parents there. Especially after they'd spent the entire week eating Mr. M's health food. Their blood would be full of iron—they'd just be more puppets for Merlin to control. "I'm sure it'll be very dull. Not worth seeing at all."

"Really, Jack?" His father raised an eyebrow. "I've seen on the news they have a massive animatronic dragon. That might be interesting to look at, surely?"

Jack's mother joined in. "Yes, I could take the day off work. We could come down with a picnic and meet you for lunch. I mean, I take it you'll be going along? To support David?"

Jack slouched back into his chair. He wasn't sure what was worse—having to face a crazy scientist-carpenter who planned to destroy England and Wales or having to have a picnic with his parents in front of his classmates.

DRAGONS
POOR EATING HABITS

Over the years many people have asked if dragons are related to dinosaurs. The answer to this question is, obviously, yes.[98] Asking if dinosaurs and dragons are related is somewhat akin to meeting identical twins at a cocktail party and asking if they've met before.

Many years ago, paleontologists used to contend that dinosaurs and dragons were two different species. However, this is ridiculous, because they are both enormous lizards that are covered in thick scales and both have certain varieties that are capable of flight.

---

[98] In fact, this is one of the very few occasions when the answer to the question is soooo very obvious that it would be perfectly acceptable and polite to answer this question with "Well, duh!"

Some paleontologists have maintained that dragons must be different because they can breathe fire.[99] Dragons can do this because of their incredibly poor diet rather than any physical difference between them and dinosaurs. When dining, dragons were rather opportunistic—they very rarely phoned ahead and made reservations. Instead they swooped out of the sky, landing on farms and swallowing pigs and cows whole. When pigs and cows weren't available, they would circle mountaintops and then dive down with their mouths open, swallowing up sheep and frequently half of the ground beneath them.

Additionally, from time to time a local king would send a knight out in full battle armor to try to defeat a dragon.[100] Naturally, all too often

[99] Technically dragons don't breathe fire. They breathe oxygen and they burp fire. But dragons are frightfully formal and well-mannered in general, and so they don't want people thinking that they go around burping all the time.

[100] It is interesting to note that in sending out a knight, kings were actually making dragons even more deadly than they already were. Which just goes

the knight would be swallowed whole, including sword, shield, armor, and saddle.

You can imagine that this relentless eating played havoc with dragon digestive juices, which were continually frothing and foaming inside a dragon's gut. (In point of fact, this is why dragons were so often ferocious and mean-tempered—imagine how cheerful you would feel if you had been suffering from indigestion for the last fifty decades.)

The problem of dragon digestive juices was only made worse by the fact that their cattle-heavy diet meant that they were often swallowing animals that contained huge amounts of explosive methane. Once the methane mixed with the digestive juices you can imagine that this created a rather volatile case of heartburn.

Of course, this would not be a problem if not for all the knights that the dragons had also swallowed. Swords, shields, and spiky armor are difficult to digest, and frequently the points or hooks on weapons would get stuck in dragons'

---

to show you, all too often when you try to help, you're only going to end up making things worse.

throats. Then when a dragon burped up some methane-infused stomach acid, the swords and shields would strike and rattle against one another, causing sparks, thus igniting the burp in a torrent of smoky flame.

It is suspected that even in the Dark Ages, knights knew that this was what was happening. However, this was never admitted or written down in ballads mainly because it sounds much more lyrical and heroic to say:

"Sir Edmonds was vanquished by the evil dragon Thermocales, who didst breathe terrifying brimstone breath uponst him."

rather than having to say:

"Eddie got killed when the big lizard burped in his direction."

Of course, it is interesting to note that ultimately it was dragons' interest in constantly snacking that led to many of them being vanquished by the great knight Sir Jonley the Late. More information on this is available in handbook section **Dragons: The Dangers of Snacking.**

39

ALTERNATIVE USES
OF TINFOIL
FRIDAY

When Jack got to school the next morning, buses had been chartered to take all the school to Carrickfergus Castle, where the film was to be made. Apparently, the headmaster felt that it would be an excellent educational opportunity to observe a real film set. Jack suspected that this was all part of Merlin's plan.

Jack felt incredibly sad as they traveled to the castle. Normally on these kinds of excursions he would have been sitting beside David, whom he had known since elementary school. It wasn't that Trudy wasn't great company and a good best friend. It was just that she wasn't David. David had gone ahead in a chauffeur-driven car with all the pupils who had been selected for special roles in the movie.

"You're thinking about David, aren't you?" Trudy asked.

"Yeah, partly that he isn't here, but also that we might

have to fight him. He's been eating Merlin's health food all week. His blood's going to have so much iron in it that Merlin will easily be able to use him as a puppet."

"We'll stop Merlin before that happens. The key is trying to destroy whatever sort of control panel he's using to actually 'puppet' the people," Trudy said. "There's no way we can do anything about the stone and the sword as long as they're guarded by the suits of armor."

Carrickfergus Castle was an awe-inspiring sight. It sat on the east coast of Ireland, facing toward Scotland, England, and Wales. A large, outer stone wall covered in windows and arrow slits ran around a central tower that looked out over the water and surrounding landscape.

Trudy pointed out of the bus window. "Are those electricity pylons new?"

"Yes."

"Merlin must want to make sure he has enough magnetic waves to control all the people who come to be extras in the film."

The bus had to park on the road, as all the parking lots in the town were filled to capacity. Jack and Trudy pushed their way through the crowded streets, led by a teacher in an unappealing high-visibility jacket. Half the population of the country seemed to have flocked to the castle. Many of them were being outfitted in suits of medieval armor or peasant's clothing. It was as if a massive Renaissance fair had come to town.

"Are you sure that Merlin isn't planning to create an army, Jack? Because that's what this looks like."

Jack shook his head. "I don't think it's that simple. I think there's a reason he's brought us to a castle on the coast. There's something else going on."

The teacher had started giving the class a lecture on Carrickfergus Castle, which seemed mainly to focus on the facts that it was in Carrickfergus and was a castle.[101] Jack suspected that the teacher hadn't done a substantial amount of research ahead of this field trip and that it wouldn't be as educational as the school had claimed.

"I think now would be a good time to go missing," Jack suggested.

Trudy agreed and they both took several steps backward from their school group, disappearing into the huge crowds behind them.

Jack and Trudy were standing in an alley behind a row of shops. "You really think this is a good idea?"

Jack had several rolls of tinfoil in his hands. "Yes—you see, aluminum foil isn't magnetic. If we make ourselves foil suits,[102] I think we'll be more resistant to Merlin's control."

"But I haven't eaten any of his high-iron health food, and you stopped at the beginning of the week. The levels of iron

---

[101] I've fact-checked this and can confirm that both of these facts are correct.

[102] Interestingly enough, this is only half the reason that Jack stole the tinfoil from his house. Not only would it help deflect the magnetic waves, but when his parents got up in the morning they would have to call off their picnic idea. After all, they would have no tinfoil to wrap their sandwiches and chicken legs in.

in our blood are probably low enough that we won't be affected."

Jack started wrapping the tinfoil around his legs. "Well, if you want to risk everyone's lives because you're too proud to make yourself an aluminum-foil suit, that's your own business." Jack started wrapping the foil over his shoulders. "But I take saving the world very seriously indeed, so I'm sure you won't mind if . . ."

Trudy punched Jack very hard in the shoulder. Aluminum may not have been magnetic. It may have been heat resistant. But it certainly wasn't Trudy resistant. Jack's shoulder hurt very much indeed.

"Hey, look at those kids over there! They've covered themselves in tinfoil to try to look like knights! Isn't that cute! Get a picture . . ."

"I knew this would happen." Trudy fumed as she struggled to keep her hands by her side and not punch any of the crowd they were walking through.

"Focus on what we're here to do. Sometimes when you're trying to save the world you have to look like an idiot for a while."

Trudy glared at Jack. "If that's the case, you look like you're trying to save the world pretty much all of the time."

"Hurtful, Trudy. Words hurt, you know," Jack said. Although he was mainly thinking about the fact that they hurt less than punches in the shoulder and that he should probably be thankful for that fact.

"Where do you think Merlin is hiding?"

Jack pointed across the heads of the crowd. Standing at

the entrance to the castle was the large animatronic giant. The green-black animatronic dragon was flying a hundred feet over the castle, occasionally blowing out an enormous plume of orange fire, much to the appreciation of the crowd below. "Wherever the guards are, that's where Merlin is."

"Do you think we'll have to fight a robot giant first?"

"And then a dragon. Well . . . if it sees what we're up to from that high up. Do dragons have good eyesight?"

Trudy shouldered her way through the crowd toward the animatronic giant.

MINISTRY OF S.U.IT.S HANDBOOK

TINFOIL
Use as a Hat

Some very strange people insist that you can use a tinfoil hat to stop the government from reading your mind.

However, if you're the kind of person who wears a tinfoil hat, then you don't really need to worry about it. Because it means you're the kind of person whose mind the government really isn't interested in reading.

40

GIANT PROBLEMS,
BUT NO LION OR WITCH

Jack and Trudy pressed their backs to the castle wall fifty feet away from where the massive animatronic giant stood guarding the castle gate. "Any ideas how we can get past the giant?" Jack asked.

Trudy turned and stared. "Really? You didn't have a plan for this part?"

"I didn't think about the giant guarding the gate! I thought about the dragon more...."

"And the aluminum foil suits . . . but not the giant. Great work, Jack."

"Half a plan is better than none."

"Okay, well, here's an idea—next time you can only come up with half a plan, try and come up with the half that isn't rubbish."

Most people would have felt annoyed at such a criticism,

but in his heart Jack felt happy that Trudy was admitting that on average, at least half of his previous plans hadn't been rubbish. "We could always fight our way in?" Jack suggested.

Trudy looked at the surrounding crowds. "Too many people nearby. Someone could get hurt. We need stealth. We need to try and use the Misery's training to turn invisible."

Jack gulped. Although he'd achieved it when he was alone in his bedroom, he wasn't sure if he could do it again. Apart from anything else, it meant that he would have to be completely truthful about something in front of Trudy. And that was a terrifying idea.

"Are you sure . . . ?"

"Do you have a better idea?"

Jack admitted he didn't. They both took a second to try to think of a really honest truth. The kind of truth that you wouldn't ever admit because it was too embarrassing.

"You ready?" asked Trudy.

"I think so," said Jack, who really wasn't sure if he was or not. He tried to focus on the fact that he was doing this to defeat Merlin. What he tried to *avoid* focusing on was how embarrassed he was going to be later on.

"Okay, we face each other, then on the count of three we tell our truths. And it has to be something really true and embarrassing. Otherwise it won't work."

Jack and Trudy both turned and stared at each other. If this worked, they'd be looking through each other in a few moments.

"One . . . two . . . three."

"When my mother was away I cried every night."
"Sometimes I imagine what it would be like if you were my girlfriend."

There was a *ping* and Jack watched as Trudy blurred and disappeared. He hoped desperately that he had vanished too so that Trudy wouldn't see how badly he was blushing. He looked down at his hands and was happy to see that they had vanished.

"Jack—what did you just say?"

Jack shrugged his shoulders. Then he realized that Trudy couldn't see his shoulders and decided that speaking would be more appropriate instead. "It's just that you're my best friend and everything. And sometimes I imagine what it would be like to have a girlfriend—that's all. You know what I'm like with my imagination."

"As long as it's just imagining," said Trudy. "I don't want you getting all soppy."

"I won't," Jack promised.

Jack felt a searing pain in his right shoulder. It was amazing that even when Trudy couldn't see his shoulder she still seemed to be able to sense its location. On reflection, Jack was happy that she had this ability. After all, a deliberately punched shoulder is many times better than an accidentally punched nose.

They moved slowly and silently along the wall toward the giant. Although its size would have made it a ferocious opponent in the battle, it was actually useful when invisible because it meant they could duck between its legs and get inside the courtyard. Although their tinfoil suits rustled slightly, the giant didn't move an inch.

"What now?" whispered Jack.

"Over there!" Trudy's voice seemed to come out of nowhere.

"Over where? You do realize, if you're pointing, that I can't see your finger?"

"Sorry—I mean over by the main tower."

Jack turned his head and saw Merlin surrounded by a group of five gleaming suits of full battle armor. Two were substantially shorter than the others. Merlin had changed out of the lab coat that suggested he was a scientist and was now wearing a red king's robe. It was embroidered with patterns of stags, flowers, and bears. Jack had to admit to himself that Merlin looked impressive, and more than a little frightening.

Merlin looked around the courtyard and stared directly at Jack and Trudy. Jack shuddered, but then realized that he was safe thanks to his invisibility. Once Merlin was reassured that no one was following, he walked through an oak door and into the tower of the castle. Jack and Trudy followed as quickly as they could.

The door led to an enormous medieval entrance hall. Flags and tapestries hung from the whitewashed stone walls. There was an enormous fireplace embedded into one wall, stacked full with logs. The room was lit by burning torches attached to metal brackets. The floor was made of thick flagstones and had a series of thick, red carpets that radiated from the center of the room and led to a series of doorways. Normally this was exactly the kind of thing that would have interested Jack. But at the moment the only thing he was interested in seeing was missing from the room: Merlin.

Trudy started fading back into view. "Which way now, Jack?"

"What am I? Google Maps?" Jack looked at the back of his hand and saw that it had reappeared as well.

Trudy glared at Jack. "I do think of you like Google Maps, because you only work after I've punched the information in." Trudy balled her right fist.

Jack gulped. "Point taken. Okay, let's think this through. Merlin has delusions of grandeur. So, he's laid the red carpet to walk on."

"Yes, but the red carpet leads to all the doors in here. So that doesn't really help us much."

Jack looked at the carpet. It did lead to all the doors, but it also led to several points in the wall and a wardrobe. Could Merlin walk through walls? Jack went over to the wall and pushed it as hard as he could. It didn't even budge. He wasn't surprised—walls were frequently stubborn like that. "Maybe there's some kind of secret passage?"

Trudy walked over beside Jack. "How do we find it?"

Jack noticed they were standing beside one of the flaming torches in a metal bracket. "Maybe this is it. In movies, they always pull a candlestick or a torch in a bracket and then a section of the wall slides away, revealing a secret passageway." Jack reached up and pulled at the torch bracket.

"AHHHHH!" Jack screamed. The wall remained unmoved.

"What's wrong with you? Are you really that surprised it didn't work?"

Jack was blowing on his hand. "No, it's not that at all. It's just that what the people who make movies clearly haven't realized is, if you have a flaming torch attached to a wall the metal bracket gets very hot. I think I'm going to need some ointment for my hand. And possibly a bandage."

Trudy turned and looked around the room. "Is there a possibility we're overthinking this? Should we maybe try one of the doors?"

Jack looked at the red carpet again and noticed that one branch of it led to the wardrobe. He snapped his fingers. "That's it! The wardrobe!"

"What about it?"

"Remember, Merlin was a carpenter. He made things out of wood, so if he was going to have hidden a secret passage, I bet he'll have hidden it—"

"In the wardrobe!" Trudy rushed over to the wardrobe and threw both doors open. Instead of a variety of cloaks and coats, there was a stairway leading upward. "This is bound to be where they went."

Jack followed Trudy over. He looked into the wardrobe and was slightly disappointed not to find either a lion or a witch.[103]

---

[103] Jack is, of course, referring to the classic of children's literature *The Lion, the Witch and the Wardrobe* by C. S. Lewis. Which I can thoroughly recommend. (Although, having said that, if you only have enough money to buy one of C. S. Lewis's books or one of mine, please buy mine. Because, frankly, C. S. Lewis died ages ago and he doesn't need the cash to buy a hot tub for his back garden the way I do. I know it isn't right to be

"Are you ready?" Trudy asked, putting a foot on the first step.

"Depends on what your definition of *ready* is, I suppose. I've got a horrible feeling that Merlin's going to be the hardest villain we've faced. Pirates don't plan well, and the queen of Atlantis was arrogant. But this guy's a scientist—that makes him smart and professional."

"Yeah, but we're going to take him down. He took my mother away from me. I didn't know if she was ever going to come back. I'm not going to forgive him for that."

Trudy bunched both fists together and started walking up the red-carpeted stairs. Jack followed her, thinking about his "half a plan." It was the first time that they'd ever gone into battle with only a rough idea of how they were going to defeat their enemy. Jack hoped it wouldn't be the last time as well.

---

begging like this, but I really don't have a choice, since my agent, Gemma, told me it isn't appropriate to put up a Kickstarter page to get a Jacuzzi.)

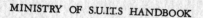

SCIENTISTS: DISCOVERERS VERSUS INVENTORS
WHO IS BETTER?

There are many different ways to divide up scientists. For example, they can be split into groupings such as evil and garden-variety scientists. However, the most important distinction is to split scientists up into those who *invent* things and those who *discover* things.

The easiest way to explain the difference is this. Isaac Newton was a man who many consider a genius because he discovered gravity. But before Mr. Newton discovered it we weren't all just floating around. Mr. Newton was smart for discovering gravity. But the real genius would be whoever actually invented it.

Despite extensive research at the patent office, we have been unable, to date, to identify the scientist who invented gravity.

41

MAGNETIC PERSONALITIES

The stairs led to a trapdoor with two huge bands of iron across it. Trudy and Jack crouched beneath it and silently listened. They could hear voices on the other side.

"I think that's Merlin," Trudy whispered.

Jack agreed. "This is the big confrontation, then."

"Yes, I don't suppose you've come up with the other half of the plan yet?"

"Umm, no. Maybe we just ask him to surrender?"

"I'm sure we'd have the element of surprise if we do that, but I'm not altogether convinced that he'll agree to it."

Jack shrugged. "Stranger things have happened."

Trudy admitted that stranger things had happened to them, but she still doubted whether Jack's plan would work. Trudy put her shoulder to the trapdoor. "On the count of three. One . . . two . . . THREE!" With a mighty shove, Trudy threw the trapdoor open and they leapt out to find themselves standing in the open air, on the ramparts of the central tower.

Merlin was standing on the far side of the tower, adjusting some switches and valves on a large brass control panel. He was surrounded by the five suits of armor. Each of them held a long sword and a shield.

"Ah, my two friends from the Ministry."

"Surrender, Merlin!" Jack shouted.

"No."

"You see, I told you that wouldn't work," Trudy muttered.

Merlin cocked his head to one side and looked at them. "Was that your plan?"

"We really only had half a plan," Jack conceded.

"That's a pity, because being alive for several hundreds of years has taught me to be prepared, and to have a backup plan just in case. As you can see I have my knights with me— Plan A. And if they fail? I have my dragon above—Plan B."

Jack and Trudy looked up and saw an enormous green-black shadow circling in the sky. It continued to belch huge clouds of smoky, orange flame.

Jack leaned over to Trudy. "This is going exactly as I expected."

"Oh," said Trudy, slightly surprised. "That's good!"

"Not really"—Jack paused—"because I expected it to go very badly indeed."

Trudy took up a fighting stance. "I'm going to use The Speed to defeat Merlin. I'm going to remember how sad I was when my mother went missing."

Jack wondered what sad memory he should think of. And

then he realized that he suspected they were going to be defeated by Merlin. . . . For once he didn't need to think of a sad thought for The Speed to work—he was *actually just sad*.

Trudy ran along the red carpet toward Merlin. Turning, Merlin stabbed at buttons on the control panel, which caused three of the empty suits of undefeatable armor to race toward her. The two smaller suits of armor remained standing next to Merlin. "Let's see how you cope with my 'knights.'"

The first knight swiped at Trudy with its enormous sword. Trudy ducked under it, grabbing the knight's shoulder. She pulled hard on its arm and sent the knight sprawling to the ground. Jack ran forward and kicked the sword away, feeling that he had played his part.

Merlin jabbed at more buttons on his control panel and two suits of armor closed in on Trudy from either side. Trudy swiveled, keeping both of them in view. The second knight lunged forward, forcing Trudy backward as the third knight swung his sword. Trudy saw it coming and backflipped over the blade at the last instant. She stood up, ramming the knight's arm with her shoulder. Its blade clattered to the ground. Jack dived forward and caught the sword by the handle, very happy with himself that he hadn't accidentally caught the blade and rendered himself left-handed for the rest of his life.

Trudy stepped forward and squared up against the remaining normal-sized suit of armor. It chopped, stabbed, and swung at her, but Trudy easily avoided each attack. "Is this the best you can do, Merlin?" Trudy mocked. "These suits are slow compared to a Ministry agent using The Speed."

Merlin didn't look rattled in the slightest. "Not to worry, young lady. Keep in mind that my 'empty knights' move through the power of magnetism. You will get tired. You will be bruised and hurt. But even if you put a sword through one of them, they won't stop fighting."

Trudy froze. She took two steps backward and stood alongside Jack. "He's right," she whispered. "What do we do?"

"Yeah, see this situation right here? This is the part that we didn't have the half plan for."

"Really?"

"Yeah, as it turns out we had a way of dealing with Merlin's Plan B rather than his Plan A."

Trudy muttered something very unladylike under her breath. "I'm still not giving up. You hear that, Merlin?"

Merlin nodded and pressed some more buttons on the control panel. All three knights stood bolt upright again. Jack felt the sword in his hand being pulled by the magnetic force. It leapt from his hand and flew back into the gauntlet of the first knight.

Trudy rubbed her hands together and rolled her shoulders to stretch them. "All right, Jack, stay out of it this time. I'm going to get serious."

Jack considered pointing out that he hadn't really done much the first time around, but decided that would probably have just been an unwelcome distraction. The three knights were heading toward them. Trudy walked five steps backward and then started running at the knights. She dived forward and flipped twice, hitting the first knight with a flying kick that sent it sprawling. Instantly, she cartwheeled as the remaining two knights swiped at her. Their swords whooshed past her and smashed into each other. Trudy did a punch front flip and landed crouched behind the second knight, slamming both hands into the back of its knee joints, which flew out. The knight crumpled and fell to the ground. Trudy was up in a flash and grabbed the knight's shield, which she spun and flung like a Frisbee. It caught the last knight in the chest, causing it to stumble a step backward, trip, and fall on the ground.

Trudy took two steps toward Merlin.

"Before you do anything too rash, maybe you want to see this." Merlin flipped up the visors of the two smaller suits of armor that were standing at his sides.

Unlike the other knights, these two helmets contained faces: Static and David. And then Jack realized that of course Merlin would have planned this—he was using their own friends against him. Well, technically he was using *one* of Jack and Trudy's friends. And Static was also there.

"How do we know they aren't just dummies?" Jack asked.

"Well, they are dummies. But I'm presuming that you want to hear my hostages speak?" Merlin twirled a finger and pressed a few buttons, which allowed David and Static to move their jaws and tongues.

"You know the way you said it was all going to come collapsing down?" David said. "I think that may have happened. Sorry."

Jack smiled at his friend's apology. "Don't worry about that, David; we're here to help you pick up the pieces."

Static looked even more sheepish. "It appears that I've

been captured by the bad guys—but that happens to heroes all the time, doesn't it?"

"Well, yes," agreed Trudy, "but generally they rescue themselves rather than having to wait for someone else to save their sorry behinds."

"Ahh," Static said. "Well, in that case I'd be grateful if you don't mention this incident if Edwyn comes and interviews you for the new Static autobiography he's working on."[104]

Trudy stood with her hands on her hips. "What's next, Merlin? Your suits of armor are too slow to defeat us. Even if you've captured our friends, you aren't going to find us quite as easy to vanquish."

Merlin considered for a moment. He glanced up in the air at the dragon, rubbing his chin. "I think that we can solve this easily." Merlin turned and punched at his console once more. David started moving forward; his eyes registered bewilderment.

"Do you really think David's going to be able to defeat me?" Trudy asked.

Merlin pretended to be confused for a minute. "Do I expect David to be able to defeat you? No, not at all, my dear. I expect David to be able to die."[105]

---

[104] Currently available in no bookstores anywhere, it's going to be titled STATIC—The Shocking Truth, obviously.

[105] Which was very similar to what he'd already said all the way back in Chapter 6. The reason for this is that Merlin spent all his time working on revenge and science and didn't pay anywhere near enough attention to his villainly dialogue.

Jack's face fell as he realized what was happening. Merlin was using his magnetic powers to force David to walk toward the castle wall. David took a step up onto the ramparts and lifted one leg over.

MINISTRY OF S.U.I.T.S HANDBOOK

INVENTORS
INSIDE-OUT INVENTIONS

Inventors often claim to be the most creative of all humans and expect to be rewarded as such. Although this can sometimes be true, it is amazing how many inventions are just inside-out versions of other inventions.

The most obvious example of this is the bath, which is nothing more than an inside-out boat. However, this is far from the only incidence of the inside-out invention. The sunlamp is nothing more than an inside-out oven. The television is just an inside-out cinema projector, and the filing cabinet is just an outside-in bulletin board.

Therefore, if you want to come up with an invention and make your fortune, just take an existing invention and turn it inside out.

42

WHEN EVEN THE
BEST CHOICE IS AWFUL

"Stop!" Jack shouted. "We give up!"

Merlin pressed a button on the control panel. David stepped back from the edge of the castle. Merlin then made him turn around and walk back.

"Thanks for that, Jack. I'm pretty sure that while armor's good for protecting from swords, it's not as helpful in a falling situation. Did you know that they didn't fit these things with airbags? Which seems like an oversight as far as I'm concerned."

Jack couldn't help laughing. Even though David had been literally one step away from death, it hadn't seemed to affect his oddness.

Trudy was still in a fighting stance. "What now?"

Jack put his hands up in the air. "I think the only thing

we can do is surrender. As long as Merlin has control of Static and David, we can't risk their lives."

Trudy clenched her fists harder for a second, but then her entire body sagged as she raised her hands up in the air. "I sort of agree with you. We can't risk *one* of their lives."

"Mean," Static muttered to himself, knowing exactly what Trudy had meant.

Merlin clapped. "You see? I always win."

"You don't always win," Jack snapped. "King Arthur banished you, didn't he?"

The smile faded from Merlin's face and was replaced with a snarl. "Oh, you found out about that, did you?"

"We know all about you, Merlin."

"You clearly don't. If you knew all about me, you would have run and hidden. You would have tried to save your own lives. But it's far too late for that now." Merlin's nimble fingers ran across the brass control panel. The gauntlets that David and Static had been wearing shot off their hands and hurtled through the air. A pair each grabbed Jack and Trudy by their wrists and pinned them to the internal wall of the tower. Their feet barely touched the ground. Merlin's hand danced across the console once more. The metal boots that David and Static wore were wrenched from their feet and flew toward Jack and Trudy. When they were a foot away they spun in the air and stamped down on Jack and Trudy's feet, pinning them in place.

Trudy turned her neck to look at Jack. "I don't suppose your 'half a plan' covers this either."

"As it turns out, it might only have been a quarter of a plan."

Merlin laughed. "What do you two know of plans? A week isn't long enough to plan anything. I have been planning my revenge on King Arthur for hundreds of years. That's planning."

"I'm sorry to have to spoil this for you, Merlin, but you've made a mistake."

"That's brave talk for a boy who's pinned to a wall and completely at my mercy."

"It is, isn't it?" said Jack. "But I don't think you'll get your revenge on King Arthur."

Merlin's face lit up with anger. "Why not?"

"Well, mainly because I'm pretty sure King Arthur's been dead for ages. I mean *really* ages—he was just a man—so he had rather a short lifespan. If you knew where he was buried we could dig him up, I suppose, but I'm pretty sure he'd be nothing but dust by now."

Trudy agreed. "Jack's right. And he probably smells awful. I mean, is it really worth getting your revenge if you have to spend all your money on air freshener afterward?"

"Very funny, you two," said Merlin, relaxing.

"I thought it was," Jack agreed.

"I know Arthur is dead. That is why I am going to have my revenge on his kingdom."

Jack whispered to Trudy. "This is the part where he gloats; they always gloat."

"Also, are you beginning to wonder how Merlin's managed to live so long?" Trudy whispered back. "Shouldn't he have died about the same time as King Arthur?"

"I'm going to kill everyone in England and Wales," Merlin

said smugly. "It took me hundreds of years to hatch this plan. And hundreds more to put it into operation."

"We know that Excalibur is Atlantean technology—an antenna that sends out waves of magnetism from your lodestone," Trudy said.

Merlin smiled as he thought of the stone. "That stone started everything for me. Funny that the legends got it so wrong and thought it was the sword that was important. It's the most powerful natural piece of lodestone in the world. Of course, it wasn't enough by itself. It was incredibly impractical to cart around an enormous stone and sword everywhere. And every time we stopped, someone wanted to try to pull out the sword to become king. It became very boring."

"I can imagine," Jack sympathized. "And that's when you came up with the idea for electricity pylons."

"It's amazing how gullible people are, isn't it?"

"In what way?" asked Trudy.

"Well, electricity pylons. They're a dead giveaway that I was up to something. Imagine how stupid people were to believe they were really there just to carry electricity. I mean, electricity is deadly. So why on earth would you carry it in lines hung above people's heads where the wind and storms could get at it?"

"But you didn't want to bury the electricity lines in the ground because that would have blocked the magnetic force."

"Exactly! It was all powered by the stone, of course, but metal lines are perfect for carrying the magnetic waves. If you put the right kind of charge through a wire, it'll cause a magnetic field."

"And the console?" Jack nodded to the console behind Merlin.

"Ah, yes. The queen of Atlantis built it for me. They really were the most advanced people, you know."

"So the entire electricity network was built by you?" asked Trudy.

"Not at all, not at all. Sometimes it does carry electricity. That's how I persuaded governments across the world to use the system."

"But you can switch it to carry either electricity or magnetic waves?"

"Precisely. It's all taken such a long time. But it will be worth it to have my revenge. I spent years trying to find that stone after Arthur buried it in Ireland. I hired archaeologists; I tried everything. But I had no luck—until I discovered that Blackbeard and his pirates were digging under the ground of Ireland, and then the queen of Atlantis asked for my help with an enormous drilling operation. With all those other digging operations it was only a matter of time before I found the stone."

Trudy tried to wriggle her wrist free of where the gauntlet had her pinned, but couldn't move it as much as an inch. "But if you want to take revenge on King Arthur's kingdom, why are there electricity pylons all over the world? Couldn't you just have them in Northern Ireland, England, and Wales?"

Merlin smiled slowly, clearly enjoying the moment. "Well, yes, Trudy—my first aim is to destroy Arthur's kingdom. My second aim is to take over the world. Before, I wanted to be king of the Britons. But now, well, emperor of the world seems like a much more satisfying title, don't you think?"

Jack's arms were beginning to hurt. Surrendering was a lot more physically painful than he realized, but his curiosity gland was working overtime as usual. "Listen, thanks for clearing up a lot of our questions. Just one more thing— how are you actually planning to destroy King Arthur's kingdom?"

Merlin pointed over the side of the battlement walls. Jack craned his neck to look. The castle was surrounded by hordes of people standing all the way down to the sea. Jack could just make out his parents standing with their picnic on the ground at their feet. They seemed dazed and unmoving, clearly under Merlin's control. A cold shiver ran down Jack's spine.

"Over the last number of years I have been genetically engineering foods to create allergic reactions in people. You must have noticed that? Years ago people were only ever allergic to grass—and yet these days there are hundreds of allergies—peanuts, wheat, cat hair, shellfish, gluten. . . ."

"Yeah," Jack agreed. "There was a guy in our class whose parents told him he was allergic to gluten. Which was odd, because he didn't even know what gluten was. So how could he have been allergic to it?"

Merlin ignored the interruption and carried on. "Everyone started worrying about their diet and started eating health food. I introduced Mr. M health foods, fortified with iron. Which allows me to control them using the lodestone and control panel . . ."

"Yeah, yeah, yeah, we know all this." Trudy faked a yawn.

Merlin frowned. "Very clever, aren't you. But thanks to my plans, and causing that boy at your school to have such a newsworthy and outlandish allergic reaction to peanuts—everyone in Northern Ireland has been eating my iron-infused foods this past week." Merlin pressed a sequence of buttons on the control panel. The front rank of the massed crowd outside the castle took a small step forward and jumped a foot in the air. When they landed, their sheer numbers and weight caused the ground to shake and vibrate. Along the shoreline a wave appeared. It slowly raised itself to five feet in height as it plowed across the sea, rocking boats and capsizing two windsurfers.

"And that was the effect when only the front line of the crowd jumps. Imagine when everyone does it together."

Jack realized what Merlin was going to do. "You're going to create an earthquake."

"An earthquake that causes a tidal wave," Trudy said.

"And the penny drops at last." Merlin pointed out at the crowd. "Half the population of Northern Ireland have come here today—because everyone wants to be famous in the movies. When I make them all jump at once it will cause a tidal wave a mile high that will cross the channel and destroy King Arthur's land."[106]

"But why?"

Merlin shrugged. "I'm really a very bitter man. I thought you'd have picked up on that by now."

Trudy grimaced and pulled against her restraints. "But

---

[106] Just like thousands of butterflies all flapping their wings at once.

you've made the classic supervillain mistake—you've explained your plot to us."

Merlin grinned. "Not at all. You see the classic mistake is when villains explain their plot and then leave the heroes to escape."

"But you just did that!"

Jack turned his head toward Trudy. "Actually, I don't think he has."

"What?"

"I mean, we're pretty much at his mercy. And I imagine he's going to kill us now."

"Well, yeah," Trudy agreed. "But this is exactly the time when you come up with one of your ideas that saves our lives and thwarts the villain."

Jack sagged a little in his restraints. "I really don't think that's going to happen this time. I'm afraid I'm a bit like one of those bank ads."

"What?" Trudy and Merlin both asked together.

Jack swiveled his head, trying to look at both of them. "You know, they have that disclaimer—past performance is not a guarantee of future results."

"You really are very annoying, you know that?" Merlin said.

"I've told him," Trudy said. "It doesn't seem to have any effect."

"He isn't annoying," David said, still unable to move. "He's my best friend."

"I think I'd side with the girl on this one. He does seem very annoying to me," Merlin said. "And that's why I'm going to finish you off before I destroy Arthur's kingdom and then use my portable human-earthquake/tidal-wave machine to take over the world."

"Right," Jack muttered. "Lesson to be learned there: Being annoying isn't a good thing."

Trudy turned to Jack. "I'm not sure that it'll be a very helpful lesson when we're dead."

"Very perceptive of you, young lady." Merlin pressed a button on the console. The swords suddenly leapt from two of the knight's hands and spun through the air, flying, powered by nothing other than magnetic force.

They spun and flew through the air. Right at Jack's and Trudy's heads.

MINISTRY OF S.U.I.T.S HANDBOOK

ARCHAEOLOGISTS
The Fiction and the Reality

It should be noted that archaeologists are not the way that they are often portrayed in films. Which is a shame, really, because the world would be a lot more exciting if they were.

The first point about archaeologists is that they don't wear fedoras and leather jackets or carry bullwhips.[107]

While that would be a fairly impressive look, it would not be very practical. First off, archaeologists spend all their time in muddy trenches, and you can't just put a leather jacket in a clothes dryer. If an archaeologist wore a leather jacket, they'd have to find King Solomon's mines every other week just to be able to afford their dry-cleaning bill. Secondly, a lot of their work takes place outdoors, sometimes in deserts or jungles. Therefore, a real archaeologist who insisted on wearing a leather jacket all the time would end up taking part in adventures called *Indiana Jones*[108] *and the Sudden Onset of Heatstroke.*

Finally, archaeologists rarely come across bulls, and even if they did they probably wouldn't whip them. After all, stumbling across a bull in a field is a terrifying enough experience without trying to make the bull really, really annoyed.

[107] I think we all know exactly to whom this is referring. If you don't, use the Internet and find out. They really are the most brilliant films.

[108] You probably don't need to look up whom I'm talking about on the Internet anymore.

43

CERTAIN DEATH

The swords were an inch from Jack's and Trudy's eyes when Merlin pressed a button on the brass console and they stopped and hung in the air. The tip of the sword was right in front of Jack's eye. "Umm, shouldn't I be wearing a pair of safety goggles or something?"

Trudy stared at the sharp point in front of her eye. "Let's really try to avoid antagonizing Merlin, okay, Jack?"

"Have you seen the error of your ways? Decided that there's no point in taking revenge on a long-dead king?" Jack asked Merlin.

Merlin shook his head slowly. "I've been in the revenge business for centuries now."[109]

---

[109] Some of you may be wondering how Merlin stayed alive for so long. The obvious answer would be magic. However, as well as being the

"You're looking remarkably well, considering," observed Trudy. "You must have really good medical care. Can you give me the name of your doctor?"

"A lot of people seem to be in the revenge business," Jack said, "but surely forgiveness is a better business. With forgiveness there's the possibility of getting repeat customers. I mean, wiping out complete groups of people—you're going to get bad feedback. A lot of negative reviews and thumbs-down."

"Enjoy your jokes. But I am an expert at revenge and that's the reason I paused the swords. You see, I just had a thought." A grin spread across Merlin's face.

Jack turned to Trudy. "I'm guessing we're really not going to like this thought."

"You think?"

Merlin pressed the buttons on the console, and David and Static began walking along the red carpet toward Jack and Trudy.

---

obvious answer, it is also the wrong answer. The truth is that Merlin has no idea what had kept him alive for so long, although it would have been obvious to an experienced Ministry operative. For many decades Merlin's entire life was all about hatred of King Arthur. As we know from the use of The Speed, negative emotions slow down time. Merlin's entire life was about hatred and revenge—therefore time slowed down around him, stretching out his lifespan to hundreds and hundreds of years. If Merlin stopped hating and plotting revenge, or even if he fell in love, there was a good chance that he would suddenly age and drop dead on the spot. Anything heartwarming could potentially be fatal for him. Therefore, it was a good thing he didn't like puppies, rom-coms, or fluffy toys.

"Guys, I don't know what's going to happen. But I'd like to take this opportunity to apologize in advance," David shouted.

"Try to resist," Jack called back.

"I'd also like to add my apology to David's," agreed Static. "I'm pretty sure whatever Merlin's going to make us do, it won't be very heroic."

A look of strain appeared on both David's and Static's faces as they tried to fight against Merlin's magnetic control. Their feet dragged along the red carpet as they tried to resist taking each step. "Keep resisting, by all means; it makes it all the more entertaining. Revenge is best when it's personal." Merlin laughed as he turned dials on the control panel.

Seconds dragged out into minutes, but although David and Static struggled as best they could, ultimately they found themselves standing in front of Jack and Trudy.

Merlin was playing with the control panel once more. David lifted his arm and slapped Jack across the face.

"Sorry!" David apologized.

Jack's face was warm and he was angry, but not with David. He was angry with Merlin. Being an evil, revenge-focused scientist who wanted to destroy a country that had rejected him as king was one thing, but there was absolutely no reason to be mean. "Merlin, is this what you're all about? Bullying children?" Jack could feel the red handprint on his face.

"Jack, you know what I'm about. Revenge. Can you imagine a better way of my getting revenge on you than making your best friend beat you up?"

"As a matter of fact, I can."

Merlin was taken aback. "I've been at this for more than a millennium and you presume to tell me you could come up with a better idea."

"Rather than getting this David guy to just slap me, you could get my best friend to actually kill me."

"Your best friend?" Merlin enquired. "You mean the girl?"

"Not the girl," Jack said quickly.

"I swear, Jack, if we get out of this, I'm going to give your shoulder such a punching for referring to me as 'the girl.'"

Jack ignored Trudy and kept on talking. "If I was trying to get revenge, I'd use my best friend and force them to push the button that would make the floating swords kill us. That way you'd be using our friend as well as involving the machinery that we were going to try and stop you from using."

Merlin didn't speak for a minute. "That would be cold, wouldn't it?" He turned his head slightly and considered Jack. "Why are you telling me this?"

Jack hung his head. "Because it's over. I'm fed up with your gloating. Why do villains always have to gloat? Just . . . just finish it."

"All right, I can be merciful. And it is a nice ironic revenge. But if the clumsy one isn't your best friend and the girl isn't either, then . . ."

"THE GIRL IS CALLED TRUDY!" Trudy shouted.

Merlin ignored her and continued, " . . . then who is your best friend?"

Jack looked up. "Static, of course. He's a bona fide superhero."

"Superhero?"

"I am a superhero," Static agreed. "That much is certainly true. I have merchandise and everything."

Trudy was about to say something, but Jack quickly shushed her. "Look at him! Can't you see he's wearing a superhero costume under his armor?"

Merlin nodded. "Actually, I did notice there was something strange earlier. He seemed to have a cloak and costume made out of school shirts."

"And I've got a hundred-percent-polyester leotard on. I made almost all of it myself. Although my mum helped me blind-stitch the inside hems; otherwise they chafe something shocking," Static admitted.

"All right, let's not get too distracted. Remember, today is about my revenge—not about your nonsense." Merlin turned back to his console and pressed buttons that made Static start walking back along the red carpet.

"Jack, I'm sorry about this. I always suspected you worshiped me. But don't worry; I'm pretty sure that I can resist the magnetic forces if I try really, really hard." Static started making groaning and moaning noises as he fought against the power of Merlin's magnetic machine. His struggles seemed to slow his movement, causing his polyester-socked feet to drag inch by inch, but he could not resist entirely.

He was less than a foot away from the machine. Merlin pointed at another button. "Now if I press *this* button, you will press *that* button, and your friends will die as the swords are driven into their heads."

Static's hand was shaking as it stretched out. "Jack, Trudy, sorry about this. I will avenge you."

Trudy gulped as she looked at the shining steel point hanging right in front of her face. Jack had never seen her look this nervous.

"Static will return in *The Revenge of Static*!" Static shouted.

Trudy couldn't help laughing. Jack was pleased that she wasn't nervous anymore.

"You know what, Jack? I'm glad we're going to be killed. Because if Static had saved the day he'd have been absolutely impossible to live with."

Jack's face twisted into a half smile. "In that case, I've got some really bad news for you."

MINISTRY OF S.U.IT.S HANDBOOK

THE REASON SCIENCE WAS INVENTED
PEOPLE WANT TO LIVE FOREVER

If you ask scientists why science was invented, they will start talking about the "quest for knowledge and truth." Which is clearly nonsense. The only reason for science to ever be invented was (a) people didn't want to feel pain and (b) people didn't want to die.

Therefore, almost 2,500 years ago, the leaders of a small village ran tests to find out who among them was the smartest. The village leaders then said to the smart people, "Hey, guys, you are going to be the scientists—we want you to solve the problem of death and stop us from ever having to feel pain." The smart people felt very proud and immediately began working on the problem, sure they would have it finished before the end of the week.

If you go and speak to the scientists today to see how they're getting on with it, they're likely to respond with, "Yeah, um, yeah, we're still working on that. Looks like it's taking slightly longer than we thought it would. . . ."

44

A SHOCKING CLIMAX

"What do you mean?" Trudy's face fell. "Please don't tell me . . ."

"Yeah, my 'half a plan' is now a whole plan. Sorry!" Jack apologized.

Static's shaking hand was less than half an inch above the button that would cause Jack's and Trudy's deaths. Suddenly there was an enormous *crack* and a blue bolt sparked from Static's finger, hitting the metal console.

"What was that?" Merlin cried.

The small blue bolt of static electricity from Static's finger caused a chain reaction. Electrical sparks started showering out from the console. It spat and fizzed and burst into flames.

The metal gauntlets and boots that had been holding Jack and Trudy in place fell away and they collapsed to the ground. Merlin was staring over the wall. The crowds of people were turning to each other, confused and suddenly able to move again.

"I expect you'll want an explanation, Merlin?" Jack asked.

"What did you do? Some kind of Atlantean technology?"

"You defeated yourself, Merlin. You pulled the metal boots off Static and David to hold us against the wall. But you didn't realize that Static's costume is made of pure polyester, so it builds up high-powered static shocks."

Static nodded. "And then when I was resisting your magnetic forces it caused my feet to slowly drag along the fluffy red carpets. Thus building up the largest static shock I've ever used. Jack and I planned it all along."

Jack sighed. "Just to clarify, Static had no idea what was going on. I only came up with the idea less than a minute ago."

Static's face fell and he turned toward Jack to remonstrate. "Come on, Jack, we're best friends. Best friends are supposed to be supportive."

Trudy laughed. Jack sighed again. "Static, we aren't best friends. I was lying about that as well so that Merlin would use you to press the button."

"Oh," said Static as this realization dawned on him. "Oh . . . this being a hero thing is very emotionally hurtful sometimes."

Trudy was flexing her arms, trying to get the blood flowing in them after being pinned to the wall. "Now, Merlin, you're going to learn what a Ministry operative can do using The Speed."

Merlin shook his head. "I'm afraid not. Remember, I have a Plan B. You may have saved King Arthur's kingdom today, but I can gain my revenge on him another day. As for you—today you die."

"Oh puleeassse, stop going on about people dying all the time," groaned Jack. "You're like a broken record with all this killing people."

Merlin whistled into the air and the enormous black dragon turned effortlessly and started flying toward the castle.

Trudy took a step backward. "But without the control panel..."

"I learned a lot from the Atlanteans about science. I used the magnetic boulder and control panel to control people, knights, and cars. But it's always good to have a backup." Merlin sneered. "My animatronic dragon is sonically activated." Merlin whistled again and the dragon turned in the air, hovering and staring down at them.[110]

Jack smiled. "This is the half part of the plan that I had prepared."

"Well, get on with it then," said Trudy.

Jack spoke directly to Merlin. "You've called your reinforcements; now we call ours. . . . CTHULHU!"

Suddenly in the air beside Jack, a glowing green slash with a black center appeared. The interdimensional monster Cthulhu stepped out of it. He screeched loudly.

Merlin took a step backward. "You have Cthulhu on your side? . . . But he's an interdimensional monster with

---

[110] If you're wondering whether Merlin really got this idea from the Atlanteans, he totally didn't. He stole it from Apple and Siri.

near-unlimited power who longs to watch the world being slowly destroyed."

"Yes," Jack agreed. "But he's OUR interdimensional monster with near unlimited power who longs to watch the world being slowly destroyed. Also, you tore up some of his files. And that didn't make him desperately happy."

Merlin looked at the dragon, which had circled and was closing in. He regained his composure. "Even if he is an interdimensional monster, he can still burn. DRAGON—INCINERATE THEM!"

Jack spoke quickly to Cthulhu. "Did you bring them with you?"

Cthulhu nodded and gestured with a bony claw toward the dimensional rift. Dozens of robot vacuum cleaners poured out of it and surrounded Cthulhu.

"That's not fair!" Merlin complained. "Those are my vacuum cleaners."

"*Were* your vacuum cleaners," Jack corrected. "The Ministry reprogrammed them. And without your magnetic control panel there's nothing you can do to stop them."

For the first time, Merlin was looking worried. He looked to the sky and was relieved to see the dragon was less than a hundred yards away. "It's over for you meddling kids. Vacuum cleaners can't defeat a dragon!"

Jack really hoped they could. He turned to the vacuum cleaners. "Okay, vacuum cleaners. Aim . . . and FIRE!"

The dragon was just overhead, and its vast canyon of a mouth opened to cover them in flame. The vacuum cleaners lifted their nozzles and switched from suck to blow. They sprayed what looked like millions of pellets into the dragon's mouth.

The pellets seemed to have no effect whatsoever. There was a click from deep inside the dragon's belly. Merlin smiled as he waited to see his enemies barbecued.

And waited. And waited.

Suddenly the dragon seemed to explode from the inside out. There was no fire, but rivets and panels from its animatronic insides shot outward and its metal and plastic body was ripped apart. Sections of metal and joints were falling to the ground as the dragon fell to pieces. There was also something that looked like large, white snowflakes falling through the air.

"What? What is this?" Merlin screamed.

Jack held out a hand, caught one of the "large snowflakes," and popped it into his mouth. "Popcorn. We got the vacuum cleaners to suck up all the corn you left in the grain container on our playing fields. Then they fired it into the dragon's mouth just as the flame was about to come out. Imagine ten tons of popcorn suddenly being exploded in what quite clearly was only a three-ton dragon." Jack stepped forward and kicked the head of the ruined dragon. "And now, Trudy, I believe you wanted to show Merlin what a Ministry agent could do using The Speed."

Trudy patted Jack on the back. "Actually, I've had a better idea." Trudy pointed at a line of birds on a nearby pylon line. "Merlin's magnetic console is broken now—so those birds won't be confused anymore by magnetic power flowing through the lines. Right?"

"Yes, they'll probably fly away soon looking for some food."

"Food's what I was thinking of."

"What are you two talking about?" Merlin raged.

"What I'm asking is, is there any corn left in the vacuums?"

Jack smiled and realized what Trudy was suggesting. "Probably—you want to . . . ?"

Trudy pointed at Merlin. "Vacuums, FIRE!"

The vacuum cleaners obediently showered Merlin with unpopped corn kernels. He shielded his face as the pellets bit into him. "Is that the best you can do?" asked Merlin.

Trudy said nothing, but merely pointed. Merlin turned and looked to see what Trudy was indicating. Hundreds of birds had noticed the pile of corn that was covering Merlin and lying at his feet. They took off as a mass flock and dived toward him, pecking, poking, jabbing, and nibbling at him.

"Arghhh!" Merlin thrashed his arms, trying to shoo the birds away, but it merely seemed to excite them. He stumbled backward as they tore his robe to shreds. He tripped, catching his knee on the battlements, and then fell off the castle.

Jack breathed in sharply. "That's going to hurt."

"He deserved it. He kidnapped my mother."

Suddenly Jack and Trudy felt a hand on their shoulders and turned to see Static. "We saved the world."

Trudy shook her head. "No, Static, *we* saved the world."

"Now, Trudy," Static said firmly, "I think you'll find that bloke in the red robe was going to take over the world with the machine that I destroyed with a static shock. . . . So, if anything—*I saved the world.* But I'm big enough to grant you both an assist."

Jack sighed. "WE saved the world."

"Sometimes," Trudy said, "I suspect the world is not enough."

MINISTRY OF S.U.I.T.S HANDBOOK

DRAGONS
THE DANGERS OF SNACKING

It should be noted that although the prevailing opinion these days is that dragons are "pretty cool," the truth is that they used to be a frightful nuisance. If you lived in a part of a kingdom that had a dragon infestation, you would be in for a truly awful time of it, generally speaking. Damsels would be kidnapped; treasure would be stolen; and sheep, goats, and other cattle would be eaten whole.

It would be nice to try to pretend that dragons were vanquished by the heroics of a group of strong and brave knights. As usual, the truth is vastly different. In fact, if there were league tables for dragons' battles against knights, it would rapidly become clear that the knights were at a distinct disadvantage.

There are various reasons for this, but the major one is simply that as an outfit for fighting dragons, shiny metal armor is worse than useless. First, shiny metal armor makes you easy to spot as a dragon flies overhead. Therefore, you lose any chance of a surprise attack. Second, as we all know, dragons breathe fire, and metal conducts heat incredibly well. Attacking a dragon in full plate armor is basically the equivalent of a turkey wrapping itself in aluminum foil before running into the oven. Finally, as has been stated previously, dragons love snacking. And as we all know, the best snacks are those that are crunchy on the outside and soft on the inside. So, when a dragon saw a knight it tended not to think of him as a mortal and dangerous enemy, but rather as an appetizer.

It is not an exaggeration to say that at one stage it looked as if humans were fighting a losing battle on the dragon front until Sir Jonley the Late turned up. Of course, he turned up late as always, because that was his name. Sir Jonley was a vain knight and always took his time getting ready for battles, because he wanted to get his hair[111] just right in case there were any comely damsels in attendance.

It turns out, showing up late gave Sir Jonley a distinct advantage, as it meant he had time to see what everyone else had done wrong and change his battle plan appropriately. After turning up late to a massed battle against a particularly ferocious dragon, Sir Jonley noted that the creature seemed to be completely impervious to arrows, spears, and swords, largely because of its rock-hard scales. He also noted how the dragon appeared to burp on his food before chewing it—clearly enjoying roasted snacks.

Sir Jonley rightly came to the conclusion that a creature that spent so much time burping was clearly one that should be attacked from the inside. After all, no weapon was going to get through its thick hide. He also surmised that the fiery inside of a dragon would be an ideal location to try to place some explosives.

His first attempt was to cover a range of sheep in gunpowder, but this proved to be ineffective,

---

[111] In *Knight Fan* magazine, Sir Jonley the Late listed his three pet peeves as trolls, evil enchanters, and helmet hair.

as gunpowder is not pleasant-tasting, and so the dragon merely spat out the poor sheep before any explosion happened.

Sir Jonley went back to the drawing board, trying to come up with an explosive that would appeal as a snack and would also taste nice when roasted. Sir Jonley consulted with the wisest people in the kingdom and discovered that you can make dynamite using extracts from peanuts. Once he had done this, Sir Jonley the Late was armed with an explosive that was delicious when roasted as well as being nutritious.

At the time a particularly vicious dragon, Owen the Terrible, was ravaging the coast of Queen Alisha's kingdom. Sir Jonley the Late made himself a fake knight-shaped decoy, stuffed the peanut-flavored dynamite inside, and waited for Owen the Terrible to come and devour it, hopefully causing it to explode upon its first burp.

Sir Jonley's plan was amazingly effective, and after the dragon was dead Queen Alisha asked Sir Jonley to marry her immediately. Sir Jonley said that though he appreciated the offer, frankly he wasn't interested in marrying anyone until he managed to get the dragon guts out of his hair.

EPILOGUE

Those of you of a nervous disposition will be glad to know that Merlin had fallen over the edge of the castle that borders on the water; and so, apart from being covered from head to toe in small peck marks, and being rather wet, he survived largely unhurt.

Static was initially very upset that Trudy and Jack refused to acknowledge that they should technically be his sidekicks. Unsurprisingly, Static became so obnoxious that Jack had to physically restrain Trudy from pushing him over the battlements. "Oh, come on, Jack, he might land on top of Merlin and that would be a win-win."

However, Static was quickly distracted when he realized that half the population of Northern Ireland was standing outside Carrickfergus Castle, feeling slightly confused and also very hungry, since they had been mainly eating health food for the past week. This, coupled with the fact that Static had access to an almost unlimited supply of popcorn, sparked his entrepreneurial spirit. Static quickly found himself a small supply of plastic bags, scooped out the insides of the dragon, and wandered around the crowds selling "Dragonfire" brand popcorn. Static was so successful that he was able to employ a professional costume designer to create his next superhero outfit.

Grey turned up and, with Cthulhu's help, dragged Merlin out of the sea. Merlin shouted and promised he would get his revenge. Jack said that he wasn't desperately worried, as given Merlin's track record they would be dead for a very long time before he actually got around to doing anything.

David discovered that wearing a suit of armor helped protect him from getting very bad bruises when he bumped into things and fell over. However, he also quickly discovered that when he fell over wearing armor, he was unable to get back on his feet and ended up just rolling around on his back. This made him realize why no one has ever tried to train a squad of attack tortoises.

In order to stop the public from realizing exactly what had happened, Ministry operatives turned up and began spreading rumors among the crowd. A whisper travels through a crowd faster than prunes travel through an elderly person, and soon everyone was applauding the amazing special effects they had just seen. A few claimed that they had felt as if they were controlled by some strange force that had stopped them from moving—in fact, some claimed that the force had actually made them come to Carrickfergus and that they had never had any intention of being in the movie. However, this was easily explained when a story appeared in the newspapers the following week revealing that Mr. M health food had been discovered to be contaminated with mind-bending chemicals, and anyone who had any of this food in their houses should destroy it immediately.

Most people followed this advice immediately and went back to having an occasional Ulster Fry.[112]

The Minister considered many different ways of punishing Merlin, but it was difficult to come up with something suitable in the modern world for a man who hated everyone and dressed in what looked like a wizard's outfit. In the end it was decided to sentence Merlin to become a children's entertainer for the next sixty years.[113] Unfortunately, it is suspected that having to deal with small groups of six-year-olds each day for the next sixty years will make Merlin have such a miserable time that the negative emotions may mean that he will eventually become immortal.

---

[112] An Ulster Fry is made up of bacon, sausages, eggs, tomato, pancakes, soda bread, and potato cakes. The cooking instructions are relatively easy—you take all the ingredients and fry them together in a pan. As an occasional breakfast meal it is absolutely delicious. However, if you try to eat one two days in a row, it's probably a good idea to have the number of your cardiologist on speed dial.

[113] Technically he was sentenced to a term of sixty years or half a million balloon animals, whichever came first.

Jack and Trudy were sitting on the edge of the castle battlements, relaxing and looking out to the sea, when Jack's parents walked up to them. "Something very strange has been going on here," Jack's father said.

Jack's mother, however, was interested in other things. "Is this your friend Trudy that you've been talking about?"

Trudy jumped off the battlements and shook Jack's parents' hands. She was astonishingly polite, which rendered Jack speechless. "It's lovely to meet you both."

Jack desperately hoped his parents wouldn't say anything to embarrass him. Sadly, he hoped this in vain. His father nudged his mother in the ribs before speaking to Trudy: "Are you Jack's girlfriend, then?"

A wicked look spread across Trudy's face. "Only in his imagination."

Jack's face turned bright red and he tried to change the subject. "What are you going to do now, Trudy?"

"I'm going home, Jack. I'm going home to do a jigsaw puzzle with my mother."

"I hate jigsaw puzzles."

"Yeah, me too," Trudy said with the largest-ever smile on her face.

Jack smiled too—although he couldn't help being slightly worried that his future was going to be very strange, unusual, and impossible indeed.

BALLOON ANIMALS
Important Safety Tips

It is important to get things the right way around.

If you take a balloon and twist it into the shape of a dog, you will get a round of applause from people.

If, however, you try it the other way around, you will get a dog bite. Which isn't as much fun and also has the potential to go septic.

THE FUTURE
Fear of It

Over the years many people have spent a great deal of time thinking about the future, how we can predict it, and how we can change it. Which is ironic, because by focusing on the future we actually miss the chance to change it by doing things right now. A good rule of thumb is that you should never trust anyone who tells you they can predict the future unless they have won the lottery at least twice.

ACKNOWLEDGMENTS

Thanks as always go to my agent, Gemma Cooper, a friend who magically appears in both my email inbox and my footnotes.

THANK YOU FOR READING THIS
FEIWEL AND FRIENDS BOOK.

The Friends who made

THE KNIGHT'S ARMOR

possible are:

JEAN FEIWEL, Publisher
LIZ SZABLA, Associate Publisher
RICH DEAS, Senior Creative Director
HOLLY WEST, Editor
ANNA ROBERTO, Editor
CHRISTINE BARCELLONA, Editor
KAT BRZOZOWSKI, Editor
ALEXEI ESIKOFF, Senior Managing Editor
KIM WAYMER, Senior Production Manager
ANNA POON, Assistant Editor
EMILY SETTLE, Assistant Editor
LIZ DRESNER, Associate Art Director
STARR BAER, Senior Production Editor

Follow us on Facebook or visit
us online at mackids.com.

OUR BOOKS ARE FRIENDS FOR LIFE